Thug in Me

D1565277

Thug in Me

Karen Williams

www.urbanbooks.net

Urban Books, LLC
78 East Industry Court
Deer Park, NY 11729

ISBN 13: 978-1-60162-443-7
ISBN 10: 1-60162-443-3

First Printing April 2011
Printed in the United States of America

10 9 8 7 6 5 4 3 2 1

Distributed by Kensington Publishing Corp.
Submit Wholesale Orders to:
Kensington Publishing Corp.
C/O Penguin Group (USA) Inc.
Attention: Order Processing
405 Murray Hill Parkway
East Rutherford, NJ 07073-2316
Phone: 1-800-526-0275
Fax: 1-800-227-9604

Dedication

This novel is dedicated to my beautiful son, Bralynn Bryce Graham. You are confirmation that life is precious, we should all believe in miracles, and dreams really do come true. I feel so blessed.

Acknowledgments

Okay, I'm back with a novel that is very special to me, so I hope you enjoy it. I have been attempting and attempting to write this story for the past five years and just never seemed to be able to bridge all the gaps and complete it. It was a challenge I took on yet again and I was able to meet this challenge. I hope you enjoy. As I wrote the story, I felt like I was fighting, crying for and loving Chance like he was a person in my world. There is something very endearing about a person who is not only able to endure the unthinkable but in enduring, continues to fight, and climb his way out. That's what I call a thug: You came from nothing and were able to build and have the ability to push through and survive no matter what.

Special thanks, hugs, and smiles go to my loved ones, Adara, Bralynn, Mom, Crystal, Terry, Mikayla, and Madison. Omari, Jabrez, Devin, and Mu-Mu, La'naya, and Tammy. And of course my fat, blue-eyed son, Bralynn, who took long naps and watched *Yo Gabba Gabba* so your mommy could get this story done. (sigh) Such a blessing to be a new mommy again and have my firstborn, Adara, who is the reason why I am what and who I am, experiencing it with me!

Thanks to all my friends, Christina W, Roxetta, Rob, Candis, Kimberly, Sewiaa, Stephanie, Linda, Cheryl, Christina T, you pushed me to write this story! Carla, Ronisha RIP , Tina, Lenzie, Valerie Hoyt, Tara,

Acknowledgments

Pearlean, Maxine, Jennifer, Barbara, Henrietta, VI, Kim, Kyle, Phillipo, Latonya, Leigh, Vanilla, Yvonne, Dena, Daphne, Sandra T, Sandra V, Marilyn, Ivy, Mondell, Daphne, Lenzie, and Lydia.

Thanks to my fellow author buddies, Mondell Pope, Rickey Teemes II, Papa Sak, Aleta Williams. Thanks, Carl, for your continued faith in me. Thanks to Kevin a good yet sarcastic editor. Thanks to Natalie for always answering my e-mails.

Thanks to Fashion Trend . . . Lori, you don't just sell cute clothes, you push my books voluntarily and I appreciate it!

Sorry if I forget anyone. Charge it to my mind, not my heart; my son is throwing milk at me from his sippy cup as we speak. I'll get you in the next book. Accept this for now.

Thanks to all my fans for your continued support. A friend of mine who works at a bookstore (no names) told me that one of their customers said that whatever I write they are going to get. I was like, wow, hearing that made me really feel valued as an author.

To all men locked behind bars for a crime you are innocent of, stay in prayer and remain hopeful you'll be set free. Like Chance said, Keep making noise until the powers that be let you out.

Prologue

Blood leaked from a gash on my lip. But it didn't stop the beating the four police officers continued to give me. One minute I was getting out of my shower after hearing a banging on the door. The next minute, four police rushed into my bathroom and I was getting fucked up. I was now lying on the floor while they all delivered punches and kicks to my head and body.

I placed my hands around my head to block some of the blows. But it didn't make a difference. They kept going.

"You fucking cop killer!" one of them yelled, stomping his black boot into my face.

I winced from the pain as he continued to slam it down on my face. When he finally retracted his foot, I cracked one of my eyelids open to get a peek at his badge. Swarovski was his name. Another cop took his baton and started hitting me in my back with it, all the while Swarovski continued to bring his foot down with the weight on his entire body onto my face.

I grunted from the pain. Being a black man from the projects, you couldn't escape getting beat by racist police, but I had never experienced a beating like this before. And most of all, I didn't know why they were attacking me or even why they were in my house.

And it only got worse.

Swarovski flipped me over on my back.

The others momentarily paused their assault.

Swarovski took the other officer's baton and jabbed me in my stomach with so much force I started breathing harshly. He then took the baton, wrapped it around my neck, and started choking me.

I grabbed his hands, hoping I could stop his assault. Because, yeah, I didn't stop the cops from beating my ass but I was gonna try and stop them from killing me!

"Get your fucking hands off of me!" His grip on the baton on my neck tightened.

Snot flew from my nose and I felt like I was going to vomit, but he continued.

I felt myself getting weak and going out. My hands started flapping at my sides and I knew in that moment I was going to die.

Spit flew from his mouth as he continued to call me names. The baton came down one more good time, hitting me in the back of my neck. My body started feeling weak, fuzzy, the way I felt just the night before when I popped an Ambien so I could get some rest.

And like the Ambien put me out, so did that blow.

Chapter 1

Now I'm here? Two days after getting my ass whipped, I sat in front of the judge and had a hard time standing to my feet, when the prosecutor laid out my crime: Murder of Devin Johnson, a police officer. A man I had never seen or heard of before. I damn near shitted on myself when I heard the charge and how much time the DA was asking for. All my fucking time: Life—plain and simple.

Without even glancing my way, the judge looked over his glasses and asked my lawyer, "How does the defendant plead?"

I stood with my public defender, angry as fuck and scared.

"The defendant pleads not guilty, your Honor."

I nodded and tried to keep calm, when inside I was dying. I ran the risk of losing everything I had: My mom, my job, my home, my girl—everything. And it pissed me the fuck off, and more importantly what pissed me off even more was that I didn't do shit.

How in the fuck did I get here?

Three Days Ago—March 2003

I turned my Suburban down my street bumping Too Short. I then pulled into my driveway. I had just bought that bad boy. It was on point too. It was black

..d fully loaded with a couple of TVs, iPod, and leather seats. My ride was a grown and sexy ride. And it was sitting on some twenty-four-inch rims that were shining on a daily. It was a gift to myself for all the hard work I had been putting in. And when I say *hard work*, no, I'm not talking about anything illegal. I did the shit the legal way. I'm not going to say I was never tempted to get in the game. Growing up in the Springdales, illegal shit was all around me and so was the opportunity to get involved in it. But I saw way too many niggas getting arrested over bullshit and too many niggas getting killed over bullshit. I was cool.

Even though my sorry-ass daddy, Curtis Redding, lived in the Springdales, he didn't live with my mother and me and he didn't help her take care of me. In fact, he didn't even claim me. And if it wasn't enough that my mama had to make a life for us alone, she had to deal with a lot of unnecessary bullshit from my daddy. He was so uninvolved my mama gave me her last name. He refused to claim me and his various women always harassed and would even jump on my mama 'cause she had something they just didn't have: me. Funny. The person he didn't give a fuck about. But the one thing my daddy did teach me, indirectly, was that your dirt always catches up with you. Case in point, my daddy ended up with full-blown AIDS, I was ten when he died. Sticking your dick in a hole just because it is open is not always a good thing. I didn't care too much when he died and I told my mother that he got what he deserved. But she always told me that it is always better to forgive, if not for anybody else, for yourself.

After seeing my mom go through all of that, the last thing I wanted to do was cause her any trouble.

So by the time I was seventeen I finished high school a year early by skipping a whole year. At the age of twenty I graduated from ITT Tech with a bachelor's degree in computer science. I knew the computer like the back of my hand, and could do any and everything to it.

A few months after graduating from college, I landed a job as a computer analyst at Microsoft, making sixty thousand dollars a year. Within my first year of employment, I bought my first home. It wasn't anything special, just a two-bedroom. But it was enough for me to move my mama out of the projects and enough for her to stop working like a slave. But she still managed to hold onto one of her jobs, being an in-home care aide for some elderly white woman named Ellen. Time and time again I told her to quit and that there was no need for her to work. But she always said that working for her wasn't like a job because they were so close.

I'm sure to most men living with their mother would probably cramp their style, but not me. I wouldn't have it any other way. My mom was why I was everything that I was. I wanted her to be comfortable and have peace of mind. She was the most supportive person in my small inner circle. And I wasn't done accomplishing stuff. I still had a ways to go. The thing about me is this: I didn't wait for anyone to give me shit. What I wanted I worked hard and got it. I was now in the process of getting a loan to open up my own business. And I knew the rules to being successful: no felonies and no bad credit.

I downed the last bottle of my Vitamin Water and put my truck in park. I had just left the gym. I had done cardio for forty-five minutes and lifted weights for an hour. It was my usual schedule when I left my job.

I hopped out of the car just as my cell phone started ringing. I pulled it out of the pocket of my sweats and glanced at the number. It was my baby Toi calling.

"Yeah, baby?" I said. I walked over to the passenger's side of my car and grabbed my gym bag.

"Hello?" was all she said.

I smiled. Toi—she was everything a brotha could ask for. She was fine, with that small waist and an onion-shaped booty, mocha brown skin, juicy lips, smoky bedroom eyes. She was sweet, could cook, and even hold down a job. The only flaw was she was too high-maintenance, which for a man can sometimes be expensive, but she was worth it. The other problem I had with her is that she wanted me to kick my mama out and move her ass right on in. It wasn't enough that I had also moved her out of the projects and into her own pad. That shit wasn't cheap. I had to work a day of overtime a week to do so.

When she said nothing further, I asked, "What's going on, baby?"

"Not much. Just wondering if I could swing by," she said.

"Yeah. Ma probably cooking now."

"I meant for later. Is your mom gonna be there?"

"She lives here; what do you think?"

"But it's your house."

"What does that have to do with anything? It's my mom. She ain't tripping off you, why you tripping off of her?"

She sucked her teeth.

"If you talking about later, I can swing by your house, baby."

"Chance, we been together for over three years. I love you. Don't you love me?"

I sighed. Oh, lord, here she go. "Toi, I wouldn't have said it if I didn't."

"Then why aren't you treating me like you do?"

"How am I not? I take you out, I'm faithful. I'm damn near paying all your bills. The only bills you pay are your cell phone and your car insurance."

"I want to move in."

"You're not my—"

She hung up before I could finish.

I chuckled. I closed the passenger-side door and slung my gym bag over my shoulder. I knew what this was about. Yeah, I loved Toi even when she had her attitude, because she sure as hell could jump ghetto when she wanted to. I had learned to adjust to it. But what she wanted at that time I just didn't. Yeah, I grew up in the projects, where guys went from girl to girl and had multiple babies, like my boy Calhoun, real name Travis, who had two kids he rarely saw because he was always roaming the streets, chasing dirty money and pussy or in jail. Time and time again, I pondered over both his and my situation. Calhoun grew up on the west side of Long Beach, CA too, but not in the Springdales. He had a mom and dad. You couldn't get more normal than his family. Calhoun's dad worked a nine-to-five as a school superintendent. His mother stopped teaching to stay at home and raise Calhoun. Despite the upbringing Calhoun had, he joined a gang, smoked weed like it was going out of style, and sometimes sherm. Calhoun's father tried to be that ideal father to him, the kind of father I had always craved. Calhoun never listened. He dropped out of high school in tenth grade and had been in and out of jail for things like selling drugs to beating up his baby mamas, and refusing to pay child support. He was an all-around fuckup. A few years ago, he talked his parents into paying off his child-support debt and when they loaned him the money, instead of paying off the debt he went and bought two bricks of cocaine that somebody robbed his dumb ass for.

I, on the other hand, had bigger plans for my life. I didn't have a problem settling down, I just wanted to make sure I was financially set. While I was sure Toi was the one, I was willing to marry her once everything in my life was in the order I wanted it in. The last thing I wanted was to bring a baby into the world and not be able to give him everything that meant quality time as well as a stable, functional home. I wanted to be a father in every sense of the word *father*. That was something I didn't have growing up. The last thing I wanted was to have to struggle and for my child to see me struggle. If Toi would just be a little more patient, I saw myself proposing to her in another year. By that time my business should be a go. I had been taking additional business classes and learned how to draft my own business plan. My plan was to open up a computer repair store.

I spied Calhoun sitting on my porch, puffing on something as I turned walked toward my house.

I sniffed and knew it was some weed.

He hopped off my porch and walked up to me.

I ignored him as he raised his free fist to give me a pound.

"What I tell you about smoking that shit near or at my house?"

"My bad. You wanna hit it before I put it out, dawg?"

"No." My job tested us for weed religiously. And the last thing I needed was to get caught up. And the funny part was it seemed that they always randomly tested all the brothas.

He smirked and wet the tip of his joint with his tongue and slipped it behind his right ear, and asked, "Aye man, what you getting into tonight?" For the life of me I couldn't understand why Calhoun of all the things chose to be a gangsta. Yeah, he was a big dude like me, with the same height, complexion, and build. Some people would say that he could pass as my brother. But I was a lot more handsome and the nigga hated on me about it and was always calling me a pretty boy. I couldn't help it cause all his front teeth were gone from all the times niggas done knocked him out for running his mouth. Or he looked aged past his years from dope and that street life. They say that's what a wild life will do to you.

"Sleep." I jogged up my steps. I had worked a sixteen-hour shift the day before and came right back at my normal time which was around 3:00 P.M. I was tired. But I never turned down overtime. Now all I wanted to do was get something good to eat, pop an Ambien, and get some sleep. I could hang out Saturday. It was only Friday. And when I did hang it wasn't going to be with Calhoun unless his ass was sober and not on any type of crime sprees.

I had loyalty to Calhoun only because we pretty much grew up together. When we were younger, he was always in the Springdales visiting his cousin Paul, who was two years year older than us but in a wheelchair. Paul and his mom lived right next door to me. Paul's mother was Calhoun's dad's younger sister. So Paul was always running with me and Calhoun, always trying to keep up in his wheelchair. And yeah, Paul couldn't walk but he could roll with the punches. We

did all kinds of shit together, stuff that you would expect young boys to do but with a little more edge to it. If
boys our age were pulling up girls' skirts, Calhoun and
I were smacking their asses after Paul rolled by in his
wheelchair and pulled their skirts or dresses up. When
niggas was stealing candy from the store, we thought
smarter: We would sell candy for the Boy Scouts and
then lie and say some bigger dudes robbed us. But
instead we took the money and bought skateboards.
When niggas our age played hide and go get it, we were
actually getting the pussy while Paul was the lookout. A
couple times, we even talked the girls into letting Paul
stick a finger in their young pussy. See, Paul couldn't
fuck, something wasn't right down there and he sure
as fuck didn't want to talk about it. Sometimes I wondered if he even had a dick; I was always too scared to
ask. But he was satisfied with us getting some.

We ran the lot we lived in and ran the other niggas
our age off. They answered to us. And yeah, Paul was
in a wheelchair but he was definitely with the business.
Whenever we had a disagreement, we fought it out
amongst each other, Paul included. To be fair, depend-
ing on which one of us had the problem, if it was with
Paul, we got on our knees so that we were the same
height as his wheelchair and we got down. Whoever
the winner was what they said was how it was going
to be. Truthfully we all got down. I beat Calhoun's ass,
Paul and I tied, and Paul packed Calhoun out. Calhoun
didn't come around for a few days after Paul gave him
a whipping. But when he did get over it and came back
around, it was just like it used to be. Our relationship
had its benefits. Calhoun couldn't fight worth a damn
so when he got into it with boys in the Springdales, I

was always there to jump in and pack the dude Calhoun was fighting out. Paul would lean over his wheelchair and throw a couple punches in too. When I didn't have decent shoes and clothes because my mama struggled with money, Calhoun would hook me up. Paul's mama got Social Security for him so he always looked fresh. And Paul was nothing nice in his wheelchair, he could pop wheelies and do the same tricks we did. One day we built a skateboard ramp and Paul wasn't even scared to jump off that shit!

I remember one day we thought we had lost Paul for good. Calhoun and I had gone to the grocery store happy as hell because Calhoun had came to me and said he had got forty dollars in food stamps from this crackhead for only ten bucks. Before we left, we went looking for Paul but he was nowhere to be found so we went to the store without him.

Calhoun wanted to buy liquor. I talked him out of it because I knew my mama would kick my ass. So instead we bought Hot Pockets, candy, ice cream, cupcakes (the good kind, Hostess), and bottles of Mountain Dew. We planned on eating everything with Paul.

Once we left the store, we walked back to the Springdales, quickly and full of excitement. Funny thing was I knew why I was excited about the goodies we had but not why Calhoun was excited. Calhoun had shit like this all the time.

As we turned to corner to the Springdales, a girl who lived in my lot rushed up to us.

She was breathing hard and her eyes were wide. "Aye! Paul got hit by a car and I think he's dead!"

"What?" we screamed in unison.

"The ambulance is at the Springdales!"

Instantly tears started falling from our eyes as we rushed back to the Springdales, crying all the way.

Chapter 2

The front of the building was blocked off. Calhoun and I both sobbed uncontrollably as we though our friend was being wheeled out on a stretcher.

The bag I was holding slipped from my hand. Calhoun tossed his bag on the ground with anger.

"This is some fucking bullshit!" he said between sniffles.

I couldn't talk, I was sobbing too hard. I instantly thought about all the good times we had all had. Things would never be the same. I knew it. I closed my eyes as hot tears spilled from them. Paul was only fourteen and was dead?

Then out of nowhere someone tapped me on my back, saying, "What happened?"

I jumped and turned to see Paul behind me.

"Aww! Nigga! We thought that was you!" I exclaimed.

"Yeah, man!" Calhoun yelled, "Where you been?"

"I went to the doctor with my mama today."

We both leaped on top of his wheelchair and started punching him, happy our friend wasn't dead.

But it turned out our good times didn't last long before we were hit with the real tragedy. Spinabifida, the disease he was born with that caused him not to walk, took his life a couple months later. Calhoun and I never got over it. Calhoun and I were never the same. Things were never the same and our fun was never the fun it used to be.

Back then Calhoun and I were inseparable. We still had a close relationship but I couldn't lie and say that the bad choices that Calhoun made didn't disappoint me. I grew up, he never did. Truthfully, I didn't have many male friends because I didn't have time to be dealing with hate or no nigga being thirsty in regards to what I had. Jealously was not just reserved for women.

I half listened to Calhoun as he went on the subject of stuff I cared very little about. Finally I told him, "I'm going to sleep."

He looked at me like I was crazy. "Sleep? It's Friday. What the fuck you going to sleep for?"

When I didn't answer, he said, "Come on."

I grabbed they keys and inserted it in the lock. "I don't have your kind of fun. You, for some reason, keep walking around acting like they can't lock your black ass up again."

He waved me off. "Man, you sound like my pops. I don't need to hear this shit."

"Well, you should listen to it." I pushed open my door.

"Man, I just wanna go ride, get some pussy."

"I'm good on that." I walked inside while Calhoun followed after me.

Chapter 3

I turned around just in time to see Calhoun shake his head at me. "You still stuck on Toi. I don't blame you, though. That bitch got a—"

I grabbed Calhoun by his neck. "Don't use that language in my house. You know my mom lives here and don't call my girl out her name. You gonna make me fuck you up," I whispered.

He pulled away from me. "Sorry, man. But you know a nigga saw her first."

I ignored him on that shit.

I dropped my stuff on my leather sectional. "Ma, you home?" The smell of cooked food wafting into the living room made my stomach grumble. I eyed a sexy painting of Toi on my wall. She was completely nude with a while silk sheath covering her private parts. The only other things that were on my walls was a picture of my mother I had blown up, pictures of Toi. There was also an painting I bought years ago with an African woman holding a basket of tomatoes in one hand and the hand of her son in the other.

"I'm in the kitchen, Chance."

I walked to the kitchen to see what my mama was cooking. She was mixing a pot on the stove.

"Hey boys," she said to us. "Chance, I made some pork chops, rice, gravy, and some cabbage with hot water cornbread. Y'all want me to fix you two a plate?"

My mama had me at the age of twenty. She was now forty-two and could easily pass for someone in their thirties. But that is usually how black women were. That "black don't crack" shit was true. My mom was dark skin with full lips and an oval-shaped face. She always had her long hair pulled back into a ponytail and simple clothes like sweat suits that always covered her body. While I took my dad's light brown complexion, strong jawline, height, and build. I was six-foot-three and had always been a big dude. I had well-toned arms and was blessed with a six-pack I tried to maintain by working out four times a week. My silky, curly hair, light brown eyes, full lips, and my set of dimples all came from my mama. I wore my hair in a set of natural curls and sported a goatee. I didn't have a problem favoring my mother more than my father. To me my mama was the prettiest woman in the world. Often other men took notice of her beauty too. A couple times I had to slap Calhoun upside his head for lusting on my mother. And even though she wasn't aging on the outside, she was on the inside. Years of stress affected my mama's health. She had high blood pressure and had already had two strokes. That's why I was trying to take as much stress off of her as I could.

I kissed her on her cheek. "Naw, Mama, I'll get it."

"Okay, well, everything is ready." She grabbed a towel and wiped her hands on it. As she walked away she stopped and said, "Before I forget, Toi called and said to call her back, that it was important."

I chuckled as my mom walked away. I frowned at my friend. "You want a plate, man?"

"You know I do."

"Come on."

I scooped two pork chops with dark brown gravy and onions, white rice and cabbage with bacon onto a plate—

one for Calhoun and one for me. I topped them off with hot watered corn bread.

We both sat down at the kitchen table to dig in the food.

My mom came back in the room. "Well, that's my ride, baby."

"Where you going, Mama?" Calhoun asked jokingly.

"Me and one of my friends are going down to Pechanga to do a little gambling."

"I need to be going with you, na'mean?" he joked.

She chuckled but said nothing else. She was never really social with Calhoun. I thought it was because he was always a nuisance and posed as a bad influence on me. When I was a kid his dad was always knocking on our door and yanking Calhoun to his car and telling my mother to keep me away from Calhoun, like I was the bad influence. It didn't matter what his father said, Calhoun always came back. His father lived to regret those words later on when while I was graduating from college, Calhoun was in jail yet again.

I swallowed the food in my mouth. "You need some money?" I asked.

"No. I got my quarters I been saving for the past couple months."

"How you expect to gamble with only quarters?" Calhoun asked.

My mom ignored him. So did I.

I reached in my wallet and grabbed two hundred-dollar bills and handed them to her. "Have fun, Ma."

"I will. I'll be back on Sunday." She pecked my cheek and was out the door.

"Play the nickel machines for me!" Calhoun joked.

I got up, grabbed two cups and filled them with some cranberry juice I had in the fridge.

I sat a cup in front of him and downed the juice in mine.

Calhoun, out of nowhere, started chuckling. "Aye remember that time we broke into Fred Sanford's house?"

I chuckled, thinking back to that day.

Christmas had just passed and my mom worked crazy hours to have a surprise for me under the Christmas tree: a bike. I was happy as hell to have one and made sure I took extra care of it. Calhoun had already lost two bikes and was on his third one. His father told him that if that one came up missing, he wouldn't replace it. During that time, a lot of kids' bikes in the Springdales were coming up missing. And no one could figure out who was taking them. Then finally it was discovered that a dude who stayed in the house across the street from the Springdales would drive around and if he saw a bike outside he would get out his beat-up old truck, hobble to the bike, grab it, put in the back of his truck, and drive away. So I made sure that I kept my bike with me at all times. I always had an eerie feeling when I saw him driving around the neighborhood. My bike meant something to me and I knew my mom got this not only for Christmas but because she saw how much Paul's death had affected me.

One day Calhoun was over my house and all we had to snack on was a bag of ninety-nine-cent Fritos. It was the end of the month so food was always scarce in my house around this time. Calhoun only had a dollar left from his allowance so we grabbed the bag of Fritos and we rode our bikes to the local store that sold chili-cheese nachos. But instead of paying three dollars for them, we gave the store our Fritos and had them put cheese and chili on them. For a dollar they did it with no problem.

We grubbed them down quickly.

I paused my eating, watched Calhoun, and said, "You probably got all kinds of snacks at home."

Calhoun didn't respond, just kept smacking. It was just something about this hood life that he liked. I didn't get it at all.

As we rode our bikes back to the Springdales, my stomach started bubbling like I had to take a shit. I looked to see if maybe Calhoun was having the same problem as me. And sure enough, he was clutching his stomach too.

"I gotta shit," I said.

"Me too. They must have gave us some fucking bad chili!" Calhoun yelled.

We pedaled as fast as we could back to Springdales and without thinking threw our bikes down out front and raced inside my house to use the bathroom.

I sat on my toilet and let loose while Calhoun banged on the door. When liquid shit wouldn't stop pouring from me, Calhoun gave up and I figured he went next door to his aunt's house to shit.

When we came back outside our bikes were gone.

I sat on my porch trying not to cry while Calhoun paced in front of me.

"I know that muthafucka got our bikes, man."

I didn't say anything.

"My daddy said if I lost this bike he's not going to buy me another one."

I nodded. "My mama can't afford to buy me another one if she wanted to."

He slapped his hand into the palm of his other hand. "Fuck that! We need to get our bikes back."

"How we gonna do that? You know he ain't gonna admit he took 'em."

"We need to get inside his house somehow."

So over the next few days we watched that man. We named him Fred Sanford because everyday, when he came home that's what he watched on TV. He didn't even watch the news. My mama said everyone should watch the news.

He didn't.

We always watched him from his bedroom window. He left every morning at seven-thirty. Every morning. Probably to go to other cities and look for other bikes to steal with his thieving old ass. Our plan was to gain access to his house from that window.

But it never failed: When he was on his way out, he always closed the window.

That is until one day when he was running late.

We watched it all through some expensive binoculars Calhoun took from his dad. We were upstairs in my bedroom window.

"Are my fucking eyes deceiving me?" Calhoun asked.

We could see him backing out of his driveway. Usually he let that piece of shit warm up. Not today.

Calhoun shoved the binoculars to the right. That's when we saw it. He left his bedroom window open.

We rushed out of my house, snuck to the backside of his house, hopped over his fence, and crept into his backyard. Good thing he ain't had no dog or we would have been fucked.

As soon as we stepped foot in that man's house my nose was hit with the funkiest of smells. I glanced at his TV that had Fred Sanford on. Fred was doing that "Elizabeth" line he always did. I chuckled, then pulled my T-shirt over my face so it covered my nose as we walked around the bedroom. He had shit everywhere. You could barely walk in the room from all the boxes and papers, plates with food on them, dirty cups and shit, dirty clothes. I scanned the room, disgusted at all the roaches that crawled on the walls. His closet door had a chair pushed upside it and the top of the chair was hooked under the doorknob. I started to open it but when a rat sped past my feet, I rushed to the living room. Calhoun was already ahead of me. This fool had stacks of bikes all over his house, mine and Calhoun along with a lot of other kids, even bikes that belonged to girls. *What a sucka.*

"Yo. He's a rotten muthafucka," Calhoun said.

"Yep," I responded as I looked all around his living room.

He even had skateboards. *What the fuck did he plan on doing with all that shit?* I thought.

He had toys that kids probably left outside like scooters, trucks, play swords and guns, girls' baby dolls and Barbie dolls.

Calhoun came back from the kitchen with four trash bags and we loaded them up with as many toys as we could.

When we were done, we were sweating.

We crept back to the bedroom, planning on going back out the window. But then we figured we couldn't get our bikes out the window, so we were going to have out the front door.

We paused in front of the closet door.

"What you think he has in there?" I asked Calhoun.

He shrugged, sat his two bags down, and tugged at the chair until it gave way.

Then I grabbed the doorknob and opened the door.

Suddenly something flew out of the closet, screeching.

"What the fuck is that!" Calhoun yelled.

Calhoun and I dropped to the floor as a fucking monkey went crazy in the bedroom, flying all around, grabbing shit and throwing it at us, from the plates and cups to clothes and boxes, he was going wild in the room.

"Come on!" I grabbed the bags one at a time and tossed them out the door with the bikes.

Calhoun was crouched in a corner, terrified.

"Come on, man!" I pulled him up and we rushed out of the room while the monkey continued to go crazy.

"Yeah, that mess was crazy." Images of the monkey flew in my head. I added, "Your bitch ass was shook by that monkey."

Calhoun shoved a piece of corn bread in his mouth and said, "Yeah, whatever nigga."

I finished up the last of my food.

"So you really don't wanna go anywhere, huh?"

"I already told you."

"Can I hold some money then?"

"The last thing you should ever ask me for is money. You could be making your own money if you wasn't so fucking lazy."

"Here you fucking go."

What I was referring to was the fact that I had tried to get Calhoun a job where I worked. But his dumb ass went crazy on the interviewer, saying, "I don't give a fuck what y'all say. I'm not working on my fucking birthday and if any white muthafucka ever ask me to clean some shit up I'm gonna blow this muthafucka up!"

"Come on, Chance. That would be some racist shit if I was cleaning up for the white man. After my ancestors did it for free."

"You have no problem doing it when you get locked up," I reminded him. And truthfully, Calhoun was a disgrace to our ancestors.

"Whatever, man."

"Yeah, whatever Calhuon. I love you but you gotta get your shit together, if not for yourself but for your kids."

He waved a hand at me.

I stood from the table. "Whatever. I'm going to sleep. Lock the door on your way out."

I pulled out my cell phone and dialed Toi's number while placing my plate in the sink.

"What?" she snapped.

"Mom said you called. What's so important, baby?" I walked out of the kitchen, ignoring Calhoun as he continued to beg me.

"I'm busy. Never mind." She hung up in my face.

I chuckled again. She was with that bullshit again. I went upstairs to get some much-needed rest. I wouldn't mine getting some from Toi but I didn't have time for all her games and drama. She had so much that it was to the point that now I simply laughed it off instead of getting annoyed. I loved her and wasn't going nowhere so I'd have to put up with it until I put a ring on her finger.

Chapter 4

I replayed that night in my head every five minutes as I sat in my cell at Twin Towers Correctional Facility. That was the last thing that I had done. It had been total of two weeks since my arraignment, where they threw that life sentence at me. I was scared out of my mind and didn't know what to do or what to say. I felt like any wrong move could cost me everything.

When the guard came to my cell he told me that I had a visit.

I took a deep breath and stood as my cell slid open. I was sure it was my mother. The thing I was surprised about was the fact that I hadn't heard from Toi in two weeks, but I had spoken to my mom almost every night since I had been there. Now was not the time for Toi to avoid me. I needed her now more than ever to get me through this shit. Even though I hadn't heard from Toi I was hoping she showed up today.

I smiled despite myself, despite the situation, and could see the worry on my mama's face when I made it to the booth where she was already seated and staring at me through the glass. No Toi. It made me feel defeated. I prayed she wasn't taking steps back from me because of my predicament. I wondered where she was and what she was doing. I hoped this didn't have her down. I hoped she wasn't with another man. But I had never ever caught Toi cheating on me. I knew she was loyal as any good woman could be. It had to be fear of losing her man to a prison term. Still, she should be here with my mother today.

The moment I sat down, her lips started trembling and tears slipped from her eyes down her face.

I tried to be strong and keep a calm face. "Aye. Don't do that, Ma." I wished I could come from behind this glass wall and give her a hug, but I knew I couldn't.

"I can't help it, Chance. They got you in here like you're some type of animal."

My mom had done everything she could to get me out of there. When she came back from Pechanga and got my collect call she rushed to the police station and told them I had nothing to do with this. The thing was, her words held no weight because she wasn't with me the night I supposedly murdered this officer. Her words held no real power as far as the powers that be were concerned. There was also no bail for me so she couldn't post. I was stuck there. But she was able to get me an attorney that I had met with a few days ago. I told him everything I knew about this case. And just that meeting cost me six hundred dollars. Crazy. That was my mother's savings. But one thing he did tell me was that the case sounded like bullshit and it would be thrown out.

"Did the attorney ask for any more money?"

"Another thousand to represent you on your court date. I'll get it to him."

"I'll give it back to you, Mama. I got it in my account but I just can't get to that sum of money. They don't let me get that much out the ATM and they won't let you withdraw money out of my account unless you are on my account."

"No worries, baby."

I looked away.

"I still don't understand how this could have happened."

I didn't either.

"And you go back to court tomorrow." She took a deep breath. "Seems so fast."

I nodded.

"Something is going to have to give, Chance. They can't lock an innocent man up. This gotta be some mistake."

"It's a mistake, Mama. But in reality you and I both know that they lock innocent men up all the time."

She closed her eyes briefly.

Instantly I regretted saying that. I was supposed to be making her feel better, not worse.

"Who knows, Mama, maybe they will see that this is a mistake and believe me when I say that night that man was murdered, I was in bed asleep and nowhere near him. Let's hope."

I leaned forward and covered my face with both my hands as the thought of spending the rest of my life behind bars hit me. My life would be over and I would lose everything that I had worked hard for. Why did this have to happen to me?

"Hey. Listen to me."

I took my hand off my face that was now watery with my tears.

"No matter how this plays out, we will get through it. You know that, right?"

I nodded.

"And no matter where this goes you gotta know that I'm gonna be in your corner, Chance."

I offered her the best smile that I could, which looked more like I was clinching my teeth than anything.

"I love you, Ma."

Just then Calhoun walked up and sat down next to my mother.

"Well, I'll let you talk to your friend."

"What's up, man?" he asked me, looking as worried as my mother.

"Can't call this shit, man." So far Calhoun had visited me about three times since I had been locked up. Every time he came he would tell me how this was some bullshit and that they had to let me out. It was crazy that he had come to a place he hated for me and Toi had not bothered to come once.

"Yo. I keep telling you that this is bullshit, man, and they're going to let you up out of here."

"Then why you look so worried?"

"Because it kills me to see you up in this muthafucka, Chance. If anybody don't deserve to be here, it's you."

"Thanks, man."

"I wish I can put some money on your books but a nigga short right now. But I'm trying to get a barbeque together so we can raise money for that lawyer of yours."

"Thanks, man."

Truth was, I wasn't concerned about money. I had money in my savings and my money market account, not an enormous amount but some. But I knew the thing that I needed was an alibi and not enough money in the world could give me that. Yes, I was home but who could testify to that? If only I had went out with Calhoun that night when he asked me to. I wouldn't be in this. I'd have someone to testify that I was with them.

"You seen Toi?"

"Naw, man, why?"

"I'm worried, that's why. She has not come to visit me and I'm unable to call her crib."

"Shit, man." Calhoun looked behind him and then back at me. "A woman is the least of your problems right now, man. Forget about her. If she can't show you any type of support then fuck her ass!"

I didn't respond and wondered where all the anger came from. But then I figured he was just mad that Toi had not come to see me.

Before I could respond, the guards came back, announcing visiting was over and flashing their lights. I quickly stood and got into the line the other inmates had formed.

I wished that I had taken the time to ask my mother or Calhoun to call Toi. Even though I tried to convince myself that it was fear that was keeping her away, it was still making me angry and hurt that she didn't make any type of effort to contact me. I mean, if I was the man who she loved why wasn't she being here for me like I was always there for her? We had been together far too long for her to just ignore me.

Chapter Five

My stomach was in knots as the attorney my mom had hired, Richard Brown, questioned me about where I was the night of the murder. I thought I had done okay. I mean, I told the truth as I knew it. But something about the district attorney made me feel like some shit was coming my way that I wouldn't be able to handle.

He clapped his hands while approaching me. "Wow. You are pretty impressive, Mr. Wallace."

The smile on his face was so tight I knew it was fake.

I licked my lips nervously and took a deep breath. I wanted to be prepared for whatever he threw at me. I didn't want my voice to crack, I didn't want to pause or to stutter on the stand.

"But I'm here to prove today that you are a murderer. Mr. Wallace, I'm not going to take up too much of your time. I am here simply to enter something into evidence: Two things that tie this man to the murder, cut and dry. Two things." He held two fingers up to the jurors.

He sat a big poster card on a wooden stand that looked like an easel for all in the court room to view. It was a photograph of my truck.

"Sir, is this vehicle registered to you?"

My eyes scanned the license plate. "Yes."

"Your Honor, I would like to enter into evidence a copy of the registration for this car, which shows

Chance Isaiah Wallace owns it. I would also like to enter the forensic report."

I wondered what was in the forensic report.

He approached the judge and passed his file to him. The judge reviewed it and nodded.

The DA spoke to the jury like he was giving a lecture at a university.

"Ladies and gentlemen, what the report states and it states it clearly is that the vehicle on that poster board that is in fact registered to the defendant had blood on the passenger seat. That was later tested and it was confirmed that the blood was that of Devin Johnson."

My heart sunk when he said that. I looked at my lawyer, lost. He looked lost too and remained silent. How in the fuck was blood in my car? That was some bizarre shit. The last place I had gone was to the gym. No one else had been in my car. The DA had to be lying about that shit.

I looked at my mother, who I knew wanted to break down but it seemed she tried to keep a straight face for me even though her lips trembled. I did not know what to say.

It turns out I didn't have to say anything.

"No further questions, your Honor."

I was told to step down from the witness stand. I stood and walked back to the chair next to my attorney and sat down.

They then questioned my mother. I scanned the faces in the courtroom. Calhoun was sitting with his face in his hands. I had suggested to my lawyer that Calhoun testify to being with me that night but he had two things working against him. One, the murder occurred at 2:00 A.M. That was way after Calhoun had left my house. And two, Calhoun was a felon so my lawyer didn't think any testimony from him would be credible.

No Toi.

My lawyer questioned my mother. "So tell me about your son, Ms. Wallace."

My mom smiled and looked at me. "He is the best son a mother could ever want. He has never been in trouble with the law. He finished college, has a good job, and is buying his own house now. He has always been a respectful kid." She added, "And he is trying to open up his own business.

"And where do you currently live?"

"I live with my son."

"Ms. Wallace, did your son commit this murder?"

"No and I put my life on it! My son wouldn't do anything like that. He has his whole life to look forward to. You see, he has no rap sheet. It is not in him to kill anybody. That night my son was in bed, asleep. You got the wrong man! It is not Chance. The murderer is out there and you're wasting time now trying to blame my son for the murder. Please let my son go!"

"No further questions, Your Honor."

That's when the DA went in on my mother.

"Ms. Wallace. You appear to be a loving mother. But in all my years as an attorney, the one thing I always learned is that no one is always as they appear to be. When you sit in that chair you give a representation of who you are and it is my job to become well acquainted with who you *really* are."

He slapped a manila folder in his hand. "And as I became more acquainted with you, I discovered, Ms. Wallace, that you are not as wholesome as you appear." His voice was stern like he was her fucking parent.

I narrowed my eyes at the DA, wondering what he was talking about.

"I have a couple questions for you, madam. You can confirm them by simply saying yes or no."

He cleared his throat and opened up the file.

"In 1980 were you not arrested for prostitution ten times?"

My eyes got wide.

My mother closed her eyes with shame. "Yes. I made some mistakes in my life—"

"In 1981, weren't you arrested for stealing?"

"They were diapers for my son!"

"Answer the question, Ms. Wallace!"

"Yes."

"And when your son was two years old, was he not taken out of your custody because you were arrested yet again for having drugs in your house?"

"But the charges were dropped for a plea bargain."

"Your Honor, can you please tell the witness to simply answer yes or no."

"Yes or no, Ms. Wallace?" the judge snapped.

"Yes."

"Ms Wallace. Do you even know who the father of your son is?" the DA asked.

Her head dropped. "No."

I gasped before I could catch myself.

The judge's eyes passed over me.

My mother turned to me and whispered, "I'm sorry."

I looked away quickly. I wanted to know why she lied to me about who my father was. I wanted to know who my father was! But I had to put that in the back of my mind and revisit it at a later time because my freedom was on the line.

"So Ms. Wallace, I guess what I'm trying to determine is what makes you a credible witness." He leaned all up in my mother's face.

"Where were you on March fifth, 2003?"

"I—I." She took a deep breath. "I was in Temecula at the Pechanga Casino."

The DA chuckled. "Then you are wasting taxpayers' time and money. You are not even a reliable witness. You're a criminal! An ex-prostitute and drug dealer. Nor can you verify an alibi for Mr. Wallace. No further questions, Your Honor."

Chapter 6

I could not stand to look at my mother as he ripped her apart. Truth be told, despite what he said about my mother and regardless if it was true or not, I wanted to beat his ass for upsetting her.

The judge instructed the courtroom to break for lunch and said we would resume in an hour.

It was the longest hour of my life.

Once the hour passed and we were back in the courtroom, I wondered what else the DA had up his sleeve.

"Your Honor, the state calls Ron Jasper to take the stand," the DA said.

I watched a man I had never seen before walk to the stand. Still, I scanned his face for any type of recognition from his neatly braided cornrows to his tall stature. Still, I didn't know this man and I wondered what he could have to say about me, why he was called to the stand and trial, and why he was really here.

He had to put his hand up the way my mother and I had to and promise to tell the whole truth and nothing but the truth. Then the punk-ass DA got started.

"Sir, state your name for the courts."

"Ronald Jasper."

"Do you know that men in front of you?"

"Yes, I do."

I narrowed my eyes at his lying ass. I had never seen him before this day!

"How are you acquainted with him?"

"We do licks together."

I bit my bottom lip to keep from shouting out.

"Sir. Could you explain to the people in the courtroom what a lick is?"

"In other words, we rob people."

"You lying muthafucka." I hissed. My eyes bored into his.

He was unaffected.

"Counsel, control your client," the judge fired at my lawyer.

"You's a lying muthafucka!" Calhoun yelled, raising up from his seat.

The judge slammed down his gavel. "Settle down!" I ignored my lawyer, who told me to be quiet. It was now making sense. The bullshit about the blood wasn't bullshit. I was being set up.

"I see." The DA had a hand under his chin.

"Can you tell me what happened March fifth, 2003?"

"Me and Chance needed something to get into. We was casing the Liquor Bank in LA 'cause it was Friday night. We saw this dude step out of an X5 BMW, it had rims and shit. We figured he had to have some ends on him and he had a nice Rolex. So we figured his crib gotta be just as nice."

"I got a nice truck and a nice crib. Why would I need to rob someone else?" I demanded, my hands in the air.

The judge hit his gavel again. "Mr. Wallace, I suggest you keep your mouth shut," he warned, locking eyes with mine.

I gritted my teeth and shook my head angrily. This man was lying on me.

"So we followed him to his house. We bust in with the burner. We asked him for his dough. At first the dude acted like he was going to give it up. But as he pulled out his wallet, he tried to be slick and instead of handing it to me the dude dropped it to the floor. I made a move to snatch it. That's when Chance yelled for the dude to get out of his pants pocket. He saw the dude reach in his pocket for something else. Chance thought he was going for a gun so he blasted away."

The DA stood with his arms crossed behind his back and nodded. "I see. Now, sir, what did he do with the gun?"

"I don't know. He never told me."

"You lying muthafucka. I didn't kill nobody and I have never seen you before!" I jumped to my feet and tried to rush after him but I was easily caught by two guards. I struggled against them both. "Get off of me."

Their hold on me tightened.

Ron winked at me.

Why the fuck didn't they all see that?

I tried to get to him but couldn't. "You fucking with my freedom. I'm gonna kill *you*. Lying-ass nigga!"

"Remove him from the courtroom!" the judge yelled.

"We the jury find the defendant, Chance Isaiah Wallace, guilty of second-degree murder of Devin Johnson."

After I heard the word *guilty*, I think I stopped listening.

I turned a deaf ear on the judge as he gave me the time I was about to serve. I grew numb inside. I couldn't stop my hands from shaking, I couldn't look at my mother, even though hearing her shrill scream brought my ears back alive.

"I don't know what to say at this point. But we can still keep working on this case, Chance." That was my lawyer.

I turned my teary eyes on him. I could hear my heart pumping in my chest. I pulled my lips in and wanted to die right there in that courtroom. I would rather be that cop I was accused of killing, than be me and have this fate laid out to me.

"Please!" my mama screamed as two police tussled with her. "My son did not do this!"

She was ignored and refused to walk so she was dragged out.

"This is some bullshit! Chance! Chance!" That was Calhoun, who was dragged out the courtroom alongside my mother.

Everything moved slowly for me and I knew this was the start of time moving slow. I also knew that the life that I had carved out for myself was over.

And just like in the movie *American Me* the prison guard said, "Nobody talks while I talk. Y'all shut the fuck up."

They shipped me from Twin Towers to Delano State Prison.

All around me all the men talked. I just kept to myself, didn't make eye contact with anyone, and kept my mouth closed.

I did the routine just as the other inmates did. I stripped naked, opened my mouth, raised my hands, lifted my balls, spread my butt cheeks wide, crouched down, and coughed. All while having several equally naked men in front of me do the same thing under the watchful eyes of the correction officers supervising us.

Then we were done. I spent the next four hours waiting in reception for them to find me a cell, after taking all sorts of tests.

I blocked out everything that was going on around me and those words, *twenty years to life* replayed over and over in my head. Part of me wished I had done something different but I didn't know what. I guess I thought this trial would play itself out and they would have to figure out—they would have to—that this person, this murderer, it wasn't me. But they never did. With all the dudes around me, I tried not to tear up again. But what man wouldn't break down and cry after hearing they would be spending the rest of their life behind bars for some shit they were no part of? I didn't even know Ron Jasper and I couldn't understand why he would get on that stand and lie on me. I had to have been set up plain and simple, by him and Lord knows who else. But why?

I was told that I could be in reception for a couple months. But it seemed like a matter a days I was sent to my bed. It was probably because of the severity of the crime.

My cell was on the second tier. I was escorted to my cell by another prison guard.

The guard didn't say much, but simply told me that I had the top bunk.

I stepped inside when the cell door slid open. It closed quickly. I looked around. It was so small. I didn't know how another man and I were going to be able to share it. There was a shelf on the wall and a thin sheet covered the tiny area the toilet sat in. I turned away and I sat my blanket roll on the top bunk, feeling like every man in there was watching me through the cell bars.

"Get the fuck away from my bed, nigga, for you get fucked up!"

I paused and turned around slowly, not knowing if I would have to fight this dude.

When I made eye contact with him, he surprised me by laughing. "I'm just fucking with you."

He stepped closer to me and held out his hand. "What's happening? They call me Tyson."

I didn't even know if I should even be talking to this dude. I inspected him quickly. He was short, light skin with tats up and down his arms. A torn shirt was wrapped around his head. And while he seemed cool, I didn't know whether to trust him or not. He could be a murderer. He could be a rapist. Point-blank, I didn't know the man. So I didn't plan on getting all friendly with him. But I told him my name.

"Chance," I said in a hoarse voice.

I shook his hand and looked down at the floor.

"I sleep on the bottom," he told me.

I nodded blankly. Then I leaped on the top bunk.

How was I going to manage to be in here with all these men? Truth be told, I didn't understand how someone could live day by day in something like this. My situation reminded me of that movie I saw called *Hurricane* about that man who was falsely accused of murder and in jail for years and years. I never thought the same shit would ever happen to me, not in a million years. This is a corrupt-ass world.

While all these people are out there killing innocent people, children are getting sexually abused, women are getting raped and beat, and here I am locked up for some shit I didn't do! I wanted to take my fist and punch it through a fucking wall. Or better yet, punch that DA and the judge for falsely putting me here. The shit they did to me should be illegal. *They* should be in fucking jail.

"Man, why you so quiet?"

I ignored him.

"Lets go over some rules in here. I mean, if we gonna get along, we gotta establish some rules. Rule number one: I'm not gay so don't even think about pushing up on me."

I shook my head. "I'm not gay either."

"Do you plan on ever changing the team you play for?"

He leaned his head over the edge of his bed so I could see him from on top of my bed.

I shook my head. "Naw."

"Rule number two: What's mine is mine, period. Don't fuck with my shit."

I nodded.

"Rule number three: Don't bring no illegal shit in here. That includes dope, pruno, lighters, weapons, and cell phones. I'm scheduled to meet with the committee next year and I'm trying to go home. I done already lost ten years of my life in here so that means I can't have no dirt on me. I've been squeaky clean since I been here and ain't no celly going to dirty me up."

I started to ask him what he did and see if maybe he could give me any type of advice on what I could do about my situation.

"Oh, and don't bring no punks in here."

"Huh?" I was confused.

"A gay dude. I do not care how much he look likes a real bitch. Fuck them somewhere else."

"Hey, man. I'm said I'm not gay." I was already tired of hearing his voice when I had so much other shit on my mind.

"And when you take a shit. You drop one turd, flush and repeat, that way our cell won't smell like shit. You got any questions for me as far as prison politics?"

I knew I should have asked to protect myself, but I didn't.

"No."

He chuckled. "I guess you want to learn the hard way."

I shrugged. I didn't want to learn nothing except that this was a bad dream and that I would wake up from the shit and go back to my normal life. Go to my job, come home, kiss my mama on her cheek, eat some of her good cooking, take my girl shopping, fuck my girl, sleep in my own bed, shit in my own toilet, and do the same thing all over again the next day. That's all I wanted.

When it was time for dinner, I followed Tyson as our cell door was mechanically opened. We fell in line with other prisoners. I didn't really know what to do, so I just copied what Tyson did. I felt eyes all on me as I walked in the line. Although I didn't put my head down in fear, I made eye contact with no one.

When we got to what they called the mess hall I picked up my tray and walked the serving line, getting my food. My face remained expressionless and when I did make eye contact with an inmate they would mean mug me, like I had really done something wrong to them.

"Keep moving," the guards said.

As I reached the edge of the serving line, a Hispanic man next to me tapped my tray.

I was confused as to what he wanted but the Hispanic man next to him said, "He wants your corn bread."

I took it off my tray and handed it to him.

I wasn't able to sit anywhere near Tyson and for the first time since I had been there and met him I wished that I could, cause he was the only familiar face and if he was next to me it would ease my comfort level somewhat. Growing up in Springdales I was never considered a punk. I knew how to handle my business when it came to fighting. But I didn't think I was built to handle this: prison. This shit was probably going to be the end of me.

I stared down at my tray that consisted of a slim amount of what looked like chili beans, some string beans, and a square of Jell-O and two pieces of bread. It was a far fucking cry from smothered pork chops, oxtail stew, enchiladas, jambalaya, lasagna, and curry chicken my mama used to cook for me

Damn, I hoped my mama was okay and I hoped she was not sitting, stressing over me. But I knew she probably was. What mother wouldn't?

Regardless of what was on the tray, it could have been some lobster. I wasn't hungry so it wouldn't have tasted good to me, not with all the stress I was dealing with. The last thing I wanted to do was eat. However, I knew that I had to put on a front with the other prisoners so I picked up my spoon and began to scoop some of the chili beans in my mouth. I didn't taste them and they felt heavy on my tongue. I chewed a few times and fought the urge to spit the shit back onto the tray. Instead, I attempted to swallow, which was hard when I had a lump in the back of my throat. After a few tries, I was able to get it down. Guards walked back and forth around us while we ate.

We were not given much time to eat the food. I gave up on the chili and ate the piece of Jell-O.

That's when dinner was called, whether you were done or not.

We all went back to our cells.

I climbed on top of my bed in silence. Just as I managed to get on top, I almost fell when I saw six black dudes crowd around our cell.

The tallest one said in a raspy voice, "Get the fuck of that bed, nigga, and come here."

I looked down, thinking they were talking about Tyson.

"You, muthafucka!" He pointed a finger at me.

I slid off the bed and stood so I was facing him. Like I said, I never considered myself to be a punk but something about six big black niggas in front of my cell had me shook. The main dude had three teardrops that were darkened in and trailed down his face.

"Aye man. Don't be giving them fucking Mexicans no food!"

At first I didn't know what he was talking about. Then I remembered at dinner how I had given a guy some corn bread on the serving line.

"I didn't want it and he asked for it. I didn't think it was a big deal." I didn't even think anyone was paying attention to what I did on the serving line. But I guess they were. That meant I had to watch my every move while I was there.

"I don't give a fuck what he asked for! And it is a big deal. You young and dumb but you need to learn the ethics of jail, or you gonna get yourself killed." He pointed a finger toward the ground while saying, "In here it's us against them."

I nodded my head at what he said. But to be honest, I didn't have a problem with Hispanics. But I had to be smart and listen to what he was saying. I wasn't home anymore. I wasn't free. The rules out there didn't apply in here.

"Next time a Mexican or white boy or anybody that ain't black ask you for something you tell them hell no. And if they got a problem with it you fuck they ass up! We'll worry about the rest. You ain't home no more, nigga. Welcome to the muthafucking jungle."

I nodded. *Hell realized* is what I wanted to call it. Maybe hell was even better than this. I couldn't imagine anything being worse. I had to get out.

"Take it to your cells!" a guard yelled.

The dudes all walked away.

Chapter 7

Sure enough, the next morning when I was passing through the serving line I was given scrambled eggs, two slices of bread, and some oatmeal.

A different dude tapped on my tray. He was Hispanic.

I glanced his way quickly and shook my head. I went to my table, sat down and started eating some of my eggs. Eating was still a struggle for me. But I knew I had to keep face in here.

I was about to put my spoon in my oatmeal when I paused, seeing the same dude that had asked for my eggs standing over me.

Out of nowhere, he stuck his finger in my oatmeal.

"What the fuck you doing?" I demanded.

The man made a *tsk* sound.

All eyes were now on him and I. Before I could make another move the dude rushed me. I flew from the metal bench from the impact and to the floor. The man got on top of me and started throwing punches. I used all the strength that I had and managed to flip him onto his back. I straddled him with my body and socked him square in the jaw. He grunted and tried to throw another punch. I ducked.

He used that as an opportunity to get me off of him.

Once he had me off of him, we both rushed to our feet. I had one fist balled and the other wide open waiting to catch one of his fists and crack him with my free hand.

I did just that, grasping his wrist and cracking him square in his face again.

There was cheering going on around the mess hall.

That's when I zeroed in on the officers who were yelling for us to stop and drop to the floor.

But if the other man wasn't going to stop, then I wasn't.

And he wasn't.

Even though he had no wins with me. And he knew it.

I was grabbing every punch and giving him one every time. His face was bloody and he was stumbling around and shaking his head weakly.

I knew I had to do this.

And if they got a problem with it you fuck they ass up!

Somebody grabbed me by the back of my shirt. It knocked me off balance and I fell to the floor. At first I thought it was one of the guards but it was an Hispanic inmate. The dude I was fighting spit in my face. The saliva splattered in my eye, making me temporarily blind for the moment.

That's when I felt his nails rake down my face. It started stinging .

Blood trickled in my eye.

I was blinking rapidly to get my eyesight back. But I still wasn't going to let this dude beat me.

I grabbed him by his neck and continued to work on him like my life depended on it.

I punched him over and over again, taking all the aggression I had inside of me out on him for fucking with me.

I gave him fist after fist after fist, breathing rapidly as I did until all he could do was lay in a heap, breathing hard.

That's when the guards finally grabbed us both and led us away.

The hole was even smaller than my actual cell. I didn't really care, though.

I was in that room all day until they let me out for an hour of exercise and that hour felt like five minutes. But even then, I was still in an enclosed space that looked like a cage.

Shortly after rec, I was sent back to solitary and a guard came to my door.

He stepped in the room and closed the door.

"You know who I am?"

"No."

I had seen him before. He was a stocky black dude with a bald cut. He had to be about six-feet-four. He was dark-skinned with a hawk's nose. His two front teeth were gold.

"I'm Roscoe. When we one-on-one you can call me Roscoe. When we with the other inmates and my peers, you call me sir. And today is your lucky day."

"Oh yeah? How is that?" I didn't have anymore more lucky days. I knew that as sure as the sun was shining.

His voice was husky. "Listen up," he told me. "You supposed to stay in here for a week for that shit you pulled in the mess hall."

What shit did I pull? I was attacked. But I didn't bother telling him this. I doubt he gave a damn.

"I can get you out today along with some money on your books."

I couldn't care less about having money on my books. And I also figured that whatever he wanted me to do it wouldn't be anything legal, else why would he come to solitary to tell me? Why would he need to speak to me in private?

My silence prompted him to continue. But I wished that he wouldn't.

"I can drop it by here and when you get released back into regular pop, you can sell it in here for me."

"Sell what?"

"Dope."

"You serious?"

"You stupid muthafucka! I read your file. You know how long you gonna be in here? For life. It's best you make some friends while you in here. And it's best you make friends with me."

It sounded like a threat more than anything.

I took a deep breath.

"Nigga, you shot a cop. The fact that you didn't get the death sentence is only 'cause you shot a black cop."

"I ain't killed nobody."

"Yeah? You probably didn't. But it don't matter. You gonna pay like you did. You know how many niggas are in here for some shit they didn't do? You know how long? All they fucking life. And you can forget about that appeal bullshit. It takes them forever to even re-spond and when they do it is denied. I done seen it happen enough to know. So fuck that keep-hope-alive. This is it for you. The only alive you gonna see is behind these fucking walls. You might as well make the best of it. And this is the best place to sling. I make a killing in here, man. Niggas in here depressed and shit about being away from their family. Niggas wondering who fucking their girl. They can't fuck. The only release they get is looking at the female guards and jacking off or fucking these *punks* in here. Then they gotta deal with how that shit makes them feel. Their form of therapy is getting high. So you need to go on and get on my team, dawg."

Deep down in the core of me, that shit he said was exactly how I felt. I did feel my life was over and whatever life I fucking had left, I felt like I was going to be spending it here. But I wasn't going to do a muthafucking thing for his crooked ass.

"I'm not slinging your shit."

"Come again?"

"You heard—"

Suddenly he took his baton and slammed it into my stomach.

I couldn't breathe for a minute. I fell onto my side and resisted the urge of fucking him up. It was just me and him in there anyway.

But I didn't. I just stayed on my side and inhaled a ragged breath.

"You stupid muthafucka. You just fucked up. Now! You on my bad side."

He left the room, closed and locked it back.

Chapter 8

It turned out that I didn't spend a week in solitary. Instead, due to a rat biting I ended up with an infection that caused a high fever. I spent nearly two weeks in the infirmary, which was the medical unit.

I was then sent back to my cell.

I figured there was no reason to act fucked up toward Tyson anymore. He wasn't the reason why I was there, and he didn't do anything to me.

So when he held out a fist for me to dap, I dapped.

He went over the politics of jail. The dos and the basic don'ts. I listened to what he had to say. I figured for someone who had been in there for ten years he knew what to do to survive.

"Hey man, you fucked dude up for disrespecting you during breakfast," he said, cracking up laughing.

I gave a small smile. "I did what I had to do. I can't have everybody else thinking I'm soft and testing me too."

"Right. Right. I like the way you think. I'm for sure getting out this place." He was doing push-ups as we talked. I was sitting on my bunk.

"What did you do?"

I paused. I knew that question was coming. Do I tell him or not? Would he look at me differently? Would he be too scared to be in the same cell with me? So instead of telling him I asked, "Man, what did you do?"

"Assault with a deadly weapon."

"What was the deadly weapon?"

He paused on his push-ups to show me his two fists. "My hands. And I tried to beat the muthafucka to death with them."

I blew out some air. "Why?"

I thought he was a probably just another gangbanger messing with people for no good reason like my dumb-ass friend Calhoun, or maybe he was just a reckless fool. But his words surprised me.

He stopped doing his push-ups and sat on the floor.

"Some sick muthafucka took my baby. My baby sister, Mia. He straddled her and forced her to go down on him while he went down on her. Then he penetrated her like she was a woman. He sodomized her." He shook his head. "There wasn't much left of my baby sister when that sick muthafucka got through with her. When he was done taking her innocence, he strangled her to death. Every time I think about it, I wanna break out of this bitch and go after his sick, twisted ass again. I was trying to kill that muthafucka! But he got saved by the bell as far as I was concerned. The cops arrested me and his ass is lying in the hospital some fucking where in a coma. She was only six-years-old. She was the only family I had."

His eyes got watery.

"Why did they call your hands deadly weapons?" I asked curiously.

He stood and bounced around the room, making jabs with his fist. "'cause I was on the U.S. Olympic boxing team, baby!"

He bobbed and weaved in front of me. "How you think I got the name Tyson? I came out the pussy swinging!"

I laughed at the comment but didn't really believe he was telling the truth about being on the Olympic team.

"Before this shit I was the man, baby!"

"Now what?" I asked, suddenly believing him. We were in prison; why would he lie?

He stopped and stood facing me. "Now nothing. I'm in here. My dream of having a career as a boxer is over." I nodded.

"But I ain't gonna be in here forever. I'm gonna get out this bitch soon."

I didn't say anything. I wanted to ask him how he pulled that off. Maybe he didn't, maybe he had pretty much done all of his time. I told myself this 'cause I didn't want give myself any type of hope and then it gets shot down. So I was scared to even ask him his opinion about my situation. I didn't even wanna bring it up.

How I felt didn't stop him from asking, "What about you, homie? You feel comfortable telling me what you did?"

After what he just admitted to me, how could I not? "Murder."

"What? Why the fuck you kill somebody? They say the quiet niggas are the ones you gotta watch out for."

"I didn't. The shit don't make a bit of sense to me. One minute I'm living my life and the next the cops are busting in my house and are beating my ass. Then I'm in jail for murder. The icing on the cake is having a man I never seen before in my life, testify against me and say that I shot an officer I also ain't never seen before in my life."

"That is some crazy shit, man." He sat on his bed while saying, "What's even crazier is the fact that it has happened to so many men in here."

I nodded. That gave me hope that someone would believe me. But then his next sentence shot me right back down.

"You know what's even crazier?" he asked me.

"What?"

"That they are never freed. They end up dying in this bitch. Dying fucking innocent."

A few hours later, during rec, I thought back to Tyson's words in the cell: the prison politics. He said in prison the only people you are allowed to congregate with are those that look just like you: black men. If I was ever caught kicking it with a white, Asian or Hispanic, I would be considered a traitor and possibly killed. It went that way for the other races as well. I saw that segregation alive and well here. And it was here on the yard. Hell, I didn't want see it now but it was my reality.

But to be honest, I kind of wanted to stay separated from all of them and not be associated with anybody. So I tried to keep a low profile and keep myself isolated on the yard. I waved a hand at Tyson, who kept gesturing for me to come over to where he was with the blacks. The dudes that came to the cell and checked me about the corn bread were present in that group. And they kept glaring at me.

I started walking the track by myself, hoping I could clear what was left of my mind. I was surprised that I hadn't went crazy yet. I missed my mom and Toi. I still had not heard from Toi. I kept telling myself that she was probably dealing with the shock of her man going from being in her face to being behind bars. Because those other thoughts, like maybe she was done with me or moved on to another man, were sure to drive me crazy. I already had enough to worry about. I had to find a way to get myself out of this prison. I had to. That is what was keeping me going: Knowing I needed to come up with some way out.

I continued to walk on the track. I kept my distance from the other men walking on it. So when I heard some sets of feet walking behind me, I increased my speed.

They increased theirs also.

I tilted my head to the right slightly, to see who was walking behind me.

Shit. It was two big corn-fed-looking Hispanic dudes.

I closed my eyes briefly. I knew they were going to give me heat for the shit that went down in the mess hall. Some shit that wasn't my fault. I was just doing what the older dude who came to my cell had told me to do. But the more I thought about it, I knew that I was defending myself. I had a right to do that.

"You think you special, *mayata*? You trying to be a shot caller? Huh?"

I kept walking.

Another one said, "*Mayata*, don't you hear this man talking to you? You better fucking answer."

"My muthafucking name ain't *mayata*."

I knew what *mayata* meant. It meant "nigger" in Spanish and I sure as fuck wasn't responding to that here or nowhere else. And if I got jumped for that shit, hey, I'd just take one for the team.

"We don't give a fuck what your fucking name is. Just answer the fucking question."

"No, I don't think I'm special. And look, I don't need this shit. I ain't asked for no shit from none of y'all"

"Well, you got it."

Chapter 9

I took a deep breath and prepared myself for whatever was about to go down. I had no choice. I couldn't stop them from whatever they had planned. I kept my back to them.

"You should have just given up the oatmeal, homes, and it wouldn't have been a problem."

The blow came from nowhere and I found myself dropping to my knees.

More blows came to my head, making me feel lightheaded. I was body-slammed and held down by one while the other continued giving me blow after blow.

The ass-kicking they were giving me was similar to the one the police had given me in my house before I had gotten arrested.

My face was in the dust in the track and I was being stomped repeatedly.

I rolled over so that I was on my back and managed to grab one of the feet stomping me and knocked one of them off their balance.

The other dropped to his knees in front of me and attempted to strangle me. I knocked his hands away then I swung with all my might, cracking another one in the jaw. He flew back from the impact.

I stood to my feet weakly, hoping they were done.

But they still came for me.

I squinted my eyes and tried to see them, which was

hard 'cause they were kicking up dirt from the scuffling, which was landing right in my eyes, blinding me and making it hard for me to fight both of them back.

Before I could get to my feet, one guy held me down so the other one could fuck me up. He punched me in one of my eyes, making up for the lucky shot I was able to toss the one holding me down over my shoulders. Then I got the other one in his jaw.

Before I could move, a fist was then slammed into my neck. I flew to the ground from the impact.

They took that opportunity to both hold me down.

"Get the fuck off of me!"

My eyes got wide when one of them took out an object that was slim and sharp around the edges. I knew it had to be a shank. He clinched his teeth and aimed it toward my face. I struggled to get my arms free but couldn't. He took a slice at the side of my face under my right eye. I had never been cut before and the shit hurt like hell.

I bit my bottom lip to keep from crying out as he cut into my skin, leaving an open gash that started bleeding.

"Don't fuck with us, *mayata*," he warned. He spit in my face. Then he pulled the shank back and aimed it toward my chest.

That's when I heard this loud sound, almost like a siren, and officers yelling for us all to get down.

My arms were released and the dude that cut me slipped away.

I remained on the ground.

I watched as they pulled the two dudes away from me but left me there.

***

That fight sent me on another trip to the medical unit to treat the cut and the other bruises. The doctor said it would be a permanent scar. It wasn't that big but it was big enough for people to see and in the shape of a moon.

Tyson was on the toilet. I was surprised they didn't put me in solitary again. But it was determined that I was attacked.

"Man, they got you again."

I didn't say anything. I just got on my bunk and stared up at the ceiling, wondering if they would come for me again.

"All that shit that nigga said about *let them deal with the other shit* and none of y'all didn't do shit to help me."

"Nigga, I couldn't. You not riding with us. I would have got fucked up if I jumped in."

I sat up in the bed. "Who is *us*?" I demanded.

"The blacks. You turned your backs on us on the yard. When you decide to join us that's when you will get protected, but you keep walking around here like we your enemies. And word is that those southsiders are planning some shit. But then again, they always planning some shit. Remember, if you ever hear them say this sound, *sur*, it's on and you better be ready to fight, 'cause them southsiders will be coming for your black ass."

"Have you been in a riot before?"

He pulled the sheet back, stood a little off the toilet, and pulled up his shirt to show me a long scar across his chest. "Yes, a couple times, and in the last one I almost didn't make it out."

"Don't they try to break it up?" I was referring to the guards and the warden.

"They let us fight for a minute, then they do what they can to contain it. They throw tear gas and eventually move on to firing shots. But they are never able to contain it without calling in outside police. Just remember this: The riots are a double-edged sword. On one hand, if a man is coming for you, you have to protect yourself, but on the other hand you don't want it to look like you're a part of it. So get as far away from it as you can. "

I frowned and placed my hands behind my head.

Tyson flushed the toilet and went to the sink to wash his hands. "Look, I hate these prison politics just as much as you do. Matter a' fact, I acted just like you did when I first got here. I was pissed off that I was even in this bitch and said fuck the world. Eventually I had to realize that I couldn't make it in here alone. I came here when I was twenty. And now I'm thirty years old. And I feel like I may be getting a year older every year, but my mentality in a sense has never caught up with how old I am because I have no real living to show for the amount of time I've been on this earth because ten years of my living has been in here. Dawg, this is a fucked-up place to be. You're in the other version of hell. That's some crazy shit. Your life is always going to be a struggle while you're in here. I mean, that's if you want to stay alive."

Maybe dying wasn't a bad alternative to being in here, I thought.

He continued. "But following the prison politics is what kept me alive. You can't be a loner here. You're gonna have to pick a side. That's how it is. This shit is more like a game and the same common sense you use on the streets you gotta use in here. Where you from?"

"I'm no thug. I have never gangbanged but I lived in the Springdales."

"Fuck gangbanging I never gangbanged either. I don't care if you ain't never gangbanged. I ain't talking about that. It's about having *thug* in you."

He took a deep breath. "Put it like this. If you grew up in the projects and you made it out, you're a thug. If your mama raised you alone and you made something of yourself, you a thug. It's not about gangbanging or going around robbing people. It's about knowing how to survive with the bare minimum. It's always about having an edge to you that gets you out of bullshit. Being able to make a dollar out of fifteen cents. Making something out of nothing, man. And if you repressed that thug in you, you better let that shit come back out 'cause it's that thug in you that's going to keep you alive in here."

Before I could say anything else a guard came to our cell with a slip of paper and told me I had a visit.

Man, nothing felt better than seeing my mama's smiling face and being able to hug and touch her hands. It gave me a type of comfort that I really needed. That was the first time I had cracked a smile since I had been in this mess. It was good seeing Calhoun too, who was sitting next to my mama.

"What's up!" He stood and hugged me. I hugged him back.

When we both pulled away he said, "I'm gonna give y'all some privacy." He went and sat at a table over from us.

I then hugged my mother tightly and sat down across from her. "Hey Mama."

"Hey baby. I—"

"Before you get into it, don't bother. Whatever you told me and didn't tell me. Whatever you kept from me all those years, I know you had a good reason for it. I'm not mad at you, Mama. I love you."

Her shoulders shook and her eyes were watery. I could tell she was trying to save face and not cry in front of me. I was trying to do the same.

"How you holding up in here?"

"Good."

But even as I said this I watched her eyes pass over all the bruises on my face and even the cut that was under my eye.

She had her hands over her mouth. She took them away from her face and asked, "Who cut you, Chance?"

I shook my head. "Mama, don't worry about it. My focus is on getting out of here if I can. Any news on the lawyer?"

"Well, I spoke to Richard Brown. He agreed to still work the case but he needs more money, Chance."

"How much?"

"He asked for fifteen thousand up front."

"Damn," I mumbled. "That's a lot of money. Why so much?"

"Well, he said something 'bout this case going to take up a lot of his time because it is going to be hard to prove you are innocent, and if he is able to get you off he wants to be assured that he gets paid for his work."

"I have six Gs in savings, that's it. I don't know of another way to get some money." I knew my mama didn't have it. Neither did Toi. I wasn't going to even bother and ask Calhoun. In that moment I regretted always shelling out dough to Toi for her rent and bills. For the Gucci and Louis Vuitton bags, the vacations and last-minute getaways, the expensive jewelry I had bought her just because. If I hadn't done all these things I would have more money saved.

So I had to make a decision quickly to get the money.

"You can put the house up for sale."

I shook my head. "No, Mama. Then where you gonna live? I rest a little better knowing you got a roof over your head somewhere safe."

"Chance, if getting you out of here meant that I had to sleep in a cardboard box, I would."

"No, Mama."

"Listen. I can go get a room somewhere. Don't worry about me. We have to get you out of here. You don't belong in here. I already spoke to someone. And you know I don't like doing things without letting you know firsthand, but Toi agreed that selling the house was the best choice to make."

Just the mention of her name made my heart speed up. I had so many questions to ask my mama about her. Was she okay? Did she mention me? Did she still love me? Why no contact? Instead I asked, "Toi? Mama, how is she doing?"

"She said she is a little shaken up with all of this. But she is being so helpful with the paperwork, since she is better with this stuff than me. She agreed to be your power of attorney. You should be getting the papers in the mail soon. Just sign them and mail them back. She told me to give you her love and apologized for not coming to court and to visit you. But that girl has really been handling business."

Relief flooded through me. I gave a half smile. So my baby did still love me. 'cause I was starting to wonder if she still did because I was now locked up and couldn't be much of a man to her and couldn't do much for her like I used to do. I mean, I was her superman before I got locked up. And I didn't have a problem with it because she was my woman. But to know the she was out there fighting for her man restored so much faith in me.

"She said she can't see you in here, that it would break her. But she is on a mission like me, baby, to get you out of here."

My smile got wider.

"As soon as we find the buyer and we get the money, Chance, we are going to get it to the lawyer."

Despite what I felt about my mother not having guaranteed housing, I accepted what Toi and my mom were putting in place for me. "Thank you, Mama."

"Now give me some love."

We both stood and I pulled my mother in my arms. I didn't want to let her go. But I knew that I had to.

She pulled away, pecked my cheek, and walked to the other table where Calhoun was at.

Calhoun walked over and gave me a bear hug. I hugged him just as tight before us both sat down.

He stared at me, smiled, and shook his head. "Man, this shit is killing me."

"What?"

"Them having you up in this bitch."

"I can't figure out how a man I have never even met would testify against me. Calhoun, have you ever seen that man before?"

"No. Matter a' fact no one from the Springdales has even heard of his ass. Trust me, I been looking."

I felt good to hear that. Truth be told, when the blood was thrown into the mix, I doubted that people would believe I was innocent.

"But don't worry, Chance. There has to be a way out this shit."

I nodded. "Well, my baby Toi and my mama are working on getting the money so my lawyer can continue. I'm relieved because I thought Toi was cool on a nigga."

"Oh yeah?"

"Yeah. But my mama said she is on it for me and that she has been spending all her time trying to get me out of here."

He changed the subject. "Who the fuck cut you?"

I touched the scar of my face. "I got jumped by a couple dudes."

"What were they? Black? White? Mexican?"

"They were Mexican."

He nodded. "Get used to that and don't take it personal. Because what you gonna see that in here is modern-day segregation."

"Oh, I have. The shit is crazy. And the prison don't do shit about that."

"Prison? You mean the guards? They just as bad as the inmates—you gonna see! Man, I hope I never have to come back here. I'd rather die!"

I looked away.

"Naw, man, it's different for you. Listen to me, Chance. They are not going to keep you in here. They can't. You didn't do nothing wrong. It's just going to take some time to get you out of here. Just look at this shit like a little vacation."

I laughed despite myself. This shit would never be a vacation to me.

"Just don't think too serious about this shit. All you need to do is kick back, wait for that lawyer to do what he need to do, and you're gonna be good."

"You really think so?"

"Come on, man. We been boys for how long? The one thing I'm never going to do is bullshit you, man. Everything is going to be okay, Chance. There is no way they going to keep your squeaky-clean ass up in here. And I'll keep a watch over Toi while you wait."

"Boy, don't make me beat your ass," I joked. I knew he was joking. Calhoun would never betray me with Toi. With anything. He was a lot of bad, but he was my boy. Our bond was too strong.

"It's good to see you with that twinkle back in your eye. The last time I saw you lose your twinkle was when Paul died."

I nodded.

We chopped it up about what had been going on since I been in here. Calhoun gave me little tips on how to get by while being locked up in there. One thing was I was going to have to show them is that I could and would get down with anybody in there. He said eventually they would stop trying to test me, but that there was always someone on some racial shit and that it would have to be a part of my life now until I got out. I even told him about Tyson and how he had been in there for ten years.

"Keep your head low, dawg. Read and work out. Stay out of bullshit." Those were his last words to me and a promise to come back again to see me.

Chapter 10

When the guard ended our visit I didn't bother arguing like some of the other men did. The officer that had assaulted me, Roscoe, was also running visiting. The men didn't say anything smart to him.

As I got in the line my name was called.

It was Roscoe. "Aye. Your girl finer than a muthafucka, man."

I locked eyes with him, but refrained from anything extra except, "That's my mom."

"Damn, that bitch fine. What you white boys say? *Milf?*" he asked the white, bald officer next to him.

The white officer nodded.

"Yeah," Roscoe said. " She's a muthafucking *Milf*, man."

They both laughed.

I didn't respond, just looked the other way. I wanted to beat his ass for disrespecting my mom like that. But I didn't. He had the power. I didn't.

I knew that situation in solitary wasn't gonna be the last run-in with him.

Now I had a little shred because I knew Toi was working on selling the house. But another month had passed and I had not heard from her and she still had not visited me. This made me start to worry again.

My mom and Calhoun visited me religiously.

I had called my mama because I spent the night before worrying about the whole situation with Toi.

"Mom, are you sure Toi is still working on getting that money?"

"That's what she said. She said she had three buyers so far and that they were going to make a decision in the next few weeks."

I took a deep breath. That was good to know. But it wasn't all that was bothering me.

"It's not just that, Mama."

"What is it, Chance?"

"I know you my mama. But she is my girl. The woman I planned on marrying. It hurts me that she doesn't bother coming to see me."

"Jail is a horrible place. I can't blame her for not coming there."

"Mama, I don't. If she never visits me, I'm okay with that as long as I know she is still with me. I just don't want to feel like I'm losing her behind this shit. I don't want to feel like she is slowly distancing herself to be done with me for good."

"I understand, son."

"I write her letters and she doesn't bother to respond."

"Have you tried calling her?"

"No." I said, not wanting to explain my reason why I hadn't called, because it probably wouldn't make sense to my mama. See, the thing is I wasn't ready to let go. I needed to feel like my baby was still with me. And if I called her and she ended things with me, I don't know if I would be able to handle it. As much support as my mama and Calhoun gave me and the tight bond I had managed to form with Tyson, I needed to feel it from Toi. Pride is why I couldn't bring myself to call her.

"Toi has not told me anything different than what I told you."

"Yeah, but she showing me something different."

"It may just be in your head, Chance. You got so much going on right now you're probably not thinking straight."

I had gotten the power of attorney papers, signed them, and mailed them back. And still Toi had not contacted me.

"I tell you what, Chance. Hang up with me and give her a call. Call her, Chance, and let her tell you for herself whether or not she can do this. And if she can't, you're just going to have to accept that. And what I'll do is become your power of attorney. No need for her to do it if she don't plan on being a part of your life any more."

"Aye. Wallace."

I glanced at the guard Roscoe. He was fucking with me again.

"Hang the phone up, nigga. You ain't the only one who needs to use it."

"Mama, I gotta go."

"Call her, Chance."

"All right, Mama."

And regardless of the punk-ass guard rushing me off the phone, I couldn't bring myself to call Toi anyway.

I went back to my cell and chopped it up with Tyson instead, trying to keep my mind off of her.

Three days later I didn't have to worry anymore. I got a letter from Toi that made me feel so much better.

Hey baby,
Your mother said that I should write you so

I'm doing this now. I'm not too good at writing letters. But if I need to write one to put you at ease, baby, then that's what I need to do. First of all . . . Are you crazy? Of course I'm still with you! You my man, baby. I love you. Why would you even think I wouldn't be in your corner? That's what a woman does, they don't turn their back on their man when things get bad. They stick it out like a ride-or-die chick. And that is what I am, all day, everyday, baby. I haven't come to visit you because I have been busy dealing with this greedy-ass lawyer and selling the house. You don't belong in there, baby! So I hope this letter puts your mind at ease and gives you one less thing to worry about. I got you.

   Toi

   Oh. One other thing . . . I'm pregnant!

I couldn't help but crack a deep smile when I read that part.

"Tyson!" I held the letter in my hand in the air. "My girl wrote me and she's pregnant!"

Tyson paused on his bobbing and weaving, took the letter from me and scanned the paper. He laughed. "Congratulations, my nigga!"

"Thanks, man."

We slapped fist.

"I bet that gives you something to look forward to, huh?"

I chuckled. "Yeah, my baby didn't quit on me after all. She's in my corner and to know that I'm about to be a father is the best feeling in the world."

"Seems like everything is going to work out for you."

I got on my bunk and nodded. I was the happiest I had been since I had gotten there.

Tyson stood by my bed as I talked. "At first I thought she had given up on me. You know. I mean, I'm in prison. That's enough to scare any woman. I should have known better."

"How long have you been with her?"

"Three years. I've never cheated on her and I have always treated her well. I'm talking about taking her out to eat once a week, sending flowers to her job, getting her hair and nails and feet done. That's my baby." I chuckled. "Matter a' fact, she really doesn't have to work. I pay pretty much all her bills, anyway. I moved her out of the projects. And when she has my baby she is not going to have to work."

"Well, shit, that's why she ain't going nowhere. You can't get any better than that." He held his arms out.

I nodded.

"But don't you think you spoiled her?"

"Spoiled her? Hell, yeah! She's my woman. My queen. I wouldn't have the shit no other way." I licked my lips and said, "I'm gonna marry her one day."

"What makes her worth marrying?" he asked.

It was a question I had never been asked before.

I shrugged. "I love her."

"Yeah, but it has to be more than that." He swallowed and said, "How is she qualified to be your wife?"

Before I could answer, he said, "Don't get me wrong. Sounds like a good woman you got there, based on her being by your side and all." He waved his hand as if he wanted me to disregard his question.

"How did you meet her?"

I chuckled and thought back to the day I had met Toi. It was spring break and I was trying to have fun so I rolled with Calhoun, who had borrowed his mother's car. We were only driving through the Springdales.

We were trying to look like we had dough, but we didn't have shit.

That's when I saw a big, firm ass and sexy thighs that instantly had me drooling. I was praying her face looked just as fine as her body did.

Not taking my eyes off of her, I told Calhoun, "Aye. Get baby attention for me."

He was eyeballing her too. "For you?"

"Yeah."

Calhoun honked the horn at her and yelled out the window of the car, "Aye baby? What it do?"

She turned around, looked at him, giggled, and walked up to the car. She was fine as hell with mocha brown skin, dimples, and a gap in her teeth. Her hair was slicked in a ponytail. She was wearing a pair of shorts and a pink tank top with some flip-flops.

Before I could lean over and tell her to come to the passenger side, Calhoun cock blocked.

"What's your name, baby?"

"Toi."

"Well, my name Calhoun. Let me take you out and wine and dine you, baby."

I was fuming in my seat.

"Oh, you gonna wine and dine me?"

"Yeah, baby. Where you wanna go?"

"Red Lobster. Can you hang with that?" That's when she finally looked my way. She paused for a second before turning her attention back on Calhoun. But her eyes came my way again.

"Yeah, I can hang with that cause I'm a real nigga. Now, what's your number?"

She told him her digits and Calhoun put them in his phone. "You didn't give me no fake shit, did you?"

"No!"

"Umm- hmm." He dialed her number.

We heard a phone ring. "See. I told you that's my real number," she said, giggling. She pulled her phone off of her hip and pressed a button on it, silencing Calhoun's call.

"Well, you know how y'all females do."

"Shit, you know how y'all niggas do. If you ain't got money to take me out don't even bother calling."

Her eyes locked with mine one more time before she walked away.

"Ha!" Calhoun winked at me.

Didn't matter though, I had put the number in my cell phone too so I ignored him.

When I got to my mom's house later on, I called her.

The first thing she said was, "Aye. Calhoun. You got another bitch? 'Cause some girl is calling my phone and cursing at me!"

I chuckled. Calhoun had two kids by two different women. He had his first kid at fifteen and his other at seventeen. Both lived in Springdales so it was no telling who was calling her. One of them had probably got his cell phone and was calling the numbers in it.

"Listen. I'm not Calhoun. Let me tell you who I am."

She was silent for a moment. "Oh. 'Cause he's been calling me from different numbers so I thought it was him. And some bitch has been blocking her number and calling my phone."

So I laid it on thick and some would say I hated on my homie. But I saw her first and plus what would Calhoun do with her besides get her all caught up in his baby mama drama and hurt her? I was the better pick. I would do right by her.

I wanted her. So I got her.

Next time I saw Calhoun, I told him, "Aye remember baby we swooped up on a couple weeks ago?"

"Yeah man, the redbone with the big ass?"

He was messing with so many chicks he had her mixed up with someone else.

"No, this one was dark skin. Her name was Toi. That's all me. I got that on lock. So take her number out of your phone."

Calhoun was quiet for a moment I guess trying to remember who Toi was. When he did, he looked at me like he wanted to whip my ass.

"I saw her first, nigga," I said. Then playfully, I rushed him and we ended up falling in the grass outside my mama's apartment.

Calhoun was pissed at first and yelled, "Get the fuck off of me." I kept fucking with him by throwing jabs at his upper body. We had never let women come between us. So eventually he laughed and tried to twist me up on the grass. But he ended up twisted up like a pretzel.

Tyson broke me out of my thoughts.

"If she were a celebrity, who would she look like?" he asked, all into my story like Toi was standing in front of him.

"I would say she looks like Trina, but darker and thicker."

"Damn! Thicker than Trina? She sounds like a winner, dude. You better keep her."

"She would have been a fool to pick that nigga over me. I love my boy and all but he ain't no good to women, he just ain't."

That initial conversation with Toi led to a date, the date led to us being inseparable ever since. She made the right choice.

Reminiscing about her had me feeling so good that when they let us out for rec, the first place I went was over to the pay phones. Not wanting to make her phone bill sky-high, I called my mama and had her call Toi on the three-way. I had to hear my baby's voice.

As the phone rang, all I thought to myself was what a good woman I had. I couldn't wait to hear her sweet voice.

About three rings the phone clicked on. Just as I anticipated hearing Toi say hello, I almost dropped the phone when a male's deep, husky voice said, "Yeah?"

Without thinking, I slammed the phone down.

Chapter 11

If that shit wasn't enough to kill how happy and hopeful I had been feeling over the past couple months, the fact that she would no longer take any more of my mother's calls had us both worried. Especially since my mom had said that the house had been sold and Toi was now power of attorney. Although she had promised my mother she would drop the money off to the lawyer so that he could resume my case, Toi never did. In fact, she was weeks past the day she was supposed to drop it off. Without the money, my lawyer refused to do anything to help me further with my case. My mother went to Toi's apartment to talk to her and the manager said that she had moved. Calhoun said he had not seen her either. As stupid as this may sound, my main concern was for her safety and the baby's. I prayed that they were okay. Calhoun blamed it on the pregnancy and said women were fucking psychos when they were carrying a child and not to trip. I tried not to but I started to feel that there was more to it. I got that *more* on a surprise visit.

Regular visits were on Saturdays and Sundays. My mom only came on Sundays because she had to work the rest of the week. It was also expensive as hell for my mom to get out there. So I was surprised when I was told I had a visit on a Saturday.

When I saw Toi seated at the table, I couldn't help but smile because I hadn't seen her in four and a half months. She still looked as fine as ever. That was the weak part of me. That part of me that loved and lusted after my woman. The other part of me was curious as hell as to what was going on, why no one could get in contact with her. Why another man answered the phone at her house.

As I pulled the chair out, I demanded, "Baby, what the fuck is going on?"

She pursed her lips, but remained silent.

"My mama said you ain't returned her calls. She went to your apartment and they said you moved. You didn't take the money to the lawyer and when I tried to call you a—"

My words trailed off when a man I had never seen before sat down next to her.

I narrowed my eyes at him. He was tall and lanky, brown skin with a long ponytail, a long white T-shirt and some jeans. He looked like a thug. I didn't know why he sat down next to Toi.

I looked from him to her. "Who the fuck is this?"

Toi didn't respond.

"What's happening, blood, my name is—"

My eyes stayed on Toi but to him I said, "Muthafucka, I'm talking to my woman."

"I told you to wait for me outside!" she snapped at him. '

I was losing control but I tried to stay calm.

"Toi. Listen to me. You talking to a man that has lost everything but my mama and you. I'm fighting for my life, baby. A life I know I'm going to get back. I don't care how long it takes me. Don't do this shit to me. Tell this muthafucka to get on so we can talk about this. I'll get over look the fact that you brought his ass here. *Whoever he is*. I'll even overlook the fact that he was most likely the one in your crib answering your phone the other day. Just tell him."

My eyes pleaded with her.

I felt like I only had an inch to hold on to but I was trying. She was my baby and she was carrying my baby. That's all that mattered. If she was scared and ran to another man I could understand that and I could forgive her for it. But I couldn't lose her. Not now. I needed her love. I needed her help.

She wouldn't talk.

So he did.

"Since she ain't opening her muthafucking mouth, I guess I will. You been in here for a few months now and a woman has needs. I been taking care of those needs and I didn't come here to hear this crybaby shit, feel me? I'm just gonna tell you once and for all. My name is Keon and Toi is my woman now. She ain't your girl no more. She ain't gonna help you with no bullshit case that you ain't gonna beat anyway. Nigga, you guilty. Do your time. And you can't call the crib no more. She ain't going to see you so forget about that too. I got her on lock."

He wrapped his arms around her on that part, when he said he had her "on lock."

My expression was murderous as I took all of this in. What this nigga was telling me. What Toi wouldn't say.

I glared at him. "What about my baby?"

He laughed.

"I had an abortion, Chance," Toi finally said.

That was a tough blow to recover from.

I blinked to stop my eyes from watering.

"Bitch. You killed my baby?" I whispered

Keon chuckled. "Watch ya mouth, nephew. Only nigga that gets to call her a bitch is me."

I ignored him.

"Where's my money?"

"What money?" That was him.

Toi offered no explanation.

"So you just gonna keep my shit, Toi?"

She rolled her eyes to the ceiling.

I took a deep breath and shouted, "Toi!"

"She ain't—"

"Shut the fuck up! Toi, baby, listen to me. You killed my baby and you don't wanna be with me and you wanna be with this muthafucka. Fine. It hurts 'cause I love you, baby, and probably always will. But if you take that money you are killing any chance I have of getting out of here. Don't do that to me, baby. Give me my money," I pleaded.

"She ain't got shit."

"Toi?"

"Nigga." His teeth were clinched. "She gave it to me. I'm head of household now. And I bought some bricks with it."

Without thinking, I lunged over the table, toward the dude. Toi leaped from her chair and scurried away in fear.

The muthafucka had the nerve to laugh at me. Laugh at my anger, laugh at my pain.

I managed to get my arms around his neck and started choking the life out of him. I was then grabbed by two guards, who attempted to restrain me.

"You punk-ass muthafucka!" I yelled at the top of my lungs.

They pulled my hands from around his neck but not without a struggle.

As they tried to pull me away, I struggled against them and kicked at the table.

***

So this became my life.

Toi had done me so dirty. I thought for sure I was going to wake up to that being a bad dream. But I didn't. This was the reality of my situation. She didn't want me anymore and she didn't want my baby. Why she had to go further and take my money, I will never know. I just knew the shit hurt. All of it. She crushed me. I always thought that we had been together so long that I could trust her with my life. Despite myself, despite the pain and anger I felt, I still loved her. Even after what she did, part of me wanted to call or write her and beg her back, forgive her for seeing someone else and killing my baby. But I didn't. I simply attempted to let it go. Calhoun was pissed and said she never came back to the Springdales and that he had no clue where she had ran off to. My mother was lost when it came to her as well. I had to accept the fact that she fucked off my money. All of it.

Months sped by, adding a year to the four and a half months I had already done. In that time frame I had got down with so many dudes to prove myself that the shit was ridiculous. I learned new ways to fuck a nigga up, that's for sure. And I was dirty with my shit because I just didn't care. I was gonna fight you until I knocked your ass out and I was gonna leave some type of memory of my ass-whipping even if I had to rake your face with my nails or bite a piece of your skin. I didn't give a fuck. This was my way of surviving, becoming a monster, and that's what the fuck I was. It was hard for me even to face my mother. Other changes were the way I looked. I felt like I had aged some years. I had also gotten bigger, not for any type of look or attraction but because if I lost too much weight and got too skinny niggas would think they could take my asshole. So far that hadn't happened. That shit you see in the movies about niggas getting raped was true and I didn't want it to be me.

Racial tension was constant. The segregation and racial shit wasn't just reserved for the inmates. You saw the guards doing the shit too. The white guards looked out for the white inmates, you saw the Mexican guards looking out for the Mexican inmates, and you saw the black guards turning their back on the blacks. It was crazy. In here, race always mattered. Being in here, I learned that my life depended on who I congregated with 'cause niggas were always watching. Shanks were made here and drugs were being brought in here as well. They could take pretty much anything from the top of canned goods from the kitchen, the razors we used to shave, a paper clip, a fucking toothbrush, and make a shank. As far as the drugs, sometimes family and an inmate's women brought them in. We on the outside tend to think that the powers that be were smarter than the criminals. Being in prison, I saw that the criminals were always smarter and way more sophisticated. The game was always about watching which guards were smashers, which meant the staff was no-bullshit and would fuck your shit and your world up, the guards who were new booty, which meant they didn't know shit about shit when it came to prison, and the staff who were weak or just plain out didn't care. Half the time, guards brought the dope in. I knew for a fact that Roscoe had blacks, Mexicans, and whites slinging his dope for him in prison. Another crazy part of prison were the punks, which is what we called the openly gays that looked like actual women! What I thought was strange about them was their preference when it came to the inmates. They did not fuck each other; they went after the straight-looking men. Some of the female guards also carried on relationships with some of the inmates that went as far as letting the inmates fuck them.

Every time I turned around somebody was fighting. They even had those skinhead, Aryan Nation dudes in there and every time I passed one of them, they gave me a look like they wanted to shank me on sight. I gave their evil, hateful ass the same look.

In the time I had been there, I watched Tyson get into it with one of them and he fucked his ass up. The crazy part was that dude was way bigger than Tyson. Dude was so fucked-up from the hits Tyson was giving to him that he laid on down in the shower, knocked out. After the fight, whenever he saw Tyson he gave him a murderous look and called him a nigger. Guards always acted like they didn't hear it. Tyson did too. He never responded. He didn't want any trouble in there. Hell, he didn't want that fight that day, but it was more self-defense than anything. Tyson always tried to stay clear of prison bullshit. So did I.

After the fight, Tyson was stressing hard because any month he would have his appointment with the committee to determine if he would get released. He was scared that the fight would hurt those chances. He warned me not to ever let anyone know when you're getting released or they would "smoke your date." I didn't know what that meant so he told me. "They will start shit with you to get you to fight or they plant some shit on you so you don't go home. Sometimes they go as far as trying to force you to murk someone. Haters. So if I do get released I'm going to play that shit off like ain't nothing happened. And you gotta play along."

Tyson tried to get me to do stuff there to get my mind off my situation but I always said no. Much of my day was spent sleeping and working out; that was pretty much it. Working out had to be creative too 'cause prisons no longer had weights. I sometimes worked out with Tyson. We used out sheets and towels, rolled up our mats to work out. Those items worked like any good pair of weights. Jail taught you how to improvise damn near on your whole life.

Tyson did everything from working in the laundry room to going to church services, Bible study, and playing sports on the yard. When he wasn't doing these things he was in the library reading up on different legal stuff and bringing books back to our cell for us to read. I never did. But he was really pressing the issue of getting out of there. I didn't think I'd ever see light of day again. My pessimistic attitude didn't stop him from trying to get me involved in the stuff he did, like pushing me to file an appeal. With the fact that I no longer had money for a lawyer, I thought maybe that was a shot for me. But when my public pretender—whom I eventually begin to understand why so many inmates called their public defenders "public pretender"—finally answered my calls, he broke it down to me how appeals worked. According to him, you have to have some type of evidence that you are innocent that was not included into the first trial. I had none of that. He also warned me that it could take up to two years before an appeals lawyer even responded to me. He also said that the majority of appeals that are filed are denied. Still, I was going to push and try anyway. I wrote a four-page letter detailing my whole life, how I had never been in trouble with the law, how I was innocent and would be willing to take a lie-detector test. I even let Tyson read it. He tweaked some things and I submitted the letter. I told Tyson I had fears that it wouldn't be approved. He encouraged me to stay positive and not to listen to my public pretender: He worked for the system, not really for me. I listened to Tyson and disregarded the negative words of my public pretender.

One day Tyson even dragged me to Bible study.

"Today is your lucky day, nigga," he said.

"Why?" I asked him.

"The pastor brought his wife and she's doing her pen pal service again."

"What's that for?" I asked as we walked.

"Every year they pick about fifteen inmates. And members of her women's group at her church write us back and forth."

He was all excited, like that was such a big deal.

"Yeah, you making that face, but niggas in here would kill to know they had a person who was guaranteed to write them. And that ain't all!" He lowered his voice. "If you get one of them old bitches, they like to put money on your books. What I always tell you? Let that thug in you out!"

I laughed.

"Man. Last year I couldn't get on the list! I was pissed because that nigga Dey Dey had just got out the SHU and he happened to go to Bible study on the right day and the pastor's wife was there. Man, he had this lady writing his ass and putting two hundred dollars at a time on his books!"

Tyson imitated a lady's face with no teeth. "Here's some money to help you out, *baby*. The lord told me you needed some *zus-zus and wham-whams*."

I laughed again. Zus-zus and wham-whams was a term for different kinds of snacks.

"Chance, don't tell me you couldn't use a package in this bitch. I get tired of eating the same nasty shit. All I do is sit and think about all the times I wasted food and wished I could get that shit back now."

He was right. My mother was able to put a few dollars on my books, but not often. I used that money to buy myself stamps, paper, and envelopes. There was often very little for much else. Calhoun had been promising to put some money on my books, but I knew he was always broke so I didn't expect it. I just appreciated the fact that he was still coming to visit me and he would even write me.

"But you got juice with the guards," I told him. *Juice* meant that you had gotten on the prison guards' good side and they liked you as well as looked out for you.

"I don't fuck with them like that. I'll be respectful but that about it. I don't want them thinking I'm gonna tell them shit or do shit for them. Man, you know snitches get stitches!" He swung and softly connected with my chin.

I jabbed him in his stomach.

"Plus, it don't look good to the inmates when you chummy with the staff."

I nodded and followed behind him.

"Man, I want a fucking TV, some Pepperidge Farm cookies. And one of them hams!"

I cracked up laughing.

He went on. "I need some better shower shoes, nigga, some shea butter lotion, some books and CDs! We can get all that stuff."

I shook my head at him, skeptical. "They can't send that stuff to us."

"Chance, there's a website for all that shit! All the little old ladies have to do is order it for us and they ship it straight to the prison."

When we got to the room for Bible study. Tyson quickly sat down. I sat next to him.

The pastor, an older man tall in stature, stood next to this petite woman. She reminded me of Pam Grier. I may be young, but I watched old Pam Grier movies as a kid and even jacked off to them.

He looked good next to his wife. He was the same height and stature as me, with brown skin and a long beard. They were both graying, but I guess it didn't bother either of them.

"Now, gentlemen, I'm going to leave Bible studies over to my wife." He rubbed her back as he talked.

She smiled up at him.

They were in tune with each other.

It made me swallow and try to get the lump in my throat down. Seeing them together as the happy couple reminded me of Toi and what I wanted for us: To get married, have kids, and grow old together.

That wasn't going to happen anymore. Not with her, and from the looks of it not with anyone.

"Good evening, gentlemen."

"Evening, ma'am," we all repeated in unison.

"Shit, I'll take her," Tyson whispered. "She finer than a mufucka."

I jabbed him in his stomach with my elbow, lightly.

Once the prayer started he stopped messing around.

He even grabbed my hand in his. I could tell that even though he played around a lot, his faith wasn't a joke to him.

Once the prayer was done, the lady clasped her hands together and said, "Well, today is your lucky day, gentlemen. I have about fifteen spots open for my pen pal group." She went to a table and grabbed some pieces of paper and pencils.

"Now I'm going to give you paper and a pencil, so go ahead and write something about yourself. Please refrain from cursing or talking about sex, drugs or violence. I will review them and submit to the ladies of my charity group and you should be hearing from them shortly."

When she passed the paper to me I didn't know what to write. I sat and thought for a moment. Under normal circumstances, I would be proud to write about who I was. But now things were very different.

So I kept it brief. Tyson had a hell of a lot to write. I watch his pencil brush over the lines on the paper. He ended up with a whole page to my four lines. I simply put my name, age, and what I did before I was incarcerated. I figured there was no need for me to put what I was in jail for because it wasn't like we planned on meeting face-to-face or anything. And plus, whoever this lady was, she knew I was in jail and that I had broken a crime, supposedly. To tell the truth, I didn't really care about doing the shit, anyway.

"Okay, gentlemen. Time's up," she announced, clasping her hands together.

She went around collecting the papers. When she got to Tyson, she patted him on his back.

"And how are you this week, young man?" she asked, giving him a soft smile and taking his paper.

"I'm good, ma'am. Just hanging in there, reading the good word every chance I get."

He did read the Bible sometimes, but he was laying it on pretty thick.

Her smile got wider. "Well, it's good that you are always in such good spirits and that you study the Bible in your free time. A lot of men in here could learn from you."

She turned her attention to me and collected my paper. "You must be new to our study group."

I nodded. "Yes, ma'am."

"Well, I hope you come back. You might get something helpful out of it."

I nodded, although I didn't plan on coming back.

She counted all the papers and then counted the inmates.

"Oh, gentlemen, you know what I just noticed? We are one over. The limit is fifteen for my group." She looked over at me and offered another one of her smiles. "Since you're new and all to the group, you are going to have to wait for the next round. I don't have another pen pal right now."

I nodded.

Tyson snickered at me like I was really missing out on something and whispered, "Don't' worry. I'll share my zus-zus and wham-whams with you *baby*."

I held in my laugh as the pastor's wife spoke to me. "But I will keep your paper in case we get another person. I doubt it, though. The church members are busy with their own lives. It's a struggle to get the fifteen that I have now to help me out with this charity. But I try to remind them that if it were them behind these ugly walls day in and day out, it might bring some joy to their day to get a friendly letter from someone, even if you don't know them."

She grabbed her Bible and opened it up. "'Now today, gentlemen, we will be studying the Book of Job."

It was hard for me to focus on what she was saying. I always believed in God, but I couldn't understand how he could punish me this way. He took away everything that meant something to me. I was stuck in this hell. If this is not what God wanted for me, why didn't he put a stop to this?

Chapter 12

The next week I was rolling up my mat and getting ready to tie my sheet around it so I could work out. Tyson had finally got his meeting with the committee. When the guard came to escort him we played it off like it was nothing. On one hand, I was just as excited as he was that this day was finally here and they were going to either keep him or let him go. But on the other hand, I didn't want to lose Tyson.

He rushed into the cell. "Aye yo. Chance." He was out of breath and stood in front of me.

"What's up?"

He looked around at the other cells near us to make sure no one was listening or looking. But you never could really tell, they knew how to play their ear hustling shit off.

He sat on his bunk and tossed a paper to me with his eyebrows raised.

I nodded, unfolded the letter and scanned it, knowing Tyson didn't want the info on the letter being passed to anyone else. The letter showed that he was approved for a release from prison! I kept my face normal in case I was being watched.

Tyson had already told me the night before, "I don't want anyone else knowing but you, 'cause you my boy. Remember what I told you before. I'm not trying to have no niggas in here smoke my release date," he had whispered.

I nodded again and handed him the paper back. I simply stared at him, silently saying congratulations.

He got it.

"Thanks, man."

I looked down. I'm not gonna say I wasn't happy for him—I was—but damn, I would be stuck in here by myself and more importantly I would be stuck.

"Don't trip. You got good news coming soon."

I waved a hand at him and picked up my mat. I lifted it over my head, squatted, and lowered my tone. "I'm happy for you, man. I'm gonna miss you, but it's good you're getting out. I have to admit that sometimes I don't think it will ever be the same for me."

He stood and crossed his arms over his chest. "How you know?"

I squatted again. "I don't. I'm just saying how I feel more times than not."

"Your name is Chance, not God, dude. If I had that defeated type of attitude you have, I would never have tried to get out. I would still be here."

I blew air out of my nose and inhaled through my mouth.

He shook his head at me. It was clear I wasn't trying to hear what he was saying.

I squatted and lifted the mat in the air and held it for five seconds.

"Chance, if I ain't taught you nothing, you always remember this: You let somebody else tell you no. You don't tell yourself no."

"Yeah? What if they told you that you had twenty years?"

"Then I'd fight for twenty fucking years until they let me out."

"With life?"

"I'd fight for the rest of my fucking life if I was in here for some shit I didn't do. Fuck that, they would give me my life back. I wouldn't sit around and wait to die in here. I'd fight as long as I fucking could, Chance."

I sat the mat down and tried to catch my breath all while taking in what he was saying.

"I'm just saying, man. Try. You got so much to offer this jacked-up world. You don't belong in prison. They know it, so I don't even know why they sent you here. I could give a fuck what a witness said."

I laughed at that.

Guys had been leaving left and right for their visit. I wasn't expecting one and Tyson never got a visit, so we both were surprised when a guard gave me a piece of paper with my mother's name on it.

I cursed under my breath. I had told my mom the last time she came not to come back for another visit. It was a day I didn't like to think about. I had hurt my mother really badly.

It was the same week that Toi and her dude had come. Seeing my mother that Sunday was not something I was looking forward to and to make matters worse, that punk ass Roscoe was making all kinds of comments about my mother as I walked to the visiting room.

"Your mama single, Wallace?"

I ignored him.

"Come on nigga, you can tell me."

I didn't reply, just kept walking.

"Man, I sure wouldn't mind hitting that pussy."

I stopped walking. I balled my fist and clenched my teeth. I was going to turn and swing on that muthafucka. But just as I was, I though about going back to solitary and getting another charge.

He shoved me. "Walk, muthafucka!"

I unballed my fist and walked.

"What you think, your mammy too good for a nigga like me? Shit, I heard different. The guard that was there the day you got sentenced said she don't even know who your daddy is. And if that shit ain't embarrassing enough, the bitch used to sell her box."

I stopped walking and turned to face him.

When he saw my frowned-up face, his grin faded and he looked a little shook.

"Look, muthafucka. Keep my mama name out your mouth."

Then, as if he remembered that he was the one with the power, he pulled out his baton, put it against my throat, shoved me against a wall, and got all up in my face.

"Yeah, muthafucka? And if I don't, what the fuck you gonna do about it?"

I looked at him with hatred because I did hate his ass.

"Reality is you ain't shit, nigga. You ain't got power to do shit to me or anyone else. If I want to fuck, I'll take her ass in the bathroom, fuck her, and kick her out without a visit. You gonna learn not to fuck with me. You should have just sold that shit like I asked you to, then you wouldn't be having these problems. 'Cause one way or another you gonna sell the shit for me. And believe me, your problems are just starting with me."

He pressed the baton to my neck so hard that I was choking.

My eyes continued to lock with his as he held it there.

After a few seconds, another guard yelled, "Roscoe, you need some help over there?"

"Naw. I'm good."

He moved his baton from my neck and shoved me ahead of him. "Walk, nigga."

When I finally made it to where visiting was I didn't waste any time. I sat down quickly. Calhoun wasn't with her this time. I told my mom simply, "Don't come back here to see me, Mom. Pretend that your son is dead."

Alarm and hurt hit her face but I didn't sit there long enough to hear her response. I stood, pushed the chair in, and walked away toward the guard. Nevertheless, I could not get her hurt face out of my head.

It had been a while since I had seen her. During that time, Calhoun still came and told me that I needed to stop tripping and see my mother. But when I told him the situation he understood and said he would probably fuck the guard up if he had said something like that about his mother. "But you did good just shutting up. A lot of times you're going to have to let a lot of shit roll off your shoulders in here," he said. "And your mom. I'll talk to her and I'm sure she will understand."

"Thanks, man."

"No problem."

Not being able to see my mom was killing me. She had been writing me letters, though, as if nothing bad had transpired. In her letters she told me that she was still working for that elderly woman, Ellen as her in-home health care aide. Ellen and my mom had so much history that when she found out my mother was homeless, she let her stay in her house even though Ellen's daughter didn't approve. Ellen had a block on her phone, according to my mama. But my mama said she was going to get a cell phone and sign up for some type of private service where she could put money on her phone and I would be allowed to call her. As much as

I wanted to talk to her, I couldn't help but be bothered by the fact that my mother had to stay with the person she worked for. I appreciated Ellen opening her home to my mom, but at any moment she or her family could have a change of heart and throw my mother out on the street. Then where would she live? The guilt of my mama not really having a stable home killed me.

She said she was putting her checks away for my lawyer. But with her only making minimum wage and her not getting full-time hours I knew that wasn't a possibility. We were starting from a zero balance, because not only did Toi take the money for the house but she cleaned out my bank accounts.

"Just go see her," Tyson said, snapping me out of my trance.

I stared down at the paper with my mother's name on it and nodded to myself.

"And you know what? Roscoe's not here today."

"He's not?" I asked, surprised. He was not a staff known to miss work. I knew he always worked visiting so he could check out all the ladies that would be coming in. See, the thing was I did not want my mother to come anymore because I didn't know how long I could hold myself back from fucking Roscoe up for disrespecting my mother and making the comments he made about her. It was always a struggle for me not to put hands on him. The last run-in with him I came really close to knocking the shit out of him.

When I got to the table my mother was seated at I noticed how anxious and skinny she looked. I had to look away.

I sat across from her, still not giving her eye contact. "Mama, I told you not to come back—" My voice trailed off at the sight of her shaking hands on the table in front on me.

"We have to do this quickly, Chance," she whispered.

My eyes shot to her face. I narrowed my eyes at her and asked, "Do what?"

She looked around and slid her hand under the table.

"Mama, what are you doing?"

"Shh and do what I say. Slide your hands under the table," she instructed.

But before I could even move a finger, two guards rushed my mother like she was a man!

They leaped over the table and knocked her out of the chair.

She fell to backward, crashing hard on the floor. One more rushed over to us and they all crowded around my mother. She didn't move. She just lay in the spot they dropped her in and buried her face in her forearms.

One of the guards bent over and pulled her up by her hair.

"You muthafuckas ain't gotta handle her like that!" I yelled. "That's my fucking mama!" I was grabbed by three other guards before I could rush forward. Two secured both my forearms and the other hooked his hand around my throat.

"It's okay, Chance," she said, crying.

"Shut the fuck up!" the guard who grabbed her by her hair yelled.

She nodded and closed her eyes.

I watched tears fall from them and felt some slip from my eyes. Being helpless to stop them from doing my mother like that made me feel like shit.

Every time I moved the hand around my neck tightened.

"Don't fucking move," he whispered in my ear.

They twisted my mama's skinny arms up so tight I thought they were going to pop. Then they applied handcuffs.

The guard still had her ponytail from his tight grip.

"Get off of her!" I raged.

I struggled against the guards. "Y'all some dirty-ass muthafuckas!"

"Oh yeah?" one of them whispered.

"Yeah, you bitch . . . ass . . . muthafucka!" My voice got an octave louder with each word.

I tried to twist my body out of their grasp. That's when they tased me.

Chance,

How you doing baby? Listen. Don't worry about me. I'm okay. I just hope and pray that you are okay in there. I know what I'm about to say will get you upset which is why I almost don't want to tell you. But I'm sure you are wondering why I did what I did. I had been getting calls. I was surprised because I had never given the number out to anyone. The person calling started to threaten me. They told me that if I didn't bring the drugs into the prison that they were going to hurt you and they knew where I stayed. After all the stuff you have been going through I couldn't let nothing else happen to you in there. At first I ignored the calls then they started getting more frequent and then I couldn't sleep at night because when I did close my eyes, Chance, it never failed, I would have this nightmare about a man being stabbed. That man was you. Then that person started getting worse. He wouldn't give up.

So I realized I could not let anything bad happen to you on account of me not doing what he asked me to do. I am so sorry. Maybe I should have gone to the cops. I know with me in here I can't do much for you. Anyhow, I pleaded guilty and took a deal so the judge sentenced me to only four years. They said it could have been worse with my past and all. It's not so bad in here. I work at the prison on the cleaning crew and whatnot. You know me. My regret about all of this is that I'm no help to you. All of this is killing me to know you are still in there, Chance. Lord knows you don't deserve this hell. I'd gladly take your place if it meant you could come home. What I did was dumb. But I know why I did it. You are still alive so for me it was worth it. I love you and I hope you can write back. I'm not giving up hope. You are going to get out of there.
Ma

I needed to stop reading that letter. I did. All it did was heighten my anger.

They had my mama in jail like she was a fucking convict.

I took a deep breath.

"You good, Chance?"

I nodded at Tyson.

But I was far from good. My situation was getting worse and worse.

After the incident with my mother being arrested, I was given another charge that added five more years to my time.

"I know it's hard, man. I'm not going to bullshit you. So if you want to talk, I'm here. But I'm not going to press you to if you don't want to. My mother is dead.

But if she was alive and something like that happened to her, I probably would have killed somebody."

I believed him. At first, when he told me the story about being on the Olympic team, I didn't believe him. But after seeing him whip ass I knew he was telling the truth.

Still I didn't respond. Tyson was the only friend I had in the whole prison. I was now accepted with the blacks but to me it was like I accepted them. I didn't trust any of them. I only trusted Tyson and I didn't want to take my frustration out of him.

"Who do you think did that shit, man? Threatened her?"

I shrugged. "Could be anybody." Truth was, I didn't want to think about who did it. Not knowing would stop me from going after them. The image of the guards manhandling my mama popped in my head again. I wiped away a tear that escaped before anyone could see it. "One more day for me and I'm out this bitch, man!"

I tried to offer a smile but I couldn't bring myself to. Not just because of what was going on with my mother, but because by the next morning Tyson was getting out. Now we could safely discuss it. I was losing my only friend in there. Seems like time was going by so damn fast. But then again, why did I care whether time sped up? I was spending the rest of my life in there. The sinking feeling hit me again about my situation.

To clear my mind I started asking Tyson questions. "What's the first thing you going to do when you get out?"

His head snapped back and he narrowed his eyes. "You need to ask, nigga? The fuck you think? I'm going to get knee-deep in some gushy, mushy pussy."

He crouched down low with the words *gushy, mushy pussy*.

I was lying back on my bed while he stood near me doing dips.

Sex was something I didn't think about anymore. Jacking off with fee fees or fucking the punks were the only ways to bust a nut in here. Tyson and I always reverted to the fee fees, which was getting a sock or a torn-up rag or even a latex glove, putting it over our dicks and jacking off.

"Man, I can't wait." He crouched down and came back up.

"I know."

"Then I'm gonna go to my favorite restaurant and eat. You know how long I been wanting to get into some of Roscoe's fried chicken and waffles?"

I chuckled.

"And man, I gotta have some of M and M's oxtails and rice with some corn bread, dawg."

I smiled, thinking of my mother. She cooked so good she could have opened up her own soul food restaurant. "My mom use to make the best oxtails."

He paused for a moment, regretting, I think, bringing oxtails up. 'Cause it got me all depressed all over again.

"What else you plan on doing?" I asked, trying to shake it.

"I always wanted to go to Magic City!"

"It ain't out here."

"I know! I plan on taking a trip to Atlanta. For me, the sky's the limit. God gave me a second chance. I feel like I should take the time to really start living now."

"You should."

"I'm gonna see what's left of my career too. Maybe I can coach kids or something."

I nodded.

He wiped the sweat off his brow and continued ex-
ercising.

"Maybe." I wasn't giving him a lot of conversation
back.

He could tell. So he tried to cheer me up.

He made a fist and swung on me hard but only hitting me softly in my arm. "How about you, Chance?
When they finally let your ass up out of here, what's the
first thing you plan on doing?"

I didn't comment.

He studied me before saying, "Man, what I always
tell you?"

My mom's face flashed before me again. I shook my
head as if to block her image out.

Then the guards announced that we could go outside
for rec.

I needed some air. "You wanna go out?" I asked him.
"I need some air."

He shook his head. "I'm cool in here. I'm going to
wash up and take a nap."

I rose from my bed and stood at my cell door for
them to unlock it. I didn't want to go outside but the
conversation was just getting me depressed.

Chapter 13

All was normal on the yard. I sat near a bunch of blacks and reflected on my situation. I tried to keep in mind what Tyson said. I wished I embodied the strength and hope that he did and I was going to miss the fuck out of him when he got released. I wondered how I would be ten years from now. Would I be full of positive energy, like Tyson? Or would I just be a bitter man, angry at the world for being done wrong. Who knows? I knew life would move on without me like I never even existed. Sometimes I didn't even want to exist. I was in my own thoughts and I almost missed a Hispanic dude toss his bola ball and yell at the top of his lungs, *"Sur!"*

Tyson told me what it meant before. It was the southsiders' call. And whenever it yelled out all southside gangs had to get up and fight. So they did.

And it was on.

The southsiders rushed us!

Next thing I knew all the blacks were fighting.

First it was the southsiders against all the blacks, but then others took the opportunity to get their enemies.

The whole yard was fighting despite the warning given by several guards for us to drop and the loud alarm.

Two dudes came after me. One of them swung on me. I dipped my head back and yanked him down to the ground. I got ready for the other dude, who was trying to take jabs at me.

I packed him out quickly, only to have the dude on the ground take something and stab me in my lower leg with it.

"Ahh!" I yelled in pain.

I took my other good foot and stomped his head on the ground repeatedly. Each time I did, his mouth hit the concrete and blood gushed out. I didn't want to do this shit but I wanted to survive this shit.

Dudes were everywhere on the yard and we easily outnumbered the guards.

I went to help another black that three Mexicans were fucking up. I grabbed one by the back of his shirt and tossed his ass and knocked the shit out of the other one. I had to get away from this shit if I could.

The only one standing came for me. I was backing up and fighting 'cause I remembered them always telling us that when a riot broke out to lie down on our stomachs with our hands on the back of our heads.

The dude could hang with me and was throwing blow for blow. The advantage I had over him was my height and weight. So I used the advantage.

I started working his ass.

But when two more dudes jumped in the shit to help him, wasn't nothing I could do but let them fuck me up.

Another joined in on my ass.

The warning for us all to drop was repeated over and over again.

The alarms were going off.

But the fighting continued.

Tear gas was thrown, which caused some to stop and some to keep on going. Some dropped to the ground and covered their faces. Two black dudes took their shirts off, tied them around their face, and rushed the dudes who had rushed me.

That's when they started shooting.

I thought back to Tyson's words when I first arrived the prison. I needed to get myself from all the fighting, but how? *This shit didn't make sense*, I thought frantically. If I stayed there on the yard and dropped like they said, I would continue to get attacked and have to fight. Which would mean I would be considered part of the riot. I figured the best thing for me to do was fight my way to the building and lie down in there. Why the fuck didn't I stay inside with Tyson?

I slipped away from the fighting and tried to dodge as many feet as I could along with bullets that were taking a few inmates down. I covered my face with my shirt to avoid breathing in the tear gas.

I dodged the bullets that were continuing to be fired by staying low.

My only thought was to make it to my cell. But as I rushed to the gate I wondered how I was going to get inside? Guards were the only one with access. But I saw inmates rushing inside. I followed after them. And inside the prison there was fighting going on all over the place. Still, I planned to get near my tier. I was pretty sure that's where Tyson was and probably stayed once the riot started. He didn't want to jeopardize his release.

Someone must have managed to break into the control center, which was where all the security buttons were to lock or open any part of the facility because all the cell doors were opened. But once I made it to my cell door I was horrified at what I saw. A skinhead was straddling Tyson.

Before I could stop him he took a sharp object and slit his throat.

"Tyson!" I rushed inside.

But it was too late. I watched death pass over his eyes.

I rushed toward the dude who leaped off of Tyson and took a fighting stance. It was the dude who Tyson had beat down.

"You dirty muthafucka!"

Now he was to wielding his knife at me.

I backed up some and placed my fists up.

He moved in on me and slashed my forearms.

I grimaced at the pain but I kept my hands up.

As soon as his arms moved back, I punched him in the center of his face.

He tried to lash me again but I stepped back.

Blood leaked on my shoes.

My heart was thudding in my chest and I avoided looking at the bed, at Tyson's lifeless body.

Murder was in my eyes. Nervousness was in his. It made him act too rashly.

He tried to swipe me across my face.

I ducked my head down and shot back up. As soon as he paused I gave him two uppercuts.

It made him weak.

I went in again. I delivered another blow to his jaw.

He grew weaker.

I moved to the other side, causing him to move as well, so he tried to intimidate me with his words. "I'm gonna kill you, nigger, like I killed your friend."

The next hit was to his right cheekbone.

As I drew my hand back his knife quickly pierced the flesh on my hand.

I grunted but keep going. If I didn't, he was going to kill me like he killed Tyson, who didn't have a chance to save himself.

I stepped in on him again and punched him in the Adam's apple. This momentarily stopped his breathing and his hands went for his throat.

That's when I quickly stepped in and hemmed him up against the bunk bed. My hands went around his hands that were still around his throat. I gripped them with all the power I had left in me, with my teeth gritted. It was either do this or have him kill me, which was his intention.

I continued to strangle him with my fist, tightening my hold by raising my forearms and burying his neck between them.

He flattened against the railing of the bunk bed and I continued, never easing up .

His fingers became loose and dropped somewhat underneath my hands. My grip grew stronger. His lips twitched and mucus flew from his nose. I was blocking off his windpipe and he was not getting air. His hands slipped completely from underneath mine and started flapping at his sides, getting fainter by the second.

I kept the same amount of pressure.

His hands came back and covered mine weakly.

I squeezed with all my might. His hands dropped.

Then he stopped struggling and moving, period.

The next minute he was dead.

I let his limp body slide to the floor.

But I didn't want to get caught for killing him. Self-defense did not seem to exist when you were black. So I raced from the cell.

More skinheads were coming my way.

I looked behind me. My only choice was to run the other way but that was where inmates continued to fight.

I had no choice but to jump from the tier to the next tier, which I did.

I landed hard on one of my legs. A few seconds later guards and police were rushing in, telling us all to get down and throwing more tear gas. I stayed down with my head in my forearms and screamed, one from the pain in my leg and two from losing my friend.

Chapter 14

I couldn't get his face out of my head. Three years had passed since his death and I still saw Tyson. It didn't matter if it was day or night, eyes opened or closed. His face always flashed before me. I would even hear all the jokes he used to crack, all the hope he had given me while I was there. Seems like such a fucked-up fate to me. He had spent so many years of his life in prison. How crazy was it that he dies the day before he was supposed to get released? What a sick twist of fate.

I had been going to that Bible Study Group that Tyson had talked me into joining to deal with this. I never applied for a pen pal again. I was going so I could put my focus and my thoughts into something before I drove myself crazy. I couldn't seem to get over the image of seeing Tyson lying in the bed, cut from ear to fucking ear, out of my head.

I tried to push the thoughts out of my mind but they never went anywhere but to the back of my head, forcing me to rethink them later on. When Tyson died I had learned that his death didn't just affect me—many guards were saddened by it. It was hard to dislike somebody like Tyson. He was always happy, always smiling and trying to cheer people up. And it was hard to judge the actions of someone like him. If someone raped and killed your little sister, what would you do? He didn't belong in there. He never did. They all knew it. But still, he brought a lot of good to the prison.

The funny part was a few days later, after the riot, when I came back to my cell after showers, I found a beaded rosary on his bed. I was confused because only the Hispanic inmates wore the rosaries. I guess not all of us were divided by race. And I wondered why the riot even happened. I don't even think the men in here understand what it really meant, anyway, this whole notion of race and racism. To me the Hispanics and blacks had some of the same struggles. One way or another we were both being oppressed. It just didn't make sense that we feuded with each other.

After the incident, we were on lockdown for a minute. No visits, no mail, no program, which meant no activities. We ate, took our showers, and went straight to lights out. I didn't care either way. I also found out that the dude who killed Tyson was not just an ordinary dude. He was the son of the man Tyson killed, the man who molested and killed Tyson's little sister. I couldn't believe it. Tyson never knew.

In those three years nothing improved in my life. My mother was still in prison and my appeal was denied. I pretty much left it alone at that point. I didn't have anyone pushing me to fight anymore. That person was now six feet under. Calhoun would still visit me. But he said every time he did he felt like he was looking into the eyes of a stranger, not his boy. I simply told him that's what prison will do to you. Somehow along the way of being there you forget who you are and eventually you just don't care about how you were. Shortly after Tyson's death I had often talked to Calhoun about my friendship with him and when he saw how depressed I was about his death, he warned me not to get close to any inmates again. I promised I wouldn't. I meant it.

And today, after three years, I had a new person in the bed underneath me, in Tyson's old bed. It was weird seeing it empty all those years. And no guard dared putting another body there. Until today. Sometimes I wish they had never put him there underneath me and sometimes I'm glad they did.

I mean, he seemed all right, but me myself, I wasn't too social with anybody. For one, I still felt bad about my friend, for two, my mother was still in jail and it bothered the fuck out of me. And three, I was having a hard time getting over the fate that I had killed a man. All that was just too much to handle.

So when he came to stand by my bunk and introduced himself to me I didn't have too much to say to him.

"What's up, homie? My name Randy."

He was brown skinned and lanky, with a low-cut fade. There was something weird about the look in his eyes. I couldn't put my finger on it, though.

I shook his hand. "Chance."

"What did you do?"

I didn't want to get into that, so I didn't. So I instead I said, "something stupid," and turned back to the book I was reading: *The Purpose Driven Life*.

He studied me. "You don't like niggas, do you?"

I turned a page in the book. "No."

"Well, good. 'Cause I love me some women. Man, I could eat me some pussy all day long! Clean it so good, I could put it back on the shelf. And I love fucking doggie style."

"Well, you ain't going to find that in here."

"What?"

"Women."

"Man, I know. Lord knows I need me some pussy right now."

I ignored his rambling and kept reading my book.

But when he wouldn't stop, and felt he had to tell me his whole life story, how he got here and how much money he used to make on the street, I had no choice but to put my book down and listen.

"What's your favorite sexual position?" he asked me. I narrowed my eyes.

"Aww. Come on, man. Your favorite position?"

I didn't respond, but in my head I thought, cowgirl. But to be real it just didn't feel right talking to another man about sex. And the fact that men did fuck each other in here whether they admitted it or not, made it worse. And plus, he was in the bunk underneath me. The shit just felt funny. And I wondered how many quote-unquote straight men went home and told their wives and girlfriends how they fucked these punks in here. Yeah. The powers that be made it just lovely for the black woman. You come in here, do your time, and bring something home to your woman . . . AIDS. It happened and was as common as someone giving another person a cold. Prison was a fucked-up place to be. I don't think I would ever be able to rid myself of the demons that prison had given me. I killed a man. I kept telling myself that it was self-defense and not because he killed my friend. But that shit still haunted me. I didn't think I could ever do something like that. I took someone's life. I thank God that I thought quick and hopped over the tier and didn't get caught. I also hoped God would forgive me.

"Man, what I wouldn't do for some pussy right now!"

I felt the same but didn't bother to tell him.

The mere thought of the cowgirl position reminded me of Toi and making love to her. We always made it an experience. From her sucking my fingers to her taking me all the way in her mouth. I closed my eyes and daydreamed of her riding me in reverse, which is what cowgirl was. She had a mirror in her bedroom and whenever we had sex in that position I would always see her titties bouncing up and down and her saying in a sexy voice, "Give that big dick to me, daddy."

Just thinking about it made my dick hard and I wanted to jack off right then and there. Then an image of her fucking the dude she showed up to my visit with flashed before my eyes.

It immediately made me angry. So I snapped at dude, "Do you have anything else to talk about besides fucking?"

He laughed. "I'm sorry, dawg. I just miss my girl. She is fine as hell. I call her Hershey. She got some sexy-ass lips. She rocks one of them weaves, but I'm cool with it. But at night the shit pulls off like a damn wig! What they call them, man?"

"A lace front."

Toi had one of those too. She begged me to buy her one for Christmas. The shit cost five hundred. Then she moved onto Indian hair from a spot called Pauline's in Bellflower. Damn. He kept taking me back to Toi. I wondered what she was doing right now. She was probably fucking that other dude she betrayed me with or moved on to another dude to screw. How in the fuck could she?

He was still talking. "She's built like a stallion, though, got the big booty and titties! She got her own crib, a new car, and job! I ain't gotta do shit but kick it."

I wondered what she saw in him if she was all that. As a man, I would never feel comfortable lying up while my woman worked.

"I can pull some serious bitches, man. I got two more in two other cities. They all got the same credentials and they always break a nigga off!"

This nigga was probably lying, I thought. So I didn't give what he said too much attention. He didn't have to lie to impress me. I didn't have shit no more. I was a prisoner.

He saw my lack of interest so he changed the subject. "Aye. Which guards are cool around here?"

I shrugged. "I don't fuck with any of them. That's just me. The person who used to be on your bed was always the same."

"Where he at?"

"Dead."

"Damn! How the fuck that happened to him?"

"Riot."

"Well, I feel you, but you gotta develop juice with the staff. That's how they look out for you and you get extra shit."

I didn't respond.

That's when the guard came with the mail. Despite all the times I had written my mama, she never responded anymore. So I wasn't expecting anything other than a letter from Calhoun, who always told me about what he was doing. Which was never shit. He still was not handling his business. He still didn't have a job and he still was not taking care of his kids. One thing he was still getting in abundance and always bragged about was pussy! He had also managed in these past four years to stay out of prison.

My eyes scanned the top for the letter for the name of the person sending it. It simply said Deyja, with a PO Box address.

I narrowed my eyes. The name didn't ring a bell. I opened up the letter anyway and started reading.

Hello,

My name is Deyja. I am a member of Christ Baptist Church. I am a new member of Mrs.

*Grace's charity group. Since Mrs. Grace has al-
ways been of tremendous help to me with things
I have gone through, I was given your information and agreed to become your pen pal. She said
you had applied for a pen pal a few years before
but never again. However, she said you were
someone who would really benefit from a pen
pal. Understand that my personal business, address, and phone number will never be discussed
or disclosed in these letters and I have no problem if you don't want to discuss any of your info.
Actually, I would prefer it. I have no romantic
interest in you at all and never will. That is not
the purpose of the correspondence. The purpose
of this is to assist Mrs. Grace on her mission. She,
like God, is a firm believer in forgiveness and con-
verting nonbelievers to Christianity. I will also
add a scripture for you to study in my letters. The
purpose of our letters is to also bring some type of
joy your way, with all you have to endure being
locked up. I will write you one letter a month. I
know that is not a lot, but with my job it is all that
I can do. You can send all letters addressed to me
to the address listed on the envelope.
Take care and here is a passage to get you started.
Proverbs 3:5–6*

That was really nice of Mrs. Grace to do that for
me. When I went to her Bible study I only went to get
my mind off of what happened to Tyson, the murder
I did, and the reality that I had been in prison for
four and a half years and was probably was never
going to get out. And now that I had someone to
write, I didn't really feel like I could write her. What
exactly would I tell her? I'm a convicted murderer?
I'm sure she didn't want to hear that shit. But the

more and more I sat there, the more curious I was to even see if she would respond to my letter. So after a few days of boredom, I decided to write her.

Hello,

Thank you for taking the time to write me. To be honest, I don't even know how to respond to this letter. I mean, what do I tell you? Where I come from? Why I'm here? Who I was before I got here? Who I am now? Because truthfully, after spending over four years locked up in here, I definitely don't think I'm the same person I was before this whole ordeal happened to me. Places like these will do that to a person. You end up becoming a person you never thought you'd become and end up doing things you never thought you had it in you to do. Often it is about survival. Survival day by day, period. So some of the things we do in here, I don't think anyone can judge us the way you would judge someone on the streets if they did the same thing. The reality is this: We are in a war zone worse than anywhere else, every hour of the day, and being that I was on the streets before, I can definitely testify to that. Even though you said that I can leave all personal information out, I'm sure you are at least curious about what I did to end up in here. I say that because I am curious about who you are. So I will just go ahead and tell you. I'm in here for something I did not do. I was convicted of a murder I swear I did not do. Plain and simple. I know a lot of men say this, that they are innocent, but I'm telling the truth. I'm innocent, as sure as the sun shines and the sky is blue. All I think about is who I was and what I had prior to coming here. I want it back so bad.

All the hope I had when I first got here seemed like it died. I have very little hope left. Very little. I'm going to hold onto it because without it, I feel like I'm a dead man.

I will end this here and hope to hear from you again,

Chance

I sealed the envelope and placed it under my mat.

Chapter 15

Randy was weird. I could not put my finger on what it was, but something just wasn't right about dude. Every damn day he wanted to talk about pussy. Morning, noon, and night. He also tried too hard at shit. But I have to admit, his quest to get juice and extra shit worked. Case in point, Roscoe, who was the dirtiest of all the staff I had ever seen, showed Randy love. He didn't fuck with Randy at all. Whereas when it came to me, he always took opportunities to fuck with me. But it wasn't just that. Randy had so much juice that he would come back to our bunks on a daily with shit. From food to personals, like the good shower gel and good deodorant. Not the shower gel we were issued that was like water and not the deodorant that was issued that caused us to get rashes under our armpits. He even had a CD player and CDs to play. It was all the shit Tyson wanted when he was in here.

"Aye. You want some?"

I didn't want to take nothing from no one in here. But the beef jerky and cookies he was holding out for me to take looked so good I took two cookies and a few pieces of jerky.

As I chewed I wondered who put money on his books or that stuff. He said his family didn't fuck with him and that his friends had their own struggles.

So I asked him, "Who got you that stuff?"

He laughed and chewed on a piece of jerky while standing near my bed.

"The warden. Look, man, he cool as fuck. During rec time, I go and clean out his office and do other shit he wants done."

I had to give it to him. "Man, you really do have juice."

He swallowed and chuckled. "I guess I know all the right things to say, man. I have always been able to persuade and win people over."

I laughed.

"Maybe you can go work for him too. You never know. Maybe he can talk to you about your case. Help you out and shit."

I swallowed the last piece of jerky. A few days ago I was having a bad night and I told Randy about my situation. At the time, I didn't trust him and didn't even like him. But I had no one else to really talk to. So I vented to him.

"It ain't gonna hurt to try, man."

I nodded, bit down on a cookie, and savored the taste. It was a Pecan Sandie, my all-time favorite.

"He is cooler than a fan, man. Maybe he can get your appeal approved. He is a powerful man, Chance. Nigga, you better do that shit. Did you know that wardens can overturn verdicts?"

"No, I didn't know that. With all these inmates in here why would he pick me to help him?"

"'Cause I told him about you, that's why."

I bumped fists with him. "Good looking."

Maybe he wasn't all that bad, I thought.

Our conversation was cut short when a guard came with mail.

It was from the girl from the church, Deyja and one from Calhoun. Randy put his focus on his snacks and I put mine into the two letters. I scanned through Calhoun's letter first. As usual it talked about the same bullshit: Women, women, and more women. There was no mention about his kids despite the fact that I had written him many times before and asked him how they were. He did encourage me to stay up and promised to put some money on my books. I didn't put my hope into that. That's why when he did put a few bucks, which was not often, I always stocked up on envelopes, paper, and stamps. I never had enough for snacks. He also said that he would come and see me again soon. I rushed through his letter so that I could get to Deyja's.

Hello,

I have to admit this is my first time corresponding with someone in prison and your letter was so interesting to me. Wow. It must be really hard to be somewhere day-to-day that you shouldn't be. And to know this and still nothing can be done about it. How tragic. I am so sorry. I know all about tragedy, so I feel your pain. And nothing can be done at all? You said you feel that you are not the same person you were when you were out—why? How have you changed, if you don't mind me asking. Is the change good or is it bad? You are in very harsh environment like you said. It must make the way you feel a lot worse. And believe me, I'm not judging. I leave that up to God and I'm certainly not that. Really no one is. So no one has the right to look down on you. A sin is a sin and most people sin. But again, your pain and frustration comes from the fact that you are innocent. I also wanted to applaud you on your faith in yourself and the fact that you have not given up. I am a true believer that faith can

*carry you through anything. I know firsthand. If
you feel you are really innocent (not to say that
you are not) then you should fight until you can't
fight anymore. And in the end, even if it doesn't
make a difference, it really will because you tried
to get out. I'm thinking that has got to feel better
than not trying and always wondering if you had
tried how it would have panned out. I know this
is a cliché but it is one that is really true. There
was something interesting you said in your other
letter: You said that without hope you would be a
dead man. What did you mean by that? And out
of curiosity, what were you doing before you got
locked up? I know that we said that this stuff will
not be mentioned, so I'm sorry if I have offended
you by asking. But I have to admit I'm a little curious. You don't have to answer if you don't want
to but I sure would like to know. I guess to answer
your question about what to tell me, you can tell
me whatever you are comfortable telling me.*

Here is your passage to read: Jeremiah 17:7
Deyja

I chuckled to myself. She already broke the rules she
had clearly set out for me. But I didn't have a problem
answering her inquiries.

I wrote back.

Hello, how are you?

*What I meant when I said I would be a dead
man without hope is this: If I didn't even have
a small smidgen that I would get out of here it
would make me a dangerous person. I would not
care about my own life or the life of others. That
is not a good way for any man to be because you*

wouldn't put any type of constraints on yourself and you would rule, respond, and make decisions with no morals, ethics or humility. I mean, I see it all the time in here. Yeah, I try to stay away but it is in my face. The way I don't want to be. So maybe I give myself hope so I won't turn into a monster in here, something so easy to do. I'm glad you want to know more about me and no, I'm not hitting on you or trying to be fresh. I just would rather talk about the person I was before I came here. And truthfully, to have to talk about jail when I'm here daily can be real boring. Like talking about a job you are at eight hours a day, five days a week, and you hate it. Believe it or not, I graduated from college at the top of my class. I was working for Microsoft, and was in the process of opening up my own business. I also owned my own home before I came to prison and my mother lived with me.

I paused and bit the tip of my pencil. Ours didn't come with erasers because men used them as pipes. I didn't know if I should put my mother was in prison. I didn't want anyone thinking less of my mother, so I didn't.

I continued writing.

She has been my biggest support since I have been in here. I have not heard from her so she has me a little worried. She is my best friend really and the strongest woman I have ever met. She raised me alone so I promised her I would make her proud of me. And I did, up until getting thrown in here. In all my years I have never been locked up. That is, until now. At first it hurt like hell for her to see me in a place like this. And for her to be "Shit."

I scratched *be* off. I didn't want say that my mother was in jail but once you get comfortable and start it is hard to stop.

"You okay, dawg?" Randy asked, chewing.

"Yeah." My stomach was grumbling for more snacks. But I didn't ask for any more.

I continued the letter.

Have to go through this is just as hard. I'm her only son. Anyway, that is a little more about me. I had some big plans for myself before I got arrested.

I thought of Toi and the business I was going to open.

But a lot of them are no longer possible . . . I will end the letter here and hope to hear from you soon.

Chance

I then wrote Calhoun's ass a letter. I did a lot of fussing at his ass about the fact that he didn't have his shit together and told him how lucky he was to be free and got on him for not doing anything with his life. I thanked him for the times that he put something on my books and still being there for me. The fact that he thought about me and took time out of his life to write and visit me meant something to me. And he had been doing it all these years. I placed both letters under my mat and I was still wondering why I hadn't heard from my mama.

Chapter 16

It turns out Randy did help me out. The warden called me up to his office one day early as hell.

A guard brought me up there. Once he let us in his office, the guard left. When I walked in I saw the warden was on the phone. I saw Randy walk by in the back room, pushing a cart and he waved at me, all excited.

I chuckled and nodded.

The warden was an older white man. He was short and stocky. He had graying hair, pale skin, and blue eyes.

I wondered if he really would really listen to me talk about my case and if he would be willing to help me.

Once he ended the call he turned to me and inspected me from head to feet.

"Wallace, right?" He had a strong southern accent.

"Yes, sir."

"Randy said you were good with computers."

"Yes, sir."

The next thing I knew, I was organizing files and creating new folders on his computer. For the life of me I couldn't understand why he needed inmates to do this. And for doing this it really only took me a few minutes.

"Okay, I'm done, sir."

He stood behind me and said, "Good job, Wallace."

I stood but he stopped me by placing a hand on my shoulder and gently shoving me back down.

"There are a few games on here. You are welcome to find something to do on the computer to occupy yourself and I'll be back."

"Yes, sir." He went into the back room I had seen Randy in.

I did everything from playing some games, to surfing the Web, and even saw a little YouTube. On the outs I stayed on the computer more than I watched TV. I checked out some of the old sites I used to frequent: MediaTakeOut, Concrete Loop, and Necole Bitchie. Then I watched a few videos on World Star Hip Hop. I even went on Facebook to look up Toi. I wondered how she looked, if she had gotten married, had kids. But when I tried to log on it said my user name and password were invalid. I figured Toi had probably closed my account because she was the one who opened it.

When was the ending of our relationship going to stop bothering me?

Probably never.

I closed out of the website as the warden came back into the room with Randy.

He got on his speaker and called for the guard that had brought me there to come back.

Once the guard came back and entered the office, the warden ordered, "Take them both to the canteen. Let Wallace get about fifty dollars' worth of items for the work today and give Randy eighty dollars for his work."

"Yes, sir," the guard said.

We were quickly dismissed.

It's funny how happy it made me to have all the snacks from the canteen. I had beef jerky, some pecan sandies, Top Ramen, some soup, tuna, sardines, and some nuts. I even stocked up on some more paper, stamps and envelopes. Randy and I pigged out to the point that neither one of us had an appetite for dinner. It was crazy how I got all that junk for just doing a little troubleshooting.

I went to sleep with a major stomachache.

Chapter 17

Good moments don't last long.

"Wallace? Wallace! Wake up."

I rolled over to see one of the guards in my cell standing over me. He tapped me with a baton until I stood to my feet.

It was earlier than they had ever woken me before. And instantly, I knew something was wrong. My stomach twisted in knots. Was I in trouble for something? Maybe they had discovered that I was the one who killed that skinhead.

"Do I need to get dressed?" I asked the guard.

"Naw. All that ain't necessary. Just put your shoes on and come on."

I stood there in my long johns and put on my shoes.

I was escorted to the supervisor's office. Once I made it inside, he didn't say anything. He just gestured me to come closer with one hand while holding a phone up in his other.

Once I reached him he handed me the phone.

I took a deep breath, while my eyes asked the supervisor who it was.

He was tight-lipped and put his head down.

"Hello?"

"Is this Chance Wallace?"

"Y—" I cleared my throat. "Yes it is."

"This is the warden of Valley State Prison. I am calling regarding you mother, "Rasheeda Wallace. At exactly 1:16 A.M. your mother had a stroke. She was rushed to the infirmary and they attempted CPR. It was unsuccessful. An attempt to transport her to the hospital was made. She expired on the way there. Thank you."

The phone clicked.

I dropped the phone. I replayed her words in my head. *She expired on the way there.*

I felt weak. I slid down to the floor, feeling numb as tears ran down my face.

Chapter 18

Sickening. That was the best way to describe how I felt as I was being escorted by two guards to my mother's burial at Potter's Field. It was a place for poor people to be buried. I thanked God that was at least done for my mama and she didn't have to be cremated.

Since she had no other family out here except for me, there was no real church service, though. Which I didn't care about . . . I probably wouldn't have been able to handle it.

Damn. I had lost my mama. I avoided looking at the open casket and instead kept staring down at my hands.

Come to find out, in all the time that she hadn't been writing me it was because she was really sick, bedridden actually. And all that time I didn't know. Part of me blamed myself. I figured if I hadn't been in prison and if she weren't stressing over me that she would still be here. So many thoughts ran through my head, I wondered if her death could have been prevented. Would she have gotten better medical care if she wasn't locked away? Did they simply look at her like she was just an inmate? A criminal? Did the person performing the CPR really know what they were doing?

I shook my head, feeling nothing but grief. I just wanted my mom to be here. All I wanted was to have her back. Man . . . I would spend the rest of my life in prison with no problem because I knew she would still be here, alive and well. Now I had nothing and nobody and it killed me.

I closed my eyes as the priest held his Bible and said a prayer for my mother.

"Saints of God, come to her aid. Come to meet her, angels of the Lord! Receive her soul and present her to God the most high.

May Christ, who called you, take you to himself, may angels lead you to Abraham's side. Receive her soul and present her to God the most high.

Give her eternal rest, O Lord, and may your light shine upon her forever.

Receive her soul and present her to God, the most high.

Let us pray: We commend our sister, to you, Lord.

Now that she has passed from this life, may she live on in your presence.

In your mercy and love, forgive whatever sins she may have committed through human weakness. We ask this through Christ our Lord."

I kept my eyes closed as he read this, praying along-side him. I prayed that my mother was in heaven and she didn't have to be in any more pain. I prayed that God would protect her.

I opened my eyes when a throat cleared.

The priest held out a hand for me to come to the open casket. "Please," he said.

I didn't want to. My eyes had avoided looking at the casket for the longest. To see my mama in there . . . I couldn't. But to say good-bye to her the right way—I knew that I had to.

I took a step forward, but then stopped.

I shook my head at the priest. "Never mind."

"This will be your only chance, young man."

I took a deep breath and wiped the side of my face on my right shoulder.

I nodded.

The priest held a hand out to me with a soft smile.

I stumbled, taking the steps forward. Not just because of the shackles but because of what was in front of me.

In his other hand were some flowers. They were bright yellow. My mama loved flowers. The real ones. I would always grab some when I went to the grocery store. It was funny that in that moment, I remembered the things about my mother that were so small to me before. I remembered her rich laugh, how when she smiled—man, I couldn't remember the last time I had seen her do that—but when she did, her eyes got all shiny. Her hands were always soft; her heart always was too. I always felt that she was just too soft for this harsh-ass world. But I always figured with me in her life, she would be okay. I was my mother's protection . . . her shield. I, against my will, had stopped being that when I got locked up.

I looked at her face and thought about the love my mama had shown me through the years. It didn't come out of toy or department stores, it all came from her heart.

I leaned over and pressed my face to hers. She felt so cold. I kissed both of her cheeks. I then stared at her face for as long as I could before breaking down.

I dropped to my knees, wrapped my arms around the casket, and sobbed silently. I cried like a baby and couldn't do anything about the ache in my chest.

That's when both guards grabbed me. They pulled me a few feet away from the casket.

I watched the casket being closed and slowly, slowly, my mama was lowered into the ground.

Dear Chance,
You have gone through so much these past few years. I'm so sorry about your mother dying. Sometimes life can be so cruel. But understand that God gives you nothing you can't bear and this too will pass. I'm not going to say that it won't be hard—it will. And it will always be on your heart. Trust me, I know. But I can promise you that as more time goes by, the pain will get less and less. Continue to pray for your mother. And I will continue to pray for you. Have you given up hope on your case? Chance, I hope not. I don't care what they say, you have to keep trying. You have to do it for yourself. I tried to make the oxtails the way that you instructed in your last letter. It was for a church gathering. You know, the way you said your mom used to make them with the tomato sauce, garlic cloves, and Worcestershire sauce. Chance, they came out so good. Everyone liked them. So I know your mom had some serious cooking skills. LOL. I wish things were different for you. You don't deserve to be there. You should be out in the world living your life to full capacity. But I have a feeling that something will give and you will be able to soon. Smile. Well, I have to get back to work. I will be writing you soon. Please stay positive, happy. Chance, just be.
Try to read the Psalms this week,
Deyja

Dear Deyja,
Thanks for still taking the time out of your schedule to write me. I can't say it enough but I really look forward to your letters. As far as my mother, her death sits heavily on me. It hurts like hell. But you are right. As each day passes, it gets a little better. Not completely, but better. I don't think I will ever be able to get past it completely. One thing I noticed when you write me is that you always make a statement about tragedy or loss. I was wondering if you wouldn't mind telling me what you were implying? I hope I'm not being too nosy. I have to admit that your letters are so special to me. Your words have a deep impact on my life right now. Not just the fact that you write me but what you write. You have joy around you and I could use some of it. Your letters help me get through days here. They make me blush and sometimes laugh. I read them over and over again like I'm watching my favorite movie. So they liked the oxtails? Yep. My mom was the best cook. How were they to you? Sure wish I could have tasted them. Sorry. I'm doing too much . . . I'll end the letter here. I can't wait to hear from you again,
Chance

I smiled a little. In the past couple months, Deyja's letters went from once a month to several letters in a week, almost as if she was writing me every day. That's what it felt like.

I don't know why she felt so inclined to write me so much. It could be that she had taken a liking to me or she felt sorry for me. It could be that she felt bad that my mother had passed. And although she said she wouldn't discuss any of her info, she had managed to tell me where she was from and what type of work she did: real estate. I would sit and read her letters over and over again. She had even slipped up on the envelope and gave me her last name; it was Sims. Deyja Sims. Humph.

After my mother's funeral and I was sent back to my *home*. Once there, pretty much every night I said that same prayer the priest had said the day my mama was buried. Yep, home . . .

That's pretty much what I called the prison because I never thought I'd be able to call any other place home again.

It had been exactly three months since my mother had passed.

My therapy during those months were the letters I received from Deyja. And of course my boy Calhoun was still coming to see me. It is hard to describe it, but something about Deyja's words always pushed me to not do something I had planned on doing the moment I found out my mama had died: kill myself. I mean, at that point, losing her made me feel like I had lost everything and I didn't want to exist anymore. I didn't think there was an important enough reason for me to still reside on this earth, period. But her letters kept telling me that I could get past this and that things would get better. However, when Deyja would write me, she would always mention something about God having a plan for me and didn't I want to wait around and see what that plan was.

Right after my mother died, the prison actually had me on suicide watch for two months. That's where I met Lewis. He had been with the department for five years and came straight out of college. He hated the job but he had three kids and a mortgage to pay and with the economy being so bad, people losing their jobs left and right—one of those people was his wife—he didn't want to gamble and quit, hoping to find something that just wasn't out there. He told me in those five years he had been attacked by inmates, under investigation, suspended with no pay for defending himself, and even been stabbed, almost dying. The job had put a strain on his relationship with his kids and his wife. His wife was always worried that he wouldn't come home and when he did, he was so worn out mentally by the job that all he did was sleep. He said the job had him in a severe depression. It was the first time I realized that prison didn't just feel like prison for the inmates. The thing I liked about Lewis was that he wasn't corrupt like the other prison guards here. He always told me that the way he came in is the way he would always stay, despite what went on.

"I didn't come here to be dirty," he always told me. One thing I was going to miss was talking to him. I even confessed to him about my case. He would always tell me that information was power and there were always loopholes to get things to go in my favor.

Chapter 19

I had been back in normal population and off suicide watch for a week. Calhoun had come to visit me. When I made it to the visiting room I was so happy to see a familiar face today.

"Whats up, my nigga?" He was standing near a table with his arms out, a big smile on his face and his head tilted to one side.

I chuckled and gave him a bear hug. We were the same height and weight but I was a more buffed than he was.

"Hey."

We both sat down.

He studied me and said," Aye. Man I'm still tripping off the fact that your mother is gone. I'm sorry."

"It's cool."

"You a strong-ass nigga, Chance. First you lose your boy in here and then your mom. If I lost my mother I don't know what I would do."

I nodded, not really wanting to talk about it. It was something that was still keeping me up at night. I changed the subject. "So what's going on with you? You been giving any thought to anything I said in my letters?"

He chuckled. "Oh, I give it thought. But at the end of the day I gotta be me, you know? So I do me. Chance, you should know by now that that shit is never going to change."

I chuckled. "Same old Calhoun. Hardheaded as ever."

"Yep." He cracked up laughing.

"You're going to have to one day, you know."

"One day what?"

"Grow up."

"I'll do that shit when I die. But aye. On to you. How you holding up in here?"

"I'm all right."

"Keeping yourself clean and shit?"

"Yep. I keep out of nonsense as best I can. Tyson taught me that."

"Right. Right. Funny thing is, I'm free and I can't keep myself out of bullshit. You would think that after two strikes I would. But you right, Chance. I'm so fucking hardheaded. My mama tells me that to this day. She ain't gave up on me. But my daddy. Seems like he has."

"Parents never give up on you, boy. How are your mom and dad anyway?" I asked. Deep down I always felt Calhoun was lucky for having the type of parents that he had. They were successful and supportive of him. And he treated them so bad. He continued to take them for granted. I had secretly wished that his father was my father.

"They all right. Mom's still a damn homemaker, cooking meals for twenty people and shit, baking pies cause she don't know what else to do with her time. My dad still doing the same type of work."

He tossed a hand. "But I didn't come here to talk about their ass. You know what I'm going to work on for you?"

"What?"

"Finding some lonely bitch to marry you so you can get conjugal visits."

Just then Deyja came to mind. I started to tell him about her but I figured he would probably laugh at me for having feelings for a woman I had never seen before who was only writing me.

So instead I laughed and said, "Yeah, and how the fuck you going to do that?"

"Just wait and see. You don't have any requirements, do you?"

I played along with him. "Nigga, do I look like it? I'm locked up. All I see is dick and balls all day long."

"Okay, well, let me be the jailhouse matchmaker. I could make a killing doing that shit."

The thought of having sex with another woman made me super-hard in my prison garb. But I knew Calhoun was just bullshitting. Any women he came in contact with, no matter how she looked, he was going for.

We chopped it up some more about the good old days and what was going on nowadays.

He stayed for the whole visit and promised to put twenty bucks of my books.

"All right, I'll be back in a couple weeks, Chance. Stay up."

I stood and gave him another hug. When he pulled away he had tears in his eyes. I saw his shoulders shake a little too. It made me feel good to know that I could still count on my boy to be there for me.

The next day the warden had called me to work but I had declined. I followed the normal routine on the prison. And in my downtime, I slept. At night when I felt no one could hear me I grieved over my mother's death. I was still unable to get it out of my head.

I remember how Calhoun and I felt when Paul passed away. When he died, it hurt me a lot but as more time passed and I got more hugs, back pats, and kisses from my mom, I was able to get past it. I couldn't get past her, though. Yeah, I would always tell Deyja that I was better and in a way, when I was corresponding with her I did feel better, but I really wasn't healed and probably never would be.

I was reflecting on this when I heard, "Wallace. You need to come with me to see the warden."

I looked at the guard standing by my cell and nodded. I quickly hopped off my bunk and put on my shoes.

I guess I couldn't hide from the warden for too long. Maybe it wasn't such a bad idea. He would probably give me some work to keep me busy. I figured if I did something with my time like Deyja said, I would keep my mind off my mother's death and keep me less depressed than I already was about being there.

The guard simply escorted me to the office. When we made it there, he knocked on the door.

"Come in."

I opened the door and took a few steps inside. "Sir, you wanted to see me?"

The guard stood behind me.

He nodded and waved a hand excusing him. "Come in and have a seat."

As I walked in further, the guard left.

I sat down across from the warden.

For a long time he just stared at me.

From the corner of my eye I saw Randy walk by in a back room that had the door open.

"Have you ever seen anything like this before, Chance?"

He turned the computer screen toward me.

Instantly my eyes got buck as I watched two men getting it on, on his computer screen.

I shook my head and looked away quickly, hoping this dude wasn't about to do what I thought he was about to do.

"Wow, boy it looks like you've seen a ghost!"

"Naw." I wanted to check him on calling me a boy but didn't. The word *boy* always had a racial connotation as far as I was concerned when it was said to a black child, black teenager or black man.

I put my head down instead.

"Chance, have you ever had anal sex before?"

"No, sir."

"Do you ever plan on having anal sex?"

"Only with a women."

"Do you see any women in here?" He had his arms spread wide.

I shook my head. "No, sir."

"It's the best. And when you are the receiver and the man is giving it to you right . . . It is the best orgasm I have ever had in my life." He sat back in his chair.

I was at a loss for words.

He stared at me. "I think you are very handsome, Chance. If you are willing, I will add two hundred dollars to your books."

"What?"

He chuckled. "Don't worry, boy. You get on my team I'll make sure you are well taken care of."

I was frozen. I didn't know what to tell this man. What I wanted to tell him he didn't want to hear and that was *fuck no!* I was cool on his proposition.

"Boy," he called. "Get on out here."

That's when Randy came from out of the back room.

My eyes narrowed. What did he expect was going to happen? That I was going to let him and Randy take my asshole?

"Is everything ready?" he asked Randy.

Randy nodded and refused to look at me.

"Take him back there. It's his first time. Get it started and I will be in shortly."

"Huh?" I stood to my feet.

"Come on, Chance," Randy said.

"*Come on, Chance* what?"

I looked from Randy to the warden then back to Randy. "Randy, you a part of this sick shit?" I demanded.

"It ain't sick. It's what the warden said to do," he said, chewing the side of his mouth like a little fucking kid.

That's why this fool was always talking about pussy and shit. He wasn't into pussy. "Man, fuck you and him."

I turned to walk toward the door.

"Grab him, take him to the back room, and get him undressed!" the warden ordered.

As soon as I felt a finger touch my shoulder, I spun around and cracked Randy in the jaw. "You punk muthafucka! You got me caught up in this shit?" I raged.

The panic button was pressed and the alarm sounded. I didn't give a fuck.

"Touch me again!" I threatened, towering over him as he lay on the floor near the warden's feet.

That's when three guards came in the room.

The warden simply pointed. That was all it took and they were all on me. Every region of my body was assaulted by them as they commenced to whipping my ass.

I bit my lips at all the pain, knowing I couldn't beat them. I didn't even bother to try. But I stopped the warden from whatever his plans were for me.

Fists, and boots were used to put me back in my place. Randy snuck back into the room he had emerged from earlier.

I buried in my forearms. The guards continued fucking me up until the warden said, "Take him to lockup. I don't want him out until next week!"

Chapter 20

It wasn't no week that I was in there. It was more like a month. That was the warden's language, I was told. A day to him was really a week. A week was a month. I hated to hear what a month to him was. I heard that shit was illegal, but what power did I have to do something about it? And it wasn't the only illegal shit they did, so shit, whatever.

Sitting in that absurdly small-ass room, sometimes I could swear I could see my mama's face like she was sitting next to me. That shit made me feel like I was going crazy. Then I had dreams about Tyson. His dead body, the image of the knife slicing his neck. I saw it all day long. Sometimes I dreamed about my own dead body. That the skinhead had killed me before I got a chance to kill him. These dreams always had me waking up screaming and sweating like a slave. I would beat on the door repeatedly but nobody ever came. They wouldn't even let me out for my hour of rec.

I wish I had some of Deyja's letters. They seemed to make me feel better about the shit I was going through. But I wasn't allowed to have shit in there. And I know this shit may sound crazy, but I would sit in those four corners and pretend I was talking to her. It was the only way to avoid thinking of where I really was and that I was alone. I created a fake image of her in my head. And when I jacked off, I no longer thought of Toi, I thought of Deyja, a woman I had never seen before.

When they decided to release me and some other inmates that were on lockdown, I was pulled out, given a shower and a clean set of clothes. I was surprised to see Lewis there to escort me since he worked with inmates that were on suicide watch. But he told me he was filling in for a staff that called off.

"What's up, Chance?" He handed me my mail.

It was a letter from Deyja.

"Thanks. This is just what I needed."

I tore the letter open as we walked back to our cells.

> *Chance,*
> *I have written you countless times in the past month. I don't know what is going on but I'm a little concerned. Understand that is this is not something you want to be a part of anymore that is fine. No harm done. Although I will miss reading your letters. I don't know . . . They do something for me. They motivate me to let go of some things that holding me back from really living. If you can get up everyday and function like a normal person in the environment you live in, with your circumstance, then I can as well. But Chance, understand that if I don't hear from you after this letter I will no longer write you.*
> *Here is a passage: Isaiah 38:18*
> *Deyja*

I put the letter back in the envelope. The first chance I got I was going to write her. I didn't want her to think that I was deliberately ignoring her letters.

Once we made it to my cell, we both noticed Roscoe was standing in front of it talking on a radio.

He held his hand out to us. "The warden wants to see him ASAP." He combined all four letters together.

"But he just got out the—"

"So? I don't give a fuck!" Roscoe got all up in Lewis's face and said, "Do what you told. You don't work this fucking tier anyway. Matter of fact. I got them; you just escort your fucking inmate to the warden, dumb nigga."

Lewis took a deep breath and backed up. "Come on, Chance."

Roscoe wasn't done. "Chance? What the fuck you doing, trying to hug the thugs? Call 'em by their last name."

Other guards standing by started laughing.

Lewis ignored them. "Come on, man."

Now I was worried about what was going to happen to me when they sent me to the warden. Part of me wanted to tell Lewis what had happened the last time I had come there. But I didn't think it would make a difference. He didn't have the power to stop it.

Once we made it to the door Lewis knocked. The warden told us to come in.

I took a deep breath and did, taking only two steps into the room. I stood in the doorway while Lewis stood behind me.

Lewis was excused quickly. "You can leave the inmate, sir," said the Warden.

Once Lewis did leave, I was told to step closer in the room. I did it slowly, mean mugging the warden.

Before I could say anything, someone closed the door behind me. I was then grabbed up and pushed further into the room. Then I was shoved to the floor.

I looked up at the warden standing in front of his desk and staring down at me.

I looked around the room. Whoever had shoved me stood near the warden. Then three black dudes came from the back room and approached me. From the floor I watched them circle me.

I stood back to my feet.

The warden spoke to me. "You made this hard on yourself, sir. I had planned on breaking you in easy."

I didn't respond.

He aimed a finger at me. "You need to learn something. Whether you are in a field or on your knees, you work for me. And you don't say no. Do you realize who I am? I am God around here, boy. I can do what the fuck I want to you inmates. Your life is mine! I can have you killed if I want."

I glared at him. "Then kill me, muthafucka."

He took a deep breath, looked at the guys around me, and nodded at them.

Before I could make a move they all cornered me. I was shoved in the back room.

I fought them the best I could but it didn't make a difference. I was overpowered and I was held down on a bed by two of the dudes.

"Get the fuck off of me!"

I was ignored. I watched another dude hold a camcorder up while the another dude stripped out of his clothes.

I felt his weight on the bed as he inched toward me.

I struggled and couldn't break free.

Panic rose in me as he managed to yank my pants down.

A camcorder was aimed in my face

I spit at it and twisted my body on the bed.

Still, they managed to strip me of my clothes. I continued to fight but it didn't make a difference.

The dude positioned my asshole and I couldn't fight him.

"Get off of me!"

He ignored me and asked, "Y'all got him tight?"

The two men holding me down said in unison, "Yeah."

"Good! I'm 'bout to make you one of the warden's *boys*." By "boy" he meant his bitch.

I couldn't stop him, though. I tried.

He took a deep breath and without reprieve, his shoved his dick up my asshole.

To keep from screaming out, I bit down on my lip, felt it pop and blood run in my mouth.

He tore my asshole apart and continued stuffing himself in and out of me, despite how rigid my body was. Despite how much I struggled.

And yet, despite how much it hurt, I refused to make a sound.

I saw the warden's shoes on the floor by the bed as I was rocked back and forth by the man who was forcing himself inside of me.

I could feel my skin tearing with each stroke.

The man behind me was breathing harshly like he was really enjoying this.

And somewhere along the way, they switched positions and another man was raping me.

Then another.

Then the warden.

And somewhere in the midst of the warden raping me . . .

I checked out.

Chapter 21

The doctors and nurses knew what happened to me. It did not take a fool to know I had been raped. But still, they asked me questions I didn't want to answer because I didn't want to relive it all over again. They didn't care.

They took X-rays of me and everything. They said they never saw a rape as severe as mine. I was full of blood and lacerations. They even took pictures.

I stayed in the medical unit for damn near a month. It was hard at first because it wasn't just my body that was damaged from that shit. I was damaged psychologically as well. For the first few days I wouldn't talk or eat. I would not bathe and when I took a shit, I would smear it all over my body. I figured if I smelled like shit and had it all over me no one would touch me ever again. Eventually some guards forced me to shower. Then they moved me back to suicide watch and had me in mechanical restraints.

Lewis was the only one I trusted and he was the only one I would cooperate with.

"Chance, I don't know what the fuck happened to you but I'm guessing you were raped. And I'm guessing it was bad. But either way, you can't carry on like this. Them guards can say you gassed them and that's assault, which leads to more charges," he told me.

"What the fuck I care about more charges for? I'm not getting out of here," I said. "Yeah, but you don't need to spend those days strapped down like you crazy when I know you ain't fucking crazy. And you giving these guards the green light to fuck you up and the inmates are gonna think you soft and you gonna become they *boy*." He didn't mean *boy* like a homie but it was another word for they bitch. Then they would have green light to take my ass as well.

He lowered his voice. "Look. It's fucked up, but move on, nigga. They took your ass." He held him arms wide. "You can't do shit about it now. Get your revenge like a man."

He was right. One way or another I had to. And that became my mission. And some way, somehow, I had to get the fuck up out of this prison.

Chapter 22

"Look at this shit right here."

I ignored Roscoe as he came and stood in front of my cell as I did push-ups on the floor.

"You bunking with a punk muthafucka yo," he told the guy that was next to him.

No comment from me.

After all the years that I had been incarcerated this man was still fucking with me.

"How your mama doing with her fine ass?"

He knew my mother was dead. Still he wanted to say some shit that would touch me.

But over the years, I had built up enough tolerance to not only ignore him, but not even acknowledge what he said. "Take the bottom bunk, Charleston" he ordered to the nerdy-looking black dude standing next to him who looked like he was scared for his life.

Yeah, Randy managed to be a ghost after I got off suicide watch and was sent back to normal pop. He was totally moved off of the tier that I was on. And with him went my letters and anything I had accumulated over the years. He was a dirty muthafucka. The only thing that was valuable to me were the letters from my mom, Calhoun, and Deyja. Now I had none of them. He even took my stamps and envelopes. I wanted to write Deyja so bad. But I had to put her on the back burner for now. My motivation was now on how to get the fuck out of there. I had to find a way.

The new guy, Charleston, didn't say anything to me. I watched him get punked left and right. He wasn't a kiss-ass like Randy was and he couldn't fight. I remember how I used to be. But I knew he wouldn't always stay that way. I was far different from the person I used to be. I had killed a man, had been raped. Naw. I wasn't the same, wasn't nothing innocent or trusting about me like Charleston.

I wanted to help dude but the last thing I needed was to get attached to him, like I was to Tyson and he die. Or get cool with him and he betray me like Randy did.

So I did nothing but watched. He never talked to me and I never talked to him. And at night he never went to sleep. He probably thought I was going to rape him. He didn't have to worry about that shit.

But as more time went by I watched him become subject to the same bullshit I was subjected to. So I felt like I had to say something.

It was like déjà vu, seeing him get punked for his food. Just like what happened to me, he was checked by the blacks for giving up his food. They came to our cell and cursed him out like they did me. And, yes, he was subject to getting jumped just like me.

But unlike all the blacks who sat around and watched, I tried to go over and help him but I was pulled back by the same black dude who had showed up at my cell when I had first got there.

"Get the fuck off me," I told him.

He looked at me, surprised. "You trying to run something?"

"Naw. But I can't just sit here and watched him get fucked up like y'all watched me get fucked up."

"We don't need no shit on us, that's why. Today is Sunday and I got a visit coming. It's too many of them anyway. Let them dig a hole for themselves," he said.

So I fell back.

But one day I did step in on a decision he was about to make.

A few months had passed since he had been there and we still had not developed any type of relationship. Those few months had pushed me into my fifth year of being incarcerated.

Charleston had come back like a kid in a candy store and was ushered with some other inmates that were escorted to their cells.

"Hey! The warden had me come up to his office," Charleston said, all excited. It was the first time he had tried to initiate a conversation with me.

The mention of the warden caused me to freeze up. He didn't notice and continued.

"All I had to do was fix some stuff on his computer and he put money on my books. So I got all this stuff from the canteen."

I hopped off my bed and leaned over his face.

He jumped back like he thought I was going to hit him.

"Stay the fuck out the warden's office," I whispered.

"Why?"

"Man, don't worry about why. Just do what the fuck I say or you're gonna regret the shit!"

He studied me for a long moment. "And why should I listen to you? You don't even talk to me."

I shook my head impatiently. "Because I know what I'm talking about."

He frowned. "Well, what are you talking about?"

I couldn't bring myself to mention what had happened to me. Nobody else talked about it, either. It was like a secret society among some of the inmates. I never heard them talk about it. Even the ones that it happened to. I mean, rapes happen here all the time under the staff's nose and they never know. Many get raped by other inmates and say nothing, but bear the shame. But it was a little different when the warden was doing it and taping it. I wondered if it went on in the women's prison as well. It probably did.

My silence made him doubtful. "Man, you just mad because he called me up there and not you. He knows that I'm not really a criminal. I was a straight-A student in high school on my way to an Ivy League college before this happened to me. Yeah, you probably jealous that he didn't pick you."

I looked away.

He smirked and mumbled, "hater."

"Well, muthafucka, I warned you," is all I could bring myself to say before hopping back on my bed.

And he did go . . . the next time. Bright and early in the morning.

And didn't come back to his cell. That's how I knew something had happened to him.

When a guard walked by I called him back.

"What's up, Chance?" he asked.

I nodded and asked," Where is Charleston?"

He looked at his clipboard and confirmed it for me by saying, "I don't know what happened to him, but according to the population sheet he's in the infirmary."

And instantly a plan came into motion that I had never thought of before!

Chapter 23

He was gone for a period of two weeks. Shorter than the time I was gone, but two weeks nonetheless.

The noise of him coming in the cell woke me that early morning.

When he got settled, silence was all I heard from the bunk underneath me.

"You wanna get that dirty muthafucka?" I whispered.

Then nothing. No response. No movement. It was like he froze. He was probably wondering how I knew what had happened to him. He probably felt the same mixture of emotion that I had felt. Shame, depression, anger. The desire to just not exist anymore.

So at first I didn't even think he would wanna bother with it.

So I almost gave up hope.

Then I heard his faint whisper: "Yes."

That word put the plan into motion.

Lewis had me in one of the solitary cells. He had pretended to some other guards that he was taking me somewhere else. Instead we ended up there so we could have privacy to talk in one of the cells.

That's when I told Lewis everything. How it wasn't just a random inmate who raped me, but some inmates that were instructed by the warden to rape me. How the warden also took a turn. His eyes were wide. I told him how it was taped and now the same thing had happened to Charleston.

He shook his head and said, "Corrupt muthafucka."

I nodded. "What can I do with this?"

"What do you want?"

"To get the fuck up out of here! To expose a dirty warden gotta bring some kind of favor my way, don't it? Then maybe I can bring exposure on my situation: How my trial was never fair; how I'm in this shithole for some shit I didn't do. How I ain't never done shit my whole life that would warrant me being up in here for even a day."

"Chance, you know information is power. If this shit can play out right you can use this as a bargaining tool for your freedom and if not that, then a reduced sentence. Because they are going to want to make this go away as quickly as they can. If not, it's gonna be all up in the news, it's going to launch so many investigations and civil rights suits and can cost their ass some serious money." He pointed a finger at me. "It may not work. But then again, the shit might. It may be a lot of niggas that he did this to. But how many are going to speak up?"

I took a deep breath, relieved that there was even a small possibility.

"But I need to be able to prove it, right? With medical documents? The actual video? Charleston is down. But we can't do this shit by ourselves."

He stared at me for a moment before asking, "Do you understand what you are asking me to do?"

"Look, I know the risk I'm asking you to take. But I'm trying to get out of here. And now you tell me this gives me the chance? I can't spend the rest of my life behind bars But I don't know all the proper channels to go through." I took a deep breath. "That's why I need you."

Lewis believed that I was innocent. I knew he did.

He stared at me for a long time before finally nodding. "You can't mention any of this to anybody, not in letters and not in your visits, to no one except me and Charleston!" He took a deep breath like he was regretting what he was going to say next. "What do you need me to do?"

The plan was simple but risky. I was going to go into the medical charts and get copies of my file and Charleston's. The only way to do that would be to get a job working in the infirmary, which I did with no problem once I shared with one of the doctors that I had a degree in computer science.

All Charleston had to do was keep it cool with the warden and get the videos to prove our case. He said that he was also taped being raped. I prayed he could find these. But he said he was now at a stage where he filmed other inmates doing it by choice or when they refused they were forced. He made sure he got the warden on the camcorder in the act. The warden always gave Charleston the job of putting the video onto a DVD and also placing a copy on his computer. He copied the DVDs as well. Every time he came back, he was shaken up by what he saw. But he kept his mouth closed and did it. I knew he wanted to get out just as much as I did. His crime was severe. It was armed robbery and two people were killed. Of course he didn't kill anybody, but the fact of the matter was that he was there. I asked him why he did it and he said to impress his homeboys. He had never been in trouble a day in his life up until that day.

I was desperate for this to work so I did exactly what Lewis told me to. I didn't confide in anyone about this, not in my letters, because they were read before they were sent out and the ones sent to me were read before being given to me. I didn't mention anything to Calhoun when he would come to visit me either. Guards were always standing by and listening to our conversations. I told Charleston to do the same.

Once we had all we felt we needed, we gave it to Lewis. "Who is the best person to send it to?" I asked.

"The Department of Justice and Internal Affairs."

And so it was done. And done so quietly and smoothly almost as if we hadn't done anything.

Now all we had to do was wait.

But then—that wasn't the end of shocking news for me. A few weeks after we sent off everything, I got a surprise visit.

I sat down at a table to see a white woman who I had never seen before. She was in her late forties with graying blond hair, brown eyes, and thin lips that continued to tremble. I racked my brain and continued to scan her face for some type of familiarity.

But there was none.

"Hello," I said calmly, resting my hands on the visiting table.

"I've seen you in pictures so I know what you look like," she told me.

I narrowed my eyes. "Okay."

"But you look a little different. You're a lot more muscular and your eyes . . . They look so aged, different from the pics."

"That's what prison will do to you." I wished she would tell me who she was.

"I'm sure you are racking your brain, wondering who I am."

I chuckled. "Yes, ma'am.

She smiled. "She said you were respectful. She was right. Chance, I knew your mother," she said quickly.

I looked at her, surprised.

"She—she worked for my mother Ellen. As her in-home health care aide. My mother is a lot nicer than me. And trusting."

I nodded.

"And with all the elderly abuse going on nowadays I wanted to make sure that my mother was safe. But I have my own family and kids and no time to monitor someone that worked for my mother. So the best way to insure this was to install a camcorder in my mother's house. I don't know quite how to say this. But on the tapes I never saw your mother abusing my mother. But I always saw a man abusing your mother."

"What?"

She nodded. "He would come over at night, always on Sundays and Mondays. On one of the tapes he even raped your mother."

I blinked rapidly at what she was telling me.

"It was horrifying to watch. When I confronted your mother about it, she told me all about you. She said you were in prison and said that if she told , the man would hurt you. She begged me not to go to the police. So I didn't, although I wanted to. I told her if he ever came back to the house she would have to go because I didn't want that type of thing going on in my mother's house. But I couldn't see myself putting your mother out in the streets. And I didn't want to because my mother truly loved your mother. But then one day she disap-peared. We knew something wasn't right because one day she said she was going to go and visit you and never came back. When she wrote my mother from prison we found out where she was. We were relieved because we feared she might be dead. She continued to write my mother from prison. And my mother used to beg me to put money on her . . ."

"Books?"

She smiled. "Thank you. Yes. And I did. Once a month. But one day I went and they said she was deceased."

I nodded.

"And I'm sure you know that by now. I'm so sorry, Chance. I feel your pain because just last week *my* mother passed away. Maybe a few weeks before she died, she talked about you still being in prison for a crime you didn't commit. She also had some stuff. Some letters from your mother and pictures of you and her when you were younger. I don't quite know if I'm able to give them to you now, but by the grace of God if you are ever freed, which you ought to be, I can pass them on. And not just that. I'll also hold onto the recordings," she lowered her voice, "of your mother and that man if they will help you at all."

"Thank you." I looked around quickly. "Do you remember what the guy who was coming over harassing my mother looked like?"

She narrowed her eyes as if trying to recollect. "He was a big guy. Tall, dark skin. I don't know if that helps much. I've never seen him in person. The time on the camcorder always displayed him coming after hours, sometimes two, even three in the morning."

No. It couldn't be. Why didn't I figure this shit out before? *'Cause one way or another, you gonna sell the shit for me. And believe me, your problems are just starting with me.*

I spied Roscoe to the right of me talking to another guard. In the gut the core of my being I knew who it was. I did. But I had to hear it for myself. I looked around the visiting room to see if I spied who I thought it was. I did.

"Listen to me very carefully. Do exactly what I say. Okay?"

"Okay."

"Don't panic, ma'am. I took a deep breath before continuing. "On the right side of this room near that table with the guy with a woman and kid in his lap." I licked my dry lips. "About three feet from them are two guards. I want you to look at them. If one of them is the man on those films, I don't want you to speak. I don't want you to even blink. If it is him, clear your throat. Got it?"

"Yes," she whispered.

I closed my eyes briefly and waited as calm as I could. Three seconds later her throat cleared.

Chapter 24

I was able to meet up with Lewis again.

I shared the information that the lady I now knew as Emily told me.

"Damn," was all he said.

His eyes locked with me. "I know what you thinking, Chance. Don't do shit, don't say shit. It's fucked up what he's been doing, but it may also work in your favor."

"How?"

"She has the proof."

I nodded.

"You are going to uncover two dirty-ass rats in here. Another body to throw at DOJ. So I'ma need you to keep laying low. Same for Charleston. Wait for the shit to hit the fan and we go from there."

I nodded and took a deep breath.

When it was lights-out I took the opportunity to tell Charleston what Lewis told me. He really wasn't responsive to it.

"Why you so quiet, man? I thought the news would make you happy."

He sat up in the bed. "Why? I'm not getting out of here."

***

True, there was a possibility that neither of us would. But it was worth a try and if we didn't, at least we could bring the Warden and Roscoe down.

"We can't think like that."

"I don't want to get out of here anymore anyway."

I looked at him confused.

"After what happened with the warden . . . I can't face my family. I come from a good family. A mama and a daddy, sisters and brothers who loved me and were proud of me. I don't wanna go back like this."

"Like what? If you talking about—"

"Do you know what the fuck happened to me up there? What I saw? What I was made to do?"

I shook my head as flashbacks of them raping me came back. "That's why we both need to expose his ass and maybe it will help us."

"Chance, I'm twenty years old. And I don't care how old I get. I will never be able to forget what happened in there. I think about it every day and it ain't a night so far since it happened that I ain't had nightmares about it. I can't be with a woman now. If I had just—"

I cut him off. "Well, you can't go back now. You can't change the shit. Let it fucking go. I'm not trying to fucking die in here and even if this don't do shit to help me I can expose his dirty ass."

To that he said simply, "I'm already dead, Chance. Seems like I died the day they did what they did. I will never be able to get over it. I will never be able to live like a normal man again. Never."

I took a deep breath, rolled over, and went to sleep.

The next morning, when the guard called for us to get up and dressed and groomed for breakfast, I rolled over and sat up for a second. Then I hopped off my bed and pulled my clothes on.

Charleston was still sleep.

"Wake up, Charleston," I said.

He didn't move.

He had his blanket completely over his body and head. He must be sleeping hella good, I thought.

I leaned over and I shook him gently. "Wake up," I said.

When he didn't move my brows furrowed together.

I reached over and pulled the blanket back. What I saw alarmed me so much I leaped back.

He had a torn sheet wrapped around his neck and tied around the edge post of his bed. He had strangled himself.

My eyes passed over his wide-open eyes. He was dead.

Just weeks after Charleston's death, The Department of Justice and Internal Affairs came storming through that muthafucka like a hurricane. Next thing I knew, I was in the room with some suits and they were treating me like royalty because I was exactly what they needed, to bring the punk-ass warden down.

The dude from Internal Affairs, whose name was Eric Stevenson, studied me as I sat calmly in front of him. There was also a woman who worked for the Department of Justice, Leslie Miller, a public defender, John Chester, as well as the district attorney, Stephen Yearly.

They read the letter that Lewis helped me draft. They saw the films, the copies of my and Charleston's medical charts.

They were also aware that Charleston's parents were also suing for their son's death.

"Would you be willing to testify against him?" That was the DA.

"Would you be willing to get me out of here?"

He narrowed his eyes at me, picked up my file and laid it in front of me. "Sir, I'm apologetic about what you have gone through at the hands of a vey sick man who has brought so much shame on our department. *But.* The fact of the matter is you are in prison for murder—"

"That I didn't do. Nor was my trial ever a fair one. The DA put a man on the stand that had never seen me before in my life. How was he credible to testify? Nor was I ever given an opportunity for an appeal. Look at my records, see where I came from, the person I was. I had no record. I ain't never done shit and y'all locked me up while the real killer is free."

He nodded. "I understand your position. But—"

"No. I don't think you do. If you're not willing to work with me, I'm not working with you. And that ain't all I know. I know which guard is bringing drugs into this prison. And who is making the families of inmates, like my mother, bring them in. And the shit's on tape also."

Silence. Wide eyes, was the response I got.

"You are all supposed to be so ethical. But you all reflect the wrong you are supposed to be taking down. I'm sick of y'all shit and this broken-ass system that locks up innocent men. Trust and believe I will go public with this shit. Y'all got it under wraps now. But I'm gonna expose this sorry-ass prison. You got an innocent man rotting away in here. And I'm not the only one. But I'm the one at this time that is going to kick up dust until I rightfully get the fuck out."

I leaned over and looked at all four of them. "Understand I'm not giving up until y'all let me the fuck up out of here."

"And what else? What other information do you have?" That was the lady from the Department of Justice.

"I just told you. A guard that works here coming to my mother's house, forcing himself on her, and forcing her to bring drugs here. He same guard that assaulted me for refusing to sell his drugs for him."

I got silence again.

"And at my say-so, the person who has possession of these recordings is ready to send them to the press," I threatened.

They were still silent. It made me feel like this shit was all for nothing.

"I'm a small fish in this fishbowl. If y'all want the big fish you all are going to have to get me out this fishbowl."

The DA locked eyes with me and said, "Give us a moment, Mr. Wallace."

They all stepped out of the room.

Those few minutes they were gone, I felt as nervous as I did when I was on trial five years ago. What if they just took their chances with me going to the press and offered me nothing? Fuck. I took a deep breath.

Then they all came back and sat back down calmly. That wasn't a good sign for me.

The DA spoke first. "Mr. Wallace, we've managed to talk and discuss your situation along with this case and we have an offer for you."

I was all ears.

"If you agree to testify in court against the warden and tell us who the mentioned guard is and furnish us with the proof and testify against him as well—" he took a deep breath as if what he was about to say next was going to kill him— "the earliest we can release you is in two years."

My heart sped up. I couldn't believe it. I would have been happy if they had said five years or even ten. Just to know one day I would get out. And they were offering me two years?

The DA looked at my public defender. "Does your client need more time to think about the offer?"

I waved my hand and I answered before he did. "No. I'll take it. But before I testify, I need a minute order indicating my release date."

Chapter 25

Two Years later. March 16, 2010

They made it seem like I was getting a new appeal and that from that appeal my murder conviction was changed to manslaughter. I did a total of seven years in that place and I knew I was lucky as hell to get the fuck out of there.

I touched the scar on my face the three Mexican dudes had given me when they jumped me on the track seven years ago and laughed. I stared out the windows of the bus as it passed through a town I never thought I'd see again . . . my town, where I grew up and made a life for myself before it was snatched away for prison life.

The warden was out, so was punk-ass Roscoe. They were going to be sent to prison for a long time and that is exactly what they deserved. And as for Randy, Lewis told me that Randy was shanked in the shower one day.

Somebody could not help but leak the information and news camcorders were all around the prison when they escorted the warden's punk ass and Roscoe out. Emily, like I had requested, did her part. I wondered if they had gotten a fair trial. And more importantly, I wondered what their defense would be? The shit was on videotape. What could they say? It couldn't be denied. I was so relieved and grateful for Charleston, Emily, and Lewis's help. I thought back to how good it felt testifying against the warden and Roscoe. All the while they were shackled like I was shackled. Lewis told me that the warden was sentenced to fifteen years while Roscoe got nine.

I chuckled again. I was free. I wish Tyson could have lived to see this day. The day he had told me was going to come but I never believed him. And I wished Charleston was here to see the day the punk-ass warden went down for all that trifling shit he made me, Charleston, and other inmates do. I smiled and thought about my mama. I still missed her. I wished she could be here to see this day as well. It still bothered me that she had to go through all that shit that Roscoe had subjected her to, on account of me.

After that visit with Emily when I was informed of what he had done to my mama, every time I saw him it was a struggle to not put my hands around his throat and end his life. But I managed to keep my cool and at the end he ended up in the shackles.

Lewis told me the day they arrested him he was blocked from entering the facility. He continued to argue and make a scene, saying, "What the fuck, yo?" Then the police arrived and put his ass in handcuffs. Part of me wished they would bring him to the very same prison that he had worked at, where he was so corrupt to inmates so that they could get retribution on his ass.

But I didn't have to worry about the warden, Roscoe or prison anymore. I was free of that place. And I wasn't doing shit to go back there. I never really did bad things before except maybe speed or buy bootleg CDs and DVDs. Now those things just weren't important enough for me to go to jail. I planned on taking no chances.

I took another breath of the fresh air that was blowing into the windows of the bus. Truth was, I really had nowhere to go. No house, no family, nothing. I wondered where Calhoun was. His number was no longer in service when I called him from the holding tank, before they released me. I knew he would be pissed that I kept quiet on getting released and even all the other shit. But I didn't want to take any chances. People were always watching and listening. I never forgot what Tyson had said about how once inmates found out another inmate is going to get released, they would be doing all kinds of shit so they didn't go home. Naw. I wasn't going to say shit until I was officially released. Calhoun would get over it. I made a mental note to stop by his parents' pad.

In the morning, I had to go by and see my parole officer. Supposedly he was going to help me piece my life back together; help me find a job and a place to live. Once I did that, I planned on stopping by Emily's house and get the things my mother had left for me.

Lewis made sure to say good-bye to me on my way out and even gave me two hundred bucks. I would never forget all that he had done for me. And I knew when I got myself straight I was going to pay him back.

I found a cheap hotel to stay in for the night.

As soon as I got there, I crashed on the bed, happy I was free but scared and not feeling like the old Chance I used to be. As I laid back on the bed in the hotel room I thought about how much I had lost. It made me sad, of course. But shit, now I was fucking free. Wasn't no better feeling than that!

***

The next morning I got up bright and early and went to the Long Beach office to meet with my parole officer.

He was an older black man with a Jheri curl and more gold teeth than white. Rings and bracelets adorned his arms and hands. He looked more like a pimp than a parole officer.

He looked at me and got straight to the point. "Listen, man. Plain and simple, I'm not here to babysit you so don't come with the bullshit. Come and meet with me once a damn month, stay out of trouble, stay out the hood, and go to fucking work everyday."

"Yes, sir."

He looked surprised that I didn't give him any attitude or lip.

He read from his computer screen. "Do you really have a bachelor's degree and you worked for Microsoft?"

I nodded. "Yes, sir."

"Well, you won't be going back there." He held his hands out. "And your degree sure as fuck don't matter now. You are an ex-convict, my brother! That shit's going to follow you wherever you go. The shit don't stop just because you are out of prison. So don't count on making over eight dollars an hour, if you can get that."

I nodded.

He told me what my conditions were. "Make sure you show up to your job, don't give me no dirty piss, stay out the projects 'cause you know the fucking felons are in there. In other words, use common sense if you don't want to go back to prison. If you don't use common fucking sense, your ass will go back and I won't give a fuck. 'Cause you should have done what you needed to not go back."

He didn't have to worry about me. I wasn't going to do as much a jaywalk.

He handed me some bus tokens. "That should be a month's worth. When you come back next month I will give you some more. And don't try that 'I lost them' shit 'cause you will just come up short!" Spit flew form his mouth every time his voice got loud.

I resisted the urge to laugh.

"Report to your job. You have to have a job."

He handed me a paper that read *Speedy Computer Repairs*. My eyes scanned the address. It was located off of Termino, in Long Beach. I was familiar with that street. "He only pays eight dollars an hour. He don't give a fuck about them minimum-wage laws. So you best to take that shit and not count on a raise."

I nodded. It was nowhere near what I used to make, but still, it was a job. Better than nothing.

"You said you know how to work on computers and shit."

I nodded.

"All the info should be on there. And this other paper has the address to Grace Hotel. They are kitchenettes and are affordable. If you want you can call the housing authority and try to get on the section eight waiting list. I wouldn't recommend trying to get on the list for the Springdales, Carmelitos, or any other projects. That's putting you back in bullshit."

He gave me that paper and then pointed a finger at me. "Don't fuck up."

"Yes. sir."

He drug tested me and I was on my way.

I went by the Grace Hotel like he had suggested. I signed the contract for a room. It wasn't bad. It was a lot cleaner than the room I had stayed at the night before. The plus was that it had a small kitchen. The room was small, though.

The computer repair store he sent me to was about fifteen minutes away from my room, so that was also another plus.

It was located in a small shopping center across the street from Wilson High School next to a bagel shop.

Once I walked in, I saw a short man sitting behind a computer.

I cleared my throat. "How you doing, sir? I'm Chance. My parole officer sent me for the position."

He stood. He was a Middle Eastern guy who looked like he was barely five feet. He shook my hand. "Yes, your parole officer told me I should be expecting a visit from you. I am Zalman. Have you come to work hard?"

"Yes, sir."

He clasped his hands together. "Good. Let me explain what we do here at my store."

He explained that he made a lot of money by doing computer diagnostics, repairing computers for customers, as well as taking broken computers, fixing and selling them as refurbished computers.

He showed me around the store. "You will be opening and closing the store," he said in his thick accent. "I can't afford to hire more manpower so you will be taking calls as well as doing repairs."

I nodded.

"I opened up another store in Bellflower, so I will be there most of the time. Right now my wife runs that store."

He pointed to the camcorder and said, "It is always on."

I started to tell him that I didn't steal. I never have and never will. But he wouldn't believe me so I didn't bother. Instead, I simply said, "You don't have to worry, sir. I'm here to work and that's it."

He smiled. "And I'm here to work you. You can have one or two days off a week. It is your choice."

I nodded. "Just one."

"Oh, you really are a hard worker. You need to open the store at nine and close it at five."

I nodded.

"Eventually, if I feel I can trust you, I will give you a company cell phone and the car to make home visits. We charge fifty dollars to come out to homes and whatever the price for the repairs."

I nodded. "That's fine."

He gestured toward a computer on the table. "That needs to be repaired. Let's see what you can do, Chance." He turned to walk away but stopped and pointed to the camcorder above my head.

I performed a diagnostic on the computer to see what the problem was. The drivers were bad and there was a virus on it. It didn't take me long to repair it and have it running good as new. Fixing computers was something I was always good at and I could take one apart with my eyes closed.

Once it was running, I tried to log on to verify the virus was gone. It was and the computer was even running faster.

Zalman got up from the computer he was sitting at, and inspected my work.

I scanned the screen he was on, shaking my head. The whole time I worked on the computer he was in some chat group on another computer.

He said, "I'm going to get myself lunch."

Once he walked to the door, he turned, looked at me, and pointed to the camcorder.

I shook my head and sat in the chair he had abandoned.

Chapter 26

I logged onto the Internet and instantly Deyja came to my mind. I wondered if she was listed. I remembered from one of her letters she told me that she worked in real estate. I wondered if I typed her name into a search box if she would pop up. I remembered how she had even slipped on one of her letters and written her last name.

I typed her name under Google Search, along with the words *real estate*.

Deyja Sims Real Estate website popped up. I clicked on her site. Since the business was under her name I assumed it was hers. My eyes scanned the page as it talked about the services that they offered to the public.

I printed out the address and phone number and closed out of the site.

I went to the phone and called her office. A secretary answered. "Deyja Sims Realty."

I licked my dry lips, cleared my throat and said, "Yes. Deyja Sims, please."

"She is out of the office and won't be back until three. Can I take a message for you?"

"No. No, thank you."

"All right. Have a nice day."

I hung up quickly.

***

At five I was all done and ready to go. My first day was a lot of work for me but it was the type of work I didn't mind doing. I was sweating like a slave. But none of that mattered. I never shied away from hard work. And it felt good. This was because I knew that at the end of the day, I would be free and able to go home. I wasn't going to be stuck there. Like the prison I was stuck at for the past seven years.

When I got off my plan was to go to see Deyja and see if I could catch Calhoun at his parents' house.

The location of her office was right off of Ximeno, near the traffic circle in Long Beach. So it wouldn't take too long. If I wasn't so tired from work I would have walked there and saved a token.

As the bus drove I couldn't help gaze at all the cars in traffic and remembered how it used to be when I had my nice, new car. I knew they had pretty much repossessed my car so my chances of getting another car were slim. Being in jail I had defaulted on my car loan and it was repossessed and that was on my used-to-be-perfect credit along with two American Express cards I had for myself and Toi. It made me feel a little bitter. But then I reminded myself that I still had my freedom and to count the blessings I did have.

The real estate office was in a small shopping center next to a clothing store and a nail salon.

My eyes passed over the sign with her name on it in bright purple letters. I wondered if that was her favorite color.

The closer I got the door, the more nervous I got. I started to sweat and my heart started to pound harder. Damn, that wasn't how I used to be. I never had a problem stepping to a woman. And I had always con-

sidered myself to be a good catch. I didn't feel that way
anymore. I had experienced a feeling I had never felt
before: insecurity.

I closed the distance between me and the door in a
series of three steps. My hand reached for the doorknob.

Then I paused as the reality of the situation hit me.
I was a fucking ex-convict. Yeah, she wrote me letters
while I was in prison. But that didn't mean shit now.
She probably wouldn't spit on me. She was an accom-
plished woman. And she could be anything from having a man to being married with kids.

I took a deep breath. I was probably wasting my
time. But there was so much I wanted to say to her. I
wanted to tell her how much her letters meant to me,
how much they helped me get through a very dark time.
And as crazy as it sounds, I felt like I fell in love with
her just based on what she wrote to me. When I went to
her website I didn't even bother looking to see if there
was a picture of her. I had no idea how she looked. And
I didn't care. It didn't matter if she were old, fat, and
ugly. However she looked is not what helped me. So
they were no concern to me now.

And maybe if my circumstances were different this
could be different. If I went in there and told her who
I was and her connection to me I would probably end
up embarrassed and leaving with my feelings hurt. The
fact that I tracked her down may even make me look
like a stalker and I wasn't. But that's probably how it
would look from her standpoint.

So with a feeling of defeat, I turned and walked away.

I instead, hopped on a bus to take me to the Westside,
to go to Calhoun's house. The ride took me about a
good twenty minutes.

I figured that since it was the evening someone had to be home.

When I knocked on the door, Calhoun's father answered. He was the same build and height as Calhoun. But Calhoun, like me, had a lot of his mother's features. In all my years of being friends with him I often wished he and I could trade places. He had everything I had ever dreamed of . . . a father. Over the years, while Calhoun continued to disappoint him, he saw my accomplishments and always applauded me on them in front of Calhoun, which didn't make him too happy. At a very low point, when Calhoun had gotten arrested and used his father's name, his father came looking for him at my house. At that time I was in my second year of college. He looked so frustrated when I couldn't tell him where Calhoun was. Since when we were kids Calhoun's dad made it seem like I was the bad influence on his son. It felt good to show him that Calhoun was actually the bad influence. But I just never allowed myself to be influenced.

He blurted out, "You know what I don't understand, Chance."

"What, sir?"

"You came from nothing. I saw how your mother struggled to take care of you with no father and here you are trying to make something of yourself. I'm trying to figure out where I went wrong with Travis."

"Well, you didn't, sir. What Calhoun is doing is more of a reflection of him and not you or your wife, so you can't beat yourself up for it. Calhoun has a lot more growing up to do. I try to talk to him as much as I can but he doesn't want to hear anything that makes sense."

His eyes were watery and tears were sliding down his cheeks. He bowed his head in defeat.

"Calhoun is just hardheaded. You are a good father, Mr. Parks. So good that growing up and being around Calhoun I always wished you were my father."

He looked up at me when I said that and smiled. "Thank you. That means a lot coming from such a smart young man like you, Chance."

"Just don't give up on him, Mr. Parks."

"I won't. I won't give up on my son." He patted me on my back and walked out of me and my mother's apartment.

I wondered now after seven years if he had given up on Calhoun and what types of crazy things Calhoun had sent his parents through.

Mr. Parks paused for a moment, taking my face in for familiarity. When he realized who I was he said, "Chance?"

"How you doing, sir?"

He cracked up laughing and pulled me into his arms for a hug.

I laughed and hugged him back.

"Praise God, you are home!" He slapped my back and continued to chuckle. When he pulled away he grabbed my face in his hands before shaking my hands.

"Is Calhoun here?"

"No. But come in."

A few minutes later, we were sitting in his living room, drinking cans of Coke. All it made me think was how lucky Calhoun was to still have both his parents.

"So how have things been?" I asked him

"Work is good, my wife is well when she isn't stressing about Travis."

I chuckled and said, "Same ol' Calhoun." Calhoun wasn't bullshitting when he told me when I was in prison that he was still on the same tip.

"Yep, same ol' Travis." He refused to call him Calhoun.

"My wife and I try not to stress out anymore, but that is hard in itself with the things that he does. But we spend a lot of time with our grandchildren."

"And how are they?"

"Well. Very well. But what about you, son? You spent seven years of your life locked away. I would imagine that would have had to be hard, harder than any other challenge you have ever faced."

"It was. But I had to find a way out."

"And how were you able to do that?"

I wasn't able to answers those questions yet. I wasn't strong enough yet. To talk about the rape and how it led me to my freedom.

He saw and said, "Travis told me that it was for something you were innocent of. I believe him and I'm sorry for always making you out to be the bad guy when the bad guy was my son all along."

"I understand, Mr. Parks."

"He was never really able to move past you being in there."

"Neither was I."

"Does Travis know you're out?"

"No. I just got out yesterday."

"Wait until he does, he's going to go crazy. Right now I'm sure he is hanging in those projects."

He paused for a moment and then said, "Chance, I'm sorry about your mother. Travis told me."

He looked away quickly and I was glad he did because the mention of my mother and her not being there momentarily choked me up.

I could only manage to get out, "Thanks."

"You bet." He studied his Coke can.

"Well, I have to get going. If he comes by tell him I came over and I will try to swing by again."

"Take care, Chance."

He stood and I did as well. He gave me another hug and I was out the door.

I knew I would run into Calhoun eventually. Long Beach was too small. He would probably be pissed that I kept the fact that I was to get released on a hush. But I had to.

Chapter 27

With the free time I had at work after I got all my repairs done I did some further research on the Internet to find a private investigator. Yeah, I was out and free but still, the case and how it panned out with me losing seven years of my life was going to forever bother me until I found out the truth. Why that dude who I never met before testified against me? Why? What were his motives? Unless I found out, that shit would forever be on my mind. I wanted answers, plain and simple. So with a little research on the web, I got the number to several investigators in my area.

I stopped by *Jump Street Investigations* in the city of Lakewood.

Once I got there and was informed of their rates I did a quick about-face and exited the office. They wanted one hundred dollars an hour. I couldn't afford that. I visited two more offices that were even more expensive than him.

So I was hoping I would have more luck with the next dude.

His name was Mateo Garcia and he was located in north Long Beach.

When I arrived at the address from my printout, I almost thought I had the wrong address because the one I had was actually a Mexican restaurant.

I walked inside and asked a waitress, "Excuse me. Do you know where Mateo Garcia's office is?"

She nodded. "It is in the back, behind the kitchen, sir. Follow me."

I looked at the kitchen, surprised.

Part of me wanted to turn around and catch the bus home. But since I had already wasted a token coming here, I might as well see what the dude was talking about.

I followed behind the waitress.

He looked like he was in his thirties, sitting behind a beat-up desk with a cowboy hat and some cowboy boots. Looking at the whole setup, I really had doubts that he could help me.

Still, when he stood and introduced himself by shaking my hand, I shook it back and sat across from him in the chair he gestured toward, feeling doubtful as hell.

He sat back in his chair, crossed his legs, and laced both his hands over one of his knees.

"So tell me about how I can help you?" He had a strong accent. I cleared my throat. "About seven years ago, I was getting out of my shower at my house. The next thing I knew, cops were dragging me out and whipping my ass. I was arrested for murder of a police officer, Devin Johnson. I was sentenced to twenty years to life in prison."

He looked surprised.

"My murder was third-degree."

"I see. Not with the intent to kill."

"Anyway, when I was there, I got the warden on some shit and a guard." I didn't bother telling him about what had happened to me there.

"They agreed if I testified against the warden and the dirty guard that they would bargain with me. They dropped the murder charge to manslaughter and I served only seven years."

He nodded.

"Okay, you're out. He spread his arms. "Why start an investigation? Wouldn't it be better to move on with your life? Seven years have passed since this murder, no? Maybe the better thing to do is to let it go."

"If I had had the power and the money to fight it when I was in prison I would have, but all the cards were stacked against me. My lawyer dropped the case when I couldn't get money to him. I filed an appeal but it was denied because I had no evidence that supported that the trial was unfair and to support that I was innocent."

"That doesn't answer my question. You are out, you're free. Again I ask you, Chance, why not just let this go?"

"Because I lost my mother, my girl, my baby, pretty much my life. And I want to do something about it."

"What makes you think that you can do something about this?"

"Because I didn't do it. Look, it makes no sense. If I didn't do it, somebody else did and I wanna know why in the hell he didn't got caught?"

"Because you did."

We were going in circles. I shook my head and stood. "You know what?" I said impatiently. "I'm wasting my fucking time."

He rolled one of his hands in a circular motion, saying, "easy, easy."

I shook my head, preparing to walk out. His words stopped me.

"Wait and listen. The system is fucked up. We know this but there has to be some type of substantial evidence as to why they pinned you for the murder." His tongue rolled over each word.

"All they had was a fucking witness. And some blood in my car."

His eyes got wide. "That is all they needed. Sit down." I did. " But it was a man I have never seen before."

That's when his interest was piqued. He started jotting something down on a notepad, while singing, "*Vido mas. Vido mas.*"

"So I still don't get why this murder was pinned on me."

"But he does."

"Huh?"

"The witness."

I nodded.

"What do you hope to gain out of this? I mean, you're free now, you got your life back."

"Not really," I said dryly. I lost what mattered to me the most. I'd never have my life back.

"Then . . . "

"I want fucking answers. I lost too much to just go on as an ex-convict, living in a motel room, and making minimum wage. I want answers. And I want my name cleared."

He was silent before sitting down the notepad and asking, "Do you remember the name of the witness?"

I thought back to that day. I saw his face and remembered how casually he lied on me on the witness stand.

"Yeah. Ron Jasper."

He scribbled it down. "The way to figure this out is to find him. I charge forty dollars an hour. If you can commit to three hours a week then I will throw in an extra hour for free. I can't guarantee my fee will stay that price. Most private investigators charge more."

But they probably weren't in the back of a Mexican restaurant, I wanted to say.

"You determine how many hours a week you want my services. And listen, I may not have a real office and may not look like I know what I'm talking about, but I can get you the answers you are looking for."

I was real doubtful that he could. "And suppose that I do chose you. What would you do?"

"Figure out who killed the cop. It's not openly complicated. I'm gonna lead you to the person who has all the answers and get him to open his fucking mouth. Bang bang."

I narrowed my eyes at him and I calculated in my head how much I would be paying. I made only three hundred and eighty dollars a week. After taxes I took home three hundred a week. Since I was staying at the Grace Hotel they charged me one hundred and seventy five dollars per week for my room. I had gotten paid last week and paid for my room for the next two weeks, bought myself some clothes, food and bath items I needed, and an electric skillet. So all I had left to my name was only one hundred bucks for the next two weeks. Still, I peeled out eighty dollars and handed it to him.

"That is all that I can afford. When I have more I will give you more."

He stuffed the money in his pockets.

"We will go from there. Is there a number where I can reach you?"

"No. But I will stay in contact with you."

I shook his hand and stood to leave.

"Would you like something to eat? I'm the manger here so it will be on me."

I wanted to decline but the thought of going back home and eating crackers with tuna, sardines or top ramen, made me say yes. Although my room was a kitchenette, I was trying to stretch my money.

I sat down at one of the tables in the restaurant after he walked me out. I scanned the menu and picked the first thing I saw: a *carne asada* burrito, with everything.

A few minute later the waitress who had helped me earlier brought it to my table.

My mouth watered as she sat it on front of me.

Red sauce and cheese covered it. Yes, I had been out of jail for a couple weeks but I still hadn't had a decent meal because of my penny-pinching.

I picked up the fork and dug in. Steak, beans, cheese, rice, guacamole, and sour cream filled my mouth. I scooped another piece in my mouth. I was so into the burrito that I almost didn't look up when my name was called.

"Chance?"

I knew who it was before I even got the chance to look at her. I could not forget that voice.

My eyes instantly locked with Toi's.

Chapter 28

I scanned her quickly, putting a pause on my chewing, and swallowing hard. She looked the same except her face was a little rounder and her hips had spread out. She wore her hair long on one side and shaved on the other with stars carved on it. Did I miss the new trend while I was in prison? Women were shaving the side of their head now?

She smiled.

Memories came back. When we were together, making love . . . how she broke me by leaving me when I needed her the most. My eyes watered a little. So I looked away from her and scanned the guy. It wasn't the dude she had brought with her when she came to visit me in prison, but he looked no better than him. He looked like a loser straight up, from the braids on his head to the way he dressed. With all the anger inside of me I tried to reconcile it by asking myself, 'Could I really blame her for leaving me with the time I was facing?' No, but it was the way she got down, the way she did it. It was plain-out dirty.

She walked over to my table and stood in front of me.

"I knew that was you!" she said in an excited voice.

I nodded.

"I never thought you would get out." She looked away and then looked back at me. "Does Calhoun know?"

I shook my head. "I haven't seen him yet."

"I have his number if you want it."

Before I could begrudgingly say I did, the dude with her demanded, "Man, are we going to eat or what? And who the fuck is this nigga anyway?"

"None of your fucking business," I said, picking my fork back up.

"What the fuck you say?"

I scooped some burrito in my mouth. "You heard me."

She shoved him back. "Just go sit down, damn!"

He sucked his teeth and walked away.

"So where are you staying, Chance?"

"Thanks to you, at a hotel."

She nodded and pulled her lips in.

Before she could say anything else the dude said, "Baby, come on so we can order!"

She backed away, continuing to stare at me as she did. "See you later, Chance."

I didn't reply. I just continued to shove the burrito in my mouth until nothing was left on my plate except a little of the rice and tomato that had fallen out the burrito while I was eating. I scooped that up as well and ate it.

And although I managed to keep my face clear of expression, to see her after all these years after she did what she did and with another man, the shit still touched me.

Although Zalman said it would be him and I working in the store only, he forgot to mention that all the women he would be tricking his money off on would be in the store too. Case in point today, while his wife was running the other store, he was here in the back room with another chick.

That's all he ever came in to do and the repairs were all mine.

I had been working there exactly a month. Dude was no joke with the women.

"If my wife calls tell her I'm out doing a service call!" he yelled

"Got it."

I shook my head at him as he ushered a woman into the back room. Guess that was his boom-boom room.

By the time he came out, I managed to clean the hard drive of a laptop, remove the viruses, and do a data transfer. Next thing I knew, he was kicking the chick right out of the store. Even after he pushed her out, the smell of her box stayed in the store.

I continued to stay busy with the laptop. I was putting the screws back on it and tightening them.

My back was to him but I could feel him staring at me.

"Did my wife call?"

"Nope." I twisted the small screwdriver in my hand.

"You keep what happens in the store between you and me, okay?"

I nodded and chuckled. I knew he was referring to the women he had coming in and out of the store.

Before I could reply, the door chimed because and someone came in and with them came the sweet scent of vanilla.

"Zalman! Oh my God. I'm so glad you are here! My laptop just crashed and I don't know what to do. Can you please fix this thing?"

He chuckled. "Deyja, don't worry. We will fix it."

I froze. Could it be?

I turned my head slightly and looked at the women standing in front of him. And when I did, my breath nearly caught in my throat.

She was beautiful. Her skin was light brown and flawless, not a mark on it. She had delicately arched eyebrows over her eyes, which were brown and almond shaped. As she continued to explain what happened to her computer her long lashes swept lightly over her perfectly carved cheekbones. Her mouth was full and lush with lipstick that was the color of plums. She twitched her button nose as Zalman talked to her.

My eyes couldn't help but travel down her body. She had full breasts hidden beneath a blazer, and the blazer showed the curve of her small waist and broad hips. Her face and body favored the actress Paula Patton, the one who played in that movie the rappers from OutKast starred in, *Idlewild*. I had seen it in prison.

I got up from my chair and walked over to the counter, keeping my eyes down and pretending to be looking for something. But instead I was trying to get a closer look at the name that Zalaman was scribbling on the work order. It read *Deyja Sims*.

It was her. So this is the woman who had been writing me all this time.

I went back over to the table I had abandoned and tried to put my focus back in what I was doing before she walked in, but I couldn't stop taking peeks at her as I tightened the last screw.

The more I studied her, the more I saw something there behind her eyes too. Pain.

When Zalman cracked his normal jokes that always had other customers laughing—not at the joke, but more at him, because you couldn't even understand the joke and because it never made sense and when he talked spit always flew. But he didn't bring any laughter from Deyja that day. She only offered a smile and said in a soft voice when he was done, "Okay, great."

"Just give us a couple hours and we will have it fixed. I will call you when I'm done"

"Thank you, Zalman!"

She did not even glance my way when she walked out of the store.

"Oh God, she is so fucking hot!" he said, watching her walk out of the store. "I love to watch those sexy lips move. I wish they would move on me!"

I watched her too, the whole time wishing I had the guts to tell her who I was. I wondered what she would have said if I told her that I was Chance.

"Hey buddy! Get to work." He ignored the fact that it was five minutes until I was scheduled to be off and that he hadn't done a lick of work that day.

"Don't worry. I will pay you for overtime. I'm not running a sweatshop."

"No. You don't have to pay me overtime. Just do me a favor, sir."

"Sure. What?"

"When she comes back to pick up her laptop don't tell her my real name."

He chuckled. "No problem. Just tell me what you want me to call you."

I thought quickly. "Isaiah is fine."

He chuckled and walked away. "Okay. As long as you keep my secrets, I will keep yours. Now get to work."

He paused in front of his camcorder, pointed, but then said, "I'm just kidding."

The solution to her problem was that her hardware overheated. But before I performed diagnostics I saved the documents on her computer on a flash.

Fixing it was simple. A can of compressed air being sprayed from a distance cooled it down.

I also downloaded a registry cleaner.

She came back to the store like clockwork.

She looked surprised when she saw me behind the counter. "Hello."

"How are you doing?" I asked her nervously.

"Good. And you?"

I simply nodded and my lips pulled in.

"Is Zalman here? He said my laptop would be repaired in a few hours."

I went from behind the counter to get it. "I have it right here. It overheated. A good thing to do is to have a can of compressed air and spray from a distance, should the same thing happen again."

She nodded.

I also slid a flash drive her way. "All of your documents are on here. Just in case."

She smiled, revealing a perfect set of white teeth. "Okay. Thanks so much. I hope that didn't take up too much of your time."

"It's no problem."

Just then Zalman walked out. I prayed he remembered not to call me Chance.

"Deyja, this is C—Isaiah. He works in the store. He will be doing home visits so if you need something repaired you can call and ask for him also." Zalman patted me on my back.

I guess he really did trust me.

She stared at me for a moment before saying, "Okay. That is good to know."

I couldn't stop staring at her. I mean, she was beautiful. And this was her.

"How much do I owe you?"

Zalman rang up the amount. It ended up being forty-five dollars.

I still couldn't stop staring at her. At one point she noticed and locked eyes with me. But I wouldn't break the stare. Again, I thought, she was here. Crazy. Small world.

Chapter 29

"What's up, my nigga, how you going to come back to town and not look me up?"

I stared at Calhoun and couldn't help but crack into a smile. He reached over the counter and hugged me. I hugged him back, happy to see him.

Once I broke the hug, I saw Toi also enter the store.

My smile dropped at her presence. Then I ignored her.

"Why didn't you come into the Springdales? You know that's where I always be!"

"A part of my parole is to stay away from known felons," I joked.

"Nigga, fuck you!"

"Nigga, fuck you! I'm not trying to go back to jail."

We both broke into laughter. I wondered how they found out that I worked here.

"Seriously, though. When I got out I went to your parents' house, you weren't there."

"Why didn't you come to the Springdales? You know that's where I always be."

"I ain't going in there for shit."

"Aww nigga! Yeah, Toi swung through the Springdales one day and told me a nigga was fresh out."

"How did you know I worked here?" I asked him.

"Shit, I didn't." He pointed to her. "She did. So I had to see the shit for myself."

"Chance, you know Long Beach is a small city," was all she said.

I frowned and figured she probably saw me in the company car. For the past month I was doing home visits for Zalman on my day off. I didn't mind because the extra money I made I was using to pay the private investigator. He didn't mind 'cause it gave him the opportunity to trick and ho more than he was already doing. And he made extra money off of my labor.

"Aye. My nigga, when you get off work we gotta go and celebrate."

I shook my head. "Naw."

"Have you got some pussy yet?"

Toi hit him on his shoulder.

"What? Y'all not together no more. It's been seven years!"

She rolled her eyes.

"I mean, what you expect after the way you did him?"

Her eyes locked with his and the both stared each other down. When Calhoun wouldn't back down, Toi put her head down.

"Like I said, dude. You had some pussy yet?"

"Chance know how to take care of Chance," I said, even though I hadn't been with another woman. Yes, I was on full. But I wasn't fucking with Toi again and I wasn't about to get a prostitute. So I would have to wait on that and keep doing what I been doing: jacking off.

"Well, look, nigga call me tonight. I'll borrow my baby mama's car and we can go to the strip club over on El Segundo called the *Boom Boom Room*."

I took his number down and slid the paper in my pocket.

"Calhoun. Go outside," Toi ordered.

"I'm catching up with my nigga."

"Go or you going to be on the bus."

"Man." He sucked his teeth and said, "Call me to-night, Chance."

I chuckled.

Once he left she said, "Chance, can we talk?"

I looked at the clock. It was ten minutes until I had to close the store.

I shut down the computer and pulled the bars on the two front doors and the walls adjacent to them. Then I stood in front of her. I didn't know what the fuck she wanted to talk about, but I asked, "Are you following me, Toi?"

She looked embarrassed.

"I saw you in that little car and it had a sign on it with the address and phone number to this place. If you call that following, then I guess that's what I did."

"Well, it is a little difficult to believe anything that comes out of your mouth," I said drily.

"Why are you being so cold to me?"

"Bitch. Did you forget what the fuck you did?"

Her eyes got wide. I guess she really thought I was going to look at her and get all softy like I used to be. No. Times were different now. Much different. Now I saw no need to be kind and gentle to her. She used to be my baby. My sweetie. My boo. But she wasn't none of that no more. She betrayed me. She broke my heart.

"I know I deserve that. I did you wrong, baby. I'm sorry for that." Her eyes got watery. "But I still love you, Chance. And whatever I gotta do to get you back and to get our life back to the way it used to be, baby, I will!"

"My life back to the way it used to be." I smirked. "Toi. I was an innocent man locked up. I needed you. I needed your love and your support just like I always gave you my love and support. And you didn't just turn your back on me. You stole from me, left my mama without a home. And if that wasn't enough. you killed my baby and brought another man to see me! That's enough for a man to kill you."

She nodded her head and pulled her bottom lip in.

It had no effect on me.

"I know, baby, and I'm so sorry. That's why I want to make this right. We can put the pieces back together. Buy another house. I know it won't be the same with your mother—"

"No."

She started crying. "I know you hate me, Chance. I'm so sorry. But I was just so scared. I didn't want to have to move back to the Springdales. I wanted to have the life you gave me. And with you in prison I didn't think I could maintain that on my own. I was just scared."

I shook my head at her selfish ass.

I took in her trembling lips and watery eyes.

"We can try again."

"Toi, I understand your fears about thinking that the man you love was going to be locked inside of a cage for good. It's not about that. It's the way you did it. You did me and my mama dirty. And I can't forget that. I loved you for years, Toi. But I don't love you anymore. I can't love a person who did what you did. I just can't. And the fact that you were able to move on so quickly makes me doubt that you were ever faithful to me. It takes a woman far longer to move on from a man. I'm a man and I couldn't have moved on from you that fast. Not when I loved you."

"But—"

The office phone rang. I snatched it up quickly. "Speedy Computer Repair," I said in a brisk voice.

"Hi, this is Deyja. Deyja Sims."

I stared at Toi.

Before I could respond, she said, "Listen, I know that you guys are going to be closing soon. But the same issue that happened to my computer happened to my secretary's computer. And I never got around to getting that stuff. And although it seems simple, I'm so scared I will end up making her computer worse. Is there any way you can stop by? I'll pay extra if I need to."

"Sure, no problem." I knew Zalman didn't care if I did it after-hours because it was more money for him.

"I will be there in about ten minutes."

"Wait. Don't you want the address?"

I had already known it from when I came there before and got discouraged and left. But I played it off like I didn't.

"Right. What's your address?"

She gave it to me quickly.

"I'll be there shortly," I said before hanging up.

"Who is that?"

I looked at Toi like she was crazy for even thinking that she had the nerve to question me on who the fuck I talk to.

"Why?"

"No reason. It's just that your face sparked all up the moment you found out who the caller was." She lowered her gaze and said, "The way it used to spark up for me. Whoever she is, she must be somebody special."

I didn't reply.

"Well, I'll let you go."

With that, she walked out.

I locked up and went to the beat-up car Zalman let me use to do service calls. He never let me take it home so I always dropped it right back off and hopped on the bus to go home.

As I walked to the car, Calhoun yelled, "Where you staying at?"

"I'm at the Grace Hotel on Redondo in room seven." I thought it would be good to catch up with him. He might be a lot of bad things but he was still my friend and he had my back when I was locked down.

When I remembered that Toi was out there. I wished that I hadn't yelled out where I was staying. I knew she was ear hustling.

When I got to Deyja's office, the same nerves that had kicked in the last time I had come there had managed to come right back. But I swallowed hard and opened the door.

The secretary, an older woman, was seated behind the desk.

"How are you doing ,ma'am. I'm Isaiah from Speedy Computer Repair and I'm here to repair your computer."

"Oh, it's not mine that needs to be fixed. It's Deyja's."

I was confused. Deyja said her secretary's computer needed to be fixed.

She rose from behind her desk."I'll show you to her office."

We walked down a long corridor where there were men and women behind several cubicles.

Once we got to the end, The secretary stopped behind a closed door.

"Just knock and she will let you in." With that she walked away.

I knocked on the door.

"Come in."

I took a deep breath and walked into her office.

She was seated behind a desk.

"Hi." She gave me a bright smile. "I'm sorry. What was your name again?"

"Isaiah."

She stood from behind her desk and said in a perky voice that sounded so sweet, "Well, Isaiah. This is the problem. See, I fibbed a little on the phone. My laptop didn't overheat. See, I bought a new one. And let's just say that I'm not very savvy on the computer. So I have no software installed and I needed my other documents on the new computer." She bit her bottom lip. "And I was hoping you could fix it."

"That's not a problem. Why didn't you just ask me?"

"I was embarrassed that I couldn't figure it out on my own."

I smiled. "Naw. That's nothing to be embarrassed about. I'm sure you're good at a lot of other things."

She looked at her high-heeled feet and blushed.

She was too adorable.

"Okay. I'll let you get to work on it."

She walked past me and her scent filled my nostrils. This time she smelled like strawberries. I wished she would stay in the room. But I played it off and got to work. By the time I was done I had two more other women come to her door and say something was wrong with their computers.

So I walked over to the cubicles to see what the problem is. Then I had a crowd of women standing around me.

That's when Deyja came over. "Well, it looks like you're very popular here, Isaiah. I hope they're not working you too hard." She eyed her staff as she said this.

But honestly, there was nothing wrong with their computers. They were checking me out. Because once

I was in Deyja's office I had taken off my T-shirt and had on a wife beater. Prison had made me bigger than I already was so I figured they were checking out my physique.

"Everything seems to be fine," I told the older woman from the group of women that claimed their computers needed repairs.

"Just making sure," she said, giving Deyja a guilty smile.

The rest of the women scurried back to their cubicles, while the men watched and shook their heads at them.

"I'll meet you up front. Just let me go to my office and get my checkbook." She walked away. I watched her as she walked. She had a sexy walk. Not one of them where a woman was doing too much by poking her butt out or excessively switching hips. She just moved in a naturally sexy way.

When she disappeared around the corner, I grabbed all my equipment and went up front.

Once there, I stood near the secretary. She looked at me and gestured for me to come closer with one of her hands.

"Isn't Deyja pretty?" she whispered, looking around to make sure no one was near to hear what she was asking me.

I smiled. "She's beautiful."

"And single," she added. "Why don't you ask her out?"

"I—"

Deyja walked toward us with the check.

"Thank you so much," she said, handing it to me.

I nodded and slipped the check into my back pocket.

I made a step to walk away but stopped and faced her. By the secretary suggesting what she did, it gave me a little more confidence to do something.

"I hope you don't take offense to what I'm about to say." I cleared my throat. "Would you consider letting me take you out sometime?"

She was taken aback by what I said and looked surprised.

"She'll go!" the secretary blurted out before Deyja could respond.

Deyja pierced her with a look. Her face softened when she turned back to me and she took a deep breath before she spoke. "You seem like you are a really nice man, Isaiah."

My hope sunk at that point. I knew she was just buttering me up to tell me no.

"Deyja, you haven't been out in—"

"Tia. Stop it."

The secretary put her hands up, as if in surrender.

Deyja continued. "Right now I don't have any interest in going out." She placed a hand on my sleeve. "But I do appreciate you offering."

I nodded, wanting to beg her to change her mind. But I didn't. "Have a nice day," I said gruffly.

Deyja simply nodded.

"Bye," the secretary yelled.

I tossed her a smile over my shoulder and exited the place. Maybe it was better that way, anyway. I mean, I was playing with fire by trying to date her. Eventually I would have to tell her who I really was.

I walked out of the office and toward Zalman's car. I was opening the door when I heard heels on the pavement behind me.

I turned around and spied Deyja coming my way.

I though maybe I had left some of my equipment in there.

Once she closed the space between us, she said in a low voice, "One more time."

"One more time what?" I asked, confused.

She took a deep breath and said, "Ask me out again."

I started to ask her what changed her mind but thought different. I gave her a slow smile and took a deep breath. "Can I take you out some time?"

"Yes."

Chapter 30

I didn't know where to take her. I didn't know how I was going to take her anywhere. But when I called her, she told me she wanted me to meet her at the Farmers Market so I didn't need to worry about any of this. My only worry now was her seeing me get off of the city bus.

The Farmers Market was located in downtown Long Beach. It was a nice place to go and buy fresh fruit, clothes, jewelry, accessories, and even paintings. They even played jazz out by the waterfalls. Before I went to prison, on paydays, I would take my mother and she would go crazy buying stuff.

I spied Deyja standing near a vendor who was selling different pieces of African jewelry.

I paused and allowed my eyes to scan her.

She was dressed in a spring dress that had an array of colors: hues of orange, brown, amber, and red. It was tied around her neck and crisscrossed down her back. The bottom of her dress hung in little sheaths down to the thighs. She had her hair pulled back from her pretty face. She wore a pair of gold earrings that were interlocking rings. They hung delicately from her ears. I snuck away and went to the vendor that sold roses. I bought one for five dollars and made my way over to her.

She was still studying the jewelry.

"Hi, Deyja."

She spun around quickly and spied me. She gave me another one of her smiles. "Hi, Isaiah."

I handed the flower to her.

"Thank you." She broke off the stem of the flower and placed it in her hair. All it did was make her look prettier than she already looked.

I inhaled her scent. This time she smelled like some sweet spices like pumpkin pie, no bullshit. Her hands were painted a peach color. So were her toes that were in a simple pair of opened toes with a low heel.

She turned back to the jewelry. "What do you think of these pieces?" she asked me.

I stepped closer to her, hoping she would not object to how close I was. I inhaled her scent again and looked at the softness of her shoulders bared in the dress.

Damn.

"I think this one would look good on you."

It was a necklace made from ivory pieces that were in different shapes, a turquoise rock in the center.

"You think so?" she tossed over her shoulder.

I nodded.

"Can I see that one, please?" she asked politely.

The lady handed it to her and Deyja placed it against her chest.

"It goes with your complexion." There was a mirror in front of her. She eyed me in it.

I looked back.

She dropped her eyes.

It was crazy that all she had on her face was a little lip gloss and she still looked pretty. Her beauty was natural.

"I'll take this one."

She handed it back to the lady, who wrapped it up in tissue paper for her.

The necklace came to thirty-two dollars and although I didn't have money to spare, I pulled out the money to pay for it.

"Let me buy it for you."

She lowered her eyes as the cashier took the money out of my hand.

"Thank you," she told me.

"No problem."

Once the lady handed it to her, we walked away.

"What else would you like to see?" I asked her.

She was much shorter than me, so to stop me from walking she tugged on one of the sleeves of my shirt. "Let's look at those."

We walked over to some scarves. She fingered a deep purple one.

"Let me buy that for you," I said.

"Listen, Isaiah. I appreciate you offering to buy that for me and buying the necklace. But understand that I didn't have you come here to spend your money on me. So don't think you have to impress me by buying up the market."

I had never had a woman tell me that.

I nodded. "I just wanna do something to make you happy."

She blushed at my words.

"I like when you do that."

She looked away, ignoring the comment. "Let's go over there." It was a table where a man was selling cologne.

Once at the table, she lifted one and placed it to my nostrils. "Tell me when you like a scent."

She picked a cologne off of the table and got close enough to me to lift it to my nostrils. Although it smelled good I wanted her to stay close to me. She would stand on her tippy toes and her body would brush against mine. When she lifted a third scent to my nose, I said, "I like that one."

"Cool Water," she told me.

I had worn it before. But I acted like it was a new scent to me.

And before I could say anything, she bought it for me. It didn't feel right and I tried to stop her by pulling the money out of my pocket and even thought it was my last, I would have spent my last dime and ate rice and top ramen for the next month just to be in her presence. But Deyja pushed one of my hands away.

"Thanks," I said after she handed me the bag with the cologne.

She smiled. "You need a special treat too because something tells me that you do for everybody else before you do for yourself."

I chuckled.

We walked over to the fruit section. "You know, it's been so long since I have been on a date. A long time, Isaiah. My employees say too long. My life consists of work and church."

"Oh yeah?" I followed behind her, admiring her soft thighs and calves as the edges of the sheaths of her dress swayed with the wind.

"Yep." She bit her bottom lip as if she was hesitating to tell me something. "Sometimes moving on can be—" She shook her head and turned back to the fruit. "Hey, let's get one of those and share it, so you don't have to worry about going in your pocket." She shoved me toward a bench and said, "You sit down over there and I will bring it to you."

I did as she instructed.

A few moments later, I watched her come back with a small plastic bowl. It had various types of fruit: cut-up mango, cantaloupe, strawberries, pineapple, and slivers of coconut.

She handed me a fork and said, "Get in there."

I laughed and watched her snag a pineapple. She was so into eating the fruit she didn't notice me watching her.

"So what made you accept my date offer?"

She paused her chewing and looked at me, confused. "Why is it such a surprise?"

I shrugged, rubbed my hands together, and said nonchalantly, "I don't know, I guess because you are who you are and I am who I am."

She speared a strawberry with her fork, slipped it in her mouth, chewed, swallowed, and said, "Isaiah. You are going to have to be more specific."

"You are very successful. You own your own business." I paused before saying, "Whereas I just repair computers."

"Come on, Isaiah. I don't care about those things."

"Well, at first you turned me down."

She took a deep breath. "It had nothing to do with you. I don't date. And my coworkers have been pushing me to go out on a date. It was either you or one of their old perverted uncles or one of their brothers who probably doesn't have a job at all. One way or another I had to get them off my back." She put a hand over her mouth like she had said too much. "Oh! I didn't mean to say that I used you. I in some way agree that I do need to go on and go out. You just so happen to be the one who asked when I finally got the nerve to say yes, is what I meant. "

"Don't worry about it. I'm not offended, but I am curious as to why."

"Why what?"

"Why you don't date."

She shook her head. "I don't really want to discuss it. Sorry."

"Okay. I understand."

When she bit down on a piece of cantaloupe, some of the juices slid out of her mouth and down her chin. She started laughing and said, "Look at me being a pig!"

Without thinking, I took one of my fingers and wiped it away. I slipped even closer to her face to where her breath was on mine, mine was on hers. And before she even knew what I was going to do next, before she could stop me, my lips brushed against hers. She pulled back an inch, surprised. I pulled forward an inch so her lips were on mine again.

I thought she was going to pull back or even toss the fruit over my head. But, shit, it would have been worth it to feel the softness of her mouth and taste the sweetness of her.

Then slowly, her mouth opened and she let me invade the insides with my tongue.

I found out that she tasted even sweeter than I thought when my tongue touched her tongue. My hands curved around the dip in her waist and I pulled her closer.

Soft moans came from her mouth, making me hard as fuck. I thought I was going to bust right on that bench, all over her pretty dress.

That's when she shoved me away.

She stood to her feet. "You are getting way too fresh with me and i—it's probably time for me to go."

Before I could say anything else, she rushed away from me.

I wanted to chase after her but something told me to let her go.

Damn, I thought. I probably pushed her away for good doing too damn much.

Chapter 31

I sat at the private detective's desk frustrated as hell, that all that time I had been paying his ass he had no leads.

"You mean you ain't found out shit?"

"No." He had his hands clasped and on his raggedy ass desk. "But I'm getting close. The last person I had got ahold of, who said they knew where I could find Ron Jasper was full of shit. It was a waste of gas."

"Yeah, well I'm starting to feel like this is a waste of money," I said drily, twisting my lips to the side.

He didn't get mad at my comment. He just stayed calm. "You hungry, Chance? I can have the cook make you a wet *burrito like last time.*"

"No, I don't want no damn burrito. I want you to cut the bullshit and do what I'm paying you to do."

He waved his hand in a circle again. "Easy. Easy. You don't believe me but I am telling you, I'm close to finding out where and who he is. So be careful how you treat me."

"All right, man." I placed a hundred dollars on his desk and stood.

I wasn't mad that he hadn't found the dude, but mad about the fact that he had no leads, no nothing.

Before going to see Mateo, I did a house call for Zalman, then sunk my way over to the restaurant. I was disappointed as hell in getting nothing from his ass.

I got in the car and went back to the shop

As soon as I got there, Zalman drawled, "Well, seems like you have been making an impression on somebody."

I walked past him to check out the work orders he had for me and tossed over my shoulder, "What's up, Zalman? What are you talking about?" I went behind the counter.

"Deyja called and said for you to call her back at work."

I immediately sat down the work order papers. It had been about a week since our date. I wanted to call her, even drop by her job, but I was scared that I had done too much damage by kissing her.

Zalman burst into laughter as I rushed for the phone to call her.

"Don't you need the number, *Isaiah*?"

I ignored him and dialed the number.

I knew there was excitement in my tone but that's how good it felt to hear her sweet voice on the phone once the secretary transferred me to her.

"Hey," I said.

"Hi, Isaiah."

There was silence for a second and she said, "I was wondering if you had any plans tonight?"

"Nope," I said quickly. Maybe too quickly.

"Well, I wanted to—" she paused. "To invite you over for dinner."

"I can do that. What time?"

"How about seven?"

I cleared my throat. "I can be there at seven."

She gave me the address and I jotted it down.

"See you then," she said quickly before hanging up.

When I looked up, Zalman was all in my mouth. I chuckled and shook my head. I put the paper with the address in my back pocket.

Then a dilemma hit me. I didn't have transportation to get there.

"Zalman. Can I drive the car tonight?"

"Sure, go ahead. I trust you now. As long as you fill it back up with gas."

"Oh, you trust me now?"

"You're no criminal." Then he went back to the computer and his chat with some other random chick.

If he could see that in me, why couldn't they seven years ago?

"I must admit, though, I am a little jealous. Deyja is a beautiful woman. I have asked her out many times and she turned me down. She must not like pretty boys."

He was only five feet if that, with a pot gut belly, teeth the color of coffee grinds, and more importantly, a wife. But still I said, "Did you, now? And how you know I'm going out with her?"

"I have good ears," was all he said. He then typed something on the screen about 'fucking some women hard.'

Chapter 32

I rushed and finished my work orders, which were three desktops and one laptop. I drove to my room. Once I got there, I wasted no time taking my clothes off. I stepped out of my pants and slipped my shirt over my head.

"Aye. Yo Chance."

I jumped. Then I turned around and saw Calhoun standing in my doorway.

"Damn, Calhoun. Don't scare me like that."

"My bad. What's up tonight?"

I smiled at him. "I can't help you. I'm on my way out," I told him, walking to the bathroom.

He followed after me. "But we ain't hung out since you been home."

"I know. I want to. I've just been busy." Wearing just my boxers, I shaved my five o'clock shadow.

"Too busy for your boy?"

I shook my head. "I can't hang with you too much no way, Calhoun. And I'm especially not going to be coming into the Springdales. I'm on parole."

"Well shit, we can at least hit up the strip club or something."

"I don't have money to be going out like that."

"Why not? You stay in a piece of shit, you ain't got a ride. What the fuck you spending your extra money on?"

"A private investigator."

"For what?" he asked, surprised.

"To find out why I had to spend seven years in prison for some shit I didn't commit."

"Oh. You having any luck on that?"

I wiped my face with my towel. "So far, hell no. But the PI feels that if he can find that man who testified against me, that will lead us to the real answers."

"I don't know. I remember I tried to find his ass after the trial and I couldn't. Chance, some answers are better left unknown, know what I mean? You got out. You free, nigga. That's what matters." He waved his hand. "That should be enough. Leave that shit alone and save your money."

"It ain't enough for me. I want to know."

He was silent before saying, "Anyway, man, can you hang with your boy or what?"

I laughed. "Okay. Maybe on payday. Next Friday."

"Sound like a plan, my nigga! All right, I got a honey in the car so I'm gonna go head out."

I put some toothpaste on my toothbrush. "Then why you trying to hang with me?"

"I ain't trying to kick it with her. But she got a fucking Magnum. I was going to drop her ass off at her crib and roll us around in her car!"

I laughed. "You still ain't shit."

"Ain't nothing changed. All right, I'll get at you next week."

Once he was gone, I jumped in the shower.

Ten minutes early, I was at Deyja's doorstep.

I wasn't as nervous as the first date we had, but still, I had a case of nerves.

When she opened her door, I checked her out. She looked so pretty. She wore a white, long linen dress that had a zipper that ran down the middle of it and the necklace I had bought her at the farmers market. Her feet were bare and painted in a French manicure. They looked soft. This time it looked as if she had put some gel in her hair; it was curly around her face.

This time she smelled like a honeydew melon.

"Hi." She reached up and hugged me.

I wanted to kiss her again but resisted the urge.

"Hey," I told her once she pulled away from my hug.

"Come in and have a seat. The food will be done soon."

I glanced around the house. As nice as her place was, it was very plain. She had some beige plush couches, a coffee table, and a TV. That's it. No pictures on her walls. No decor. Nothing. It was funny because I remember Toi's place was always decked out . At least every couple months she was adding something to her crib and I was footing the bill for it. She had everything from vases damn near the size of me to pictures of naked black women and men on her walls. She also had pictures of her and me on her walls. Deyja's house was more primitive. Simple.

When she noticed me checking out the decor, or lack thereof, she said, "I haven't gone about decorating the place just yet. As much as I love color, when I moved back here I just wasn't in the right spirits to do it."

I nodded. "Where did you move back here from?"

"I came back from Baltimore, Maryland. My hometown. Long story." She smiled and added, "Don't want to discuss."

I chuckled. "I understand."

"The food will be done soon. I'm making this new dish a member of my church gave me. It's chicken, marinated overnight in orange and pineapple juice. It's supposed to be really good. We will be having that with some creamy mashed potatoes and string beans."

I remained standing.

"Well, sit down."

I sat down on the couch. It sounded like Maxwell playing on her stereo, but the song was unfamiliar to me. To be sure it was him, I asked, "Is this Maxwell?"

"Yep. He finally came out with a new album last year."

Damn. I had missed that being in prison. I use to love Maxwell's music.

"You haven't heard this song yet?"

"Nope. What's it called?"

"'Pretty Wings.' Where have you been?"

I chuckled and didn't reply.

She sat down next to me and made sure her long dress covered her legs. Too bad for me.

And damn, I couldn't stop looking at her. I blew air out of my mouth.

Her eyes narrowed. "What was that for?"

I chuckled. "I don't know. It's like every time I get around you I feel like I'm a kid all over again and I'm with my first crush."

The blush came.

"And when you do that . . . " I shook my head.

One of her thighs was resting against mine.

"When I do what?"

"When you blush. You look so pretty. It makes me want to kiss—"

Out of nowhere she leaned over and kissed me. Nothing major. She just pressed her soft lips against mine.

Then she sat back down and stared at me with her eyes wide, like all of a sudden she got scared. Like she did it on a dare.

"Oh god. What am I doing?"

"It's okay," I said.

My hands ran up and down her arms.

I pressed my lips against her cheeks. Then I let my tongue run down her neck, where I placed more kisses.

And she let me. I don't know why, but she let me.

My mouth traveled down to her breast and even though she had on a dress bra and a slip I could still see her nipples pointing through as I kissed them. She was making me hard and with it being so long I didn't know if I could control myself. But I didn't want to dog her either. So I stopped, and moved to the couch across from her.

She kept her eyes on me quietly.

"Look, Deyja. I like you. And it's been—I ain't trying to rush you."

She nodded and pulled her bottom lip in.

"I'm going to go ahead and go. And if it's okay with you, I'll call you tomorrow."

"Okay."

I got to my feet and walked toward the door.

When she got up to follow me I thought it was just to lock it .

But as my hand reached for the doorknob, I was surprised when she said, "Wait."

I turned around and faced her.

"I think I want you to—to rush me."

She slid something into one of my hands.

I looked at her, confused, then at the condom in my hand. And before I could even comment she took the zipper in the center of her dress and slid it down.

I didn't hesitate. I lifted her up so her legs were wrapped around me. She didn't stop me, she just wrapped her arms around my shoulders for protection like she feared I was going to drop her. But she felt so little in my arms.

Kissing her felt so good, like it did a few seconds ago, and like it felt at the Farmers Market that day and I knew part of it was because of who I was kissing and the fact that I had not had a real kiss in seven years.

She returned it with just as much urgency as me.

I laid her flat on the couch and had her dress wide open. I wanted to touch her all over so my hands roamed over her curves.

When my palms were over her nipples, she let out soft moans in her throat.

I sucked on her nipples and slipped my fingers in her underwear so I could feel her pussy. I stroked the soft hairs and touched her pearl tongue. I wanted to taste it, but the need to bury my dick in her was too severe to wait. I would just hope I got another opportunity to do it, to taste her.

I slid my fingers up and down her opening.

Her eyes were closed and she was arching her lower body toward my hand.

I slid a finger into her and felt the warmest, tightest pussy ever. I had to feel it with my dick. I had to. I stripped out of my clothes quickly.

I slid the condom onto my dick that was so hard the veins were popping out of it. I ripped her panties off and positioned her legs. I pulled back and without delay, I slid into her.

Her moans got louder and I wanted to scream, but instead I leaned down and kissed her, drowning out her moans.

Her pussy felt so good to me. I jabbed her repeatedly and stroke by stroke, it was warm, wet, and pulsated around my dick.

Her fingertips stroked up and down my back and her eyes were closed in pleasure.

I gripped her ass in my hands and pulled her even closer to me and put myself deeper into her.

Her fingernails dug into my skin and her legs criss-crossed around my waist.

I sped up.

My stroking got rougher to the point that every time I dug in her pussy, her body was slamming against the couch. I lifted one of her legs on my shoulders and continued stroking her pussy with my dick.

She was biting her bottom lip, I guess to keep from crying out. I continued tearing her pussy up. In the midst of four more strokes I felt seven year's worth of built-up nut burst out of me and into the condom.

I collapsed on her chest and both of our breathing was heavy.

Instantly my dick got hard again and instantly I felt regret. I really hope she didn't feel like I dogged her. I specifically waited for Toi for four months after dating her because I didn't want her to think I only wanted her for sex.

Deyja stood to her feet and left the room. I guessed she was in the bathroom and confirmed when I heard the sound the shower running.

I waited for her to come back. She stepped back into the room about ten minutes later, freshly showered and in a pretty, silky white robe.

She handed me a towel. "The water is still running, Isaiah. Go down the hall straight to your right."

"Thanks." I wrapped it around my waist and went into direction she told me.

When I emerged from the shower a few minutes later Deyja was no longer in the living room. I dried off quickly, put my clothes back on, and went to look for her. "Deyja?"

"I'm in here." I found her in her kitchen at the stove.

She was placing slices of chicken on a plate next to some mashed potatoes and string beans.

She glanced at me and said, "I didn't want us to put the food to waste."

She handed me a plate.

"Thank you," I said. I sat down at her kitchen table and dug in. The chicken had a sweet and tangy flavor to it and was very moist. The potatoes were creamy, buttery, and I could taste cheese in them.

She sat down next to me.

"This is good."

She blushed and waved a hand. "Are you just saying that?" Her head was tilted to the side and her lips were curved in a smile. I was once again reminded of how pretty she was. How sweet she was.

"Naw. I don't lie when it comes to food, baby. My mom was a tough act to follow when it came to cooking."

She blushed again. "What did you say about your mama?"

"That she was a tough act to follow when it came to cooking," I repeated, sliding a piece of chicken in my mouth.

"Sorry. I'm listening to you, it's just when you said . . . *baby*."

"I'm sorry, I—"

"No. No, Isaiah. You didn't do anything wrong. I liked it. I haven't been called *baby* in so long."

I wanted to ask her why, but I didn't. I was enjoying myself with her and didn't want to bring up anything that might cause her distress. Maybe her dude had cheated on her, done something to break her heart, and she had stayed alone from fear she would be hurt again. But she didn't have to worry about that. I wouldn't do anything to hurt her.

I scooped more potatoes in my mouth.

She was watching me chew. It made me a little nervous. But her smile gave me a little comfort.

"I'm glad you like my food, Isaiah. Maybe I can cook for you again."

"Maybe I can cook for you, Deyja."

"Maybe." She picked up her fork and spooned some potatoes into her mouth.

At that point I knew I was playing with fire to continue a relationship of any kind with her. I knew it, but that didn't stop me from putting my plate aside, walking over to her, getting on my knees, and kissing her on her lips. She didn't stop me.

Chapter 33

Zalman was missing in action and he wasn't at the other store either because his wife was calling like crazy, looking for him.

The thing was, ever since he hired me he was always in and out anyway. When the wife wasn't at the other store, he was supposed to be working on orders over there, but instead he would go and bring the work orders from that store over to me. And while I was doing them he would be out doing his thing or in the back room doing his thing. I wondered if his wife would ever find out.

So I never had any real downtime at the store. I didn't bother me, though. Keeping busy always made the time go by faster.

Today was no exception to that shit either.

I reached for the phone before I started on a work order. I called Deyja again for the fifth time. Her secretary was still on some, "Deyja is unavailable but I can send you to her voice mail."

I wanted to stop by there but I didn't want to press. I figured maybe if I gave her a little time she could get past the fact that we had sex so quick. The last thing I wanted her to feel like was that I used her for sex. And I can't remember ever enjoying making love to a woman the way I enjoyed making love to her.

I hung up the phone and worked on my last work order of the day. When I was finished, I went into the back to wash up at the sink in the restroom. I was covered with dust from the last computer I had just repaired.

I grabbed a wash towel and pressed it against my face to dry the water I had just splashed on it.

Then suddenly before I could remove the face towel my head was slammed against the mirror. I could feel steel pressed against my temple.

"Yeah muthafucka. You bet not do shit. I will put a slug through you. And you won't see daylight no more."

I kept silent and listened to see what he wanted. I figured I was being robbed.

"Listen up and listen well. You need to be careful where you look, feel me? Or you just might find out some shit you better off not knowing."

He slammed the gun on the back of my skull and the hit knocked me out.

"Chance, wake up!"

My eyes fluttered open and I blinked a couple times to see Calhoun standing over me, peering down into my face.

I shook my head and sat up quickly.

"What the fuck happened to you, man?"

The back of my head was throbbing. I rubbed it and felt a knot.

Dude's words came back to me. *You need to be careful where you look, feel me? Or you just might find out some shit you better off not knowing.*

I turned back to Calhoun. "When did you get here?"

"Less than a minute ago. I came in and didn't see you up front. I walked further and seen you laid out on the bathroom floor. What the fuck happened?"

I stood to my feet with some difficulty, then I walked out of the bathroom. Calhoun followed.

I glanced at the clock; it said five-twenty. If Calhoun just got there then that meant he probably didn't catch sight of anybody. But I asked him anyway, "Was anybody leaving when you came in?"

"Naw. Why?"

I quickly told him what happened.

"Damn man." He dug in his back pocket. "Here."

He handed me a small gun. "Keep that in case he tries to come around again."

"Thanks." I tucked it into my back pocket. Then I stood to my feet and walked toward the front of the store. I didn't see anyone. Damn. I wondered who the fuck that was. "What are you doing here, anyway?"

"It's Friday, nigga. We supposed to be going to see the strippers." He took some flyers off of the counter and tossed them in the air, giving the effect of making it rain.

I laughed. "Pick that shit up."

The ache in my head was serious. I needed a Motrin to get rid of it. It was crazy. Who in the fuck would need to threaten me? I thought of one person: Ron Jasper.

"We going or what?"

"I don't know about that."

"Naw. Fuck that, you going!"

I looked Calhoun up and down. He wasn't playing. He was already dressed. I wasn't, so we would have to stop by my hotel so I could shower, shave, and throw something on. I didn't want to go, especially after the shit that just happened to me.

But once I had promised him, I had to stick to my word. I would have preferred not to go. Strippers were never my thing. I understood men going for their bachelor parties and shit. But why get a complete stranger to get ass-buck naked for you when you had a woman at home? And most of the men who went to strip clubs were married or had women. I didn't have a woman but there was only one woman at this time who I wanted to see in the nude. And she wasn't at a strip club.

I locked up the store and hopped in Calhoun's ride. Or should I say, some chick's ride. As he drove in the direction of my hotel, we passed the street that Deyja's office was on.

"Wait. Turn down this street," I told him quickly. "Where, nigga?"

I directed him to the shopping center her office was located in.

I hopped out the car and jogged to the door. Once I got inside, I walked over to the secretary.

"Well, hello!" she exclaimed like she was really excited to see me.

"How you doing? Is Deyja here?"

"She is." She pressed an intercom button. "Deyja. Isaiah is here to see you."

There was a pause before she said, "Send him in."

"Go ahead."

"Thank you."

I walked down the hall, past the cubicles, to her office.

I heard a few flirtatious *"hi's."*

I chuckled and spoke back before making it to her office door.

"Come in," she said after I knocked.

I didn't know what to say or do. But I went in anyway.

She had her hair flat-ironed and it had cut layers that framed the edges of her face; not too much makeup, except for red lipstick. This time she was wearing pink and it really looked nice on her. She was standing by her office window with her back to me. The dress clung to her curves. I admired her feminine shape, where her waist dipped in and where her hips flared out, the curve of her butt. Memories of the day we made love flashed before me. I still couldn't remember having it that good before.

"How you doing?" I asked, standing behind her.

"I'm good," she said in a low voice. Her back was still turned to me.

I still didn't know what to say to her. Hell, to be honest, she still had not returned any of my calls, so maybe that was a sign that I should back the hell up and move on. But still, I couldn't even if I wanted to.

"I miss you."

She turned and faced me. She stared at me for a moment, then her lips parted. "And I can't stop thinking about you, Isaiah."

I smiled. "Baby. I can't either." I walked closer to her and placed my arms around her waist. "Then why won't you return my calls?"

She looked away. "I thought what we did would be the end of anything else."

She had me confused now. "Why would you think that?"

"The way I threw myself at you. I did it because I just I felt that I needed to push you away. I didn't know if I was ready to get involved. So on one hand I felt that if I pushed myself on you, I could see if I was really ready to move on. If I couldn't, I would have given you want you wanted. And we could have left it at that."

"But I want you."

She blushed and looked away, then her expression suddenly turned serious.

"Listen. You see me where I work, what I drive. And where I live ain't much better. I don't have a lot of money. But I have a whole lot of love to give a woman." I stared into her eyes. "I will be so good to you if you just give me the chance."

"Isaiah, it's not about what you have or don't have. There's a lot about me you just don't know." She looked down.

I wanted to tell her the same thing. But I was scared and I was sure that what she didn't know about me would push her away. I was, after all, still lying about the fact that I was the guy she was writing when I was in prison.

I pulled her face back up by placing two fingers below her chin. "I don't want to stop seeing you. I don't know. It's like you are giving me something to look forward to. I sit and pray that I get a call from you. That I can get the opportunity to be around you."

"Isaiah. I don't know—"

Before she could finish I stepped closer to her and kissed her on her lips. She parted her mouth and gave me a chance to invade it again with my tongue. Her mouth tasted fresh. She played with my tongue. I pulled it out of her mouth and planted kisses in the corners of her mouth. I walked her backward toward the wall so I could do more, kiss her some more.

But her intercom stopped any of that. "Deyja, you have Mr. Harris here to see you."

She broke away from me and went to her phone. "Give me about five minutes," she said quickly to her secretary.

She turned back to me. "You are going to have to go, Isaiah. You are interrupting me from working. Can't have that."

I chuckled. "Nope, can't have that."

She looked at me and smiled before shaking her head.

"So can I see you again tonight?" I knew it was wrong to dis a friend for a girl but I would do it in a heartbeat for her.

"I have Bible study tonight. When I get home I will give you a call."

That was enough for me. But still I walked back up to her, causing her to back up a little and kissed her. I had to taste those lips again.

I turned my back on her before she could get the chance to see a grown-ass man blush.

When I made it back out to the car Calhoun said, "Damn, nigga. What the fuck is wrong with you?"

"Why?"

"You look all happy and shit."

"I am," was my only reply as I hopped in the front passenger seat and buckled up.

"Now let's get into these strippers so I can be happy!"

I shook my head at him. "Man, don't you think it's time you either pick one of your baby mamas to settle down with or get you another woman?"

"Shiiiit. Like Mike Epps said, '*Fuck these bitches! Fuck these bitches!*' he sang.

"You ain't shit."

"Fuck you, nigga. *And fuck these bitches!* I ain't never settling down, too much pussy to be fucked. Too many hoes to keep in check out here. They get on my damn nerves." He drove down the street toward the freeway. "Just like the hoe that owns this car. I damn near cursed her ass out earlier today."

"What did she do?"

"Man, we were watching TV and do you know what she had the nerve to ask me?"

"What?"

"If I would get her a glass of water."

I laughed, thinking it would be some worse shit than that.

"I looked at the bitch like she was crazy and asked her if she was into that sadomasochism shit."

"What?"

"You know, them dominatrix bitches."

"Because she asked you for some water?"

"Yeah." He hopped on the freeway.

"Well, not me. I'm a one-woman type of dude. Before I went to prison I felt like Toi was the person I was going to spend the rest of my life with. It's crazy how things change." I shook my head. "Now I don't want any sight of her."

"Well, she sure wants you back."

"Too bad. She should have been down for me when I went to prison."

"But you was looking at a lot of time."

"Fuck that. I get that. But the way she did it was flat-out wrong. I don't care what you or anybody else say. I'm off her ass."

"Well, be off her ass and move on to some stripper ass!"

I laughed.

"Real talk: She did you dirty, taking your money and shit, aborting your baby. Then she disappeared like a ghost. I wanted to kill her ass. But as time went by I had to let that go. Just like you need to let it go."

Truthfully, I did. The shit was over now and I didn't want to think about it anymore so I didn't respond. I had other shit to worry about.

I touched the back on my head and felt the knot. It reminded me that first thing in the morning I was going to go see Mateo and tell him about this shit.

Chapter 34

When we got to the strip club I couldn't help but feel ashamed of Calhoun. I know strippers gotta make their money and I respected that. But damn, Calhoun had two kids that he could be using that money on. I'm sure they could use some things. The shit didn't make a bit of sense to me. Dollar after dollar he tossed to those women. He was trying to make it rain, like he was a rapper when in reality he didn't have a fraction of the money that rappers had.

And again, his kids could use that money.

But there he was, drinking champagne right out of the bottle. It wasn't Cristal, but still. And he had to get a lap dance. And another. And another.

When was my friend ever going to grow up?

After he came back from his third lap dance, he sat next to me.

"You need to be careful or niggas in here gonna think you got major dough and try to jack us," I warned, looking around to see if any thirsty niggas were watching us.

"Man, that's why I keep the heat in the back pocket. Speaking of that, you still got that little gun I gave you?"

I nodded. But I left it at home. I didn't feel comfortable having a gun I didn't have registered to me in my possession. Okay, stop the bullshit and tell me how in the fuck you managed to beat a murder charge?"

I ran down the whole story to Calhoun. About the crooked, sick warden and Roscoe. His eyes were wide when I was done. "I wanted to tell you everything, but I felt it was better to wait until I was out of there."

"Fucking sick!" Calhoun was still tripping off the shit I told him about the warden and Roscoe. "That's some shit that happens in the movies!"

"Well, it happened where I was."

Truthfully, the rape was an issue I still didn't feel comfortable discussing in too much detail. Calhoun saw, so he changed the subject. "Why you don't you take one of them bitches back there?" He gestured to some half-dressed strippers not too far from us.

I continued to sip my drink. "I'm cool."

"Oh, jail done turned you gay, huh?"

The rape flashed before my eyes.

I shook my head. "No. Just because I'm not all over these strippers don't make me gay."

"I'm sorry, dawg. I didn't mean it like that. I never told you this, but I was raped in prison before too."

I was surprised. "How come you never told me?"

"It's not something you go around broadcasting. I wanted to put it behind me."

"I understand. I hope to do the same."

"Well, I'm just happy you home, dawg. I love you. man."

"I love you too, with your tricking-off-money ass."

He fanned some bills in front of me. "Shit, I'm making it rain in here! Remember. It ain't tricking if you got it, my nigga."

I laughed. "*You ain't got it.*"

"Damn, nigga, I'm just fucking around. Relax and enjoy this shit. Toi said you ain't fucking with her. But hell, I understand why. She ain't shit. Springdale pussy. Even though you moved her ass out of the projects that shit was still in her. Dumb niggas like you trying to make a ho a housewife. And if you had not got arrested, your dumb ass was going to marry her too! You should have known better, anyway. You knew she was just a rat from the projects. And she is back where she belong anyway, in the Springdales."

I never considered Toi a rat. I always thought that I had a good girl. So she couldn't make it without me paying her bills, I thought. I wondered what happened to the dude who claimed he bought bricks with my money. "Well, shit, you live and you learn."

"True that."

"And I don't even know why I'm sharing this shit with your dumb ass, but I am seeing a little shorty."

"Ah yeah who is she? Is she fine like Toi?"

"Stop bringing that bitch up. But, yeah, she is better than Toi in every way."

He laughed. "How did you meet her?"

I shook my head and smiled. "The shit is crazy, Calhoun. Believe it or not, I met her when I was in prison. I know I never mentioned it to you because I thought you would have taken it as a joke. She was writing me like a pen pal and shit."

He laughed loudly. "Yeah? I done did that shit!"

I chuckled.

My laughter stopped when he said, "That shit don't last. And remember the way you get somebody is how you lose them. Shit, when you piss her off she will probably start writing another man in prison."

I disregarded his negativity by saying, "Naw. Not Deyja. She is different."

"Deyja?"

I gave a sharp look to his wide eyes.

"Don't tell me you know her." I held my breath.

He downed his drink and eyed a thick redbone walking down the aisle. "Naw. That shit just sound like a white-girl name."

I exhaled and relaxed. "Nigga, you better stop fucking with me."

He laughed again.

"She's beautiful, sweet, pure." I rubbed my hands together. "I just hope I don't manage to fuck things up between us."

He flicked his finger at the redbone. She came walking over our way.

When she got to us, Calhoun said, "My boy fresh out. Give him a lap dance."

She walked over to me but I stopped her quickly before she could even get a word out. "I'm straight, baby."

"Well fuck it! Give a nigga one," Calhoun exclaimed.

I shook my head at him as he tricked off some more money. I just sat there and sipped on my drink. I wondered what Deyja was doing and wished I was spending my time with her instead of Calhoun's dumb ass.

When I got to Mateo, I got straight to the point. I wasn't about to let him butter me up by offering me food and another promise. Today. If he didn't have any type of lead I wasn't paying him shit.

"Last week I had somebody come to my job with a gun and hit me on the head. I think it's him. Ron—"

Before I could comment further, the detective placed a cell phone in front of me. "Chance. Is that him?"

I scanned the picture on his cell phone. It brought back memories of the day he lied on me in court. I gritted my teeth and shoved the phone away. "Yeah, that's him."

He just stared at me. "I'm getting close, Chance, closer than you think. I'm in contact with someone in his circle that it a little . . . let's just say, upset with him. Trust and believe me, I'm going to find him. But when I give you that call you have to be ready to go. It's going to happen sooner than you think."

I twisted my lip to the side and forked over another hundred dollars.

"All right, man." I grabbed the pen and notepad off his desk and jotted down my cell phone. "You can reach me on this number." It was the number to the cell phone Zalman gave me for after-hours. He was so cheap that he only chirped me to save minutes.

"*Vido mas. Vido mas*," Mateo sang, taking the notepad back from me. He flicked his finger for his pen that I absentmindedly placed in my pocket. I shook my head, slipped it out of my pocket, and handed it to him.

As I left, I wondered if this was such a good idea to continue with this. I had been feeling that way ever since the guy I felt was Ron Jasper had come to my job and hit me in the head with a gun.

While I waited to hear word from Mateo, I started spending a lot of time with Deyja. We took trips to the park, mostly walked and talked. Little by little, she was getting closer to me. She started being more affectionate, hugging me and whatnot. We still hadn't crossed the line to making love again. I wanted to but I didn't want to force it. I knew it would happen again when the time was right. I was surprised one day when she brought it up to me. About a month had passed since the first time. All we had been doing was kissing and hugging. One day she asked me, "How come you haven't tried to make love to me again, Isaiah?"

We were at the farmers market again sitting on the benches where they were playing jazz.

I laughed and said, "Believe me, baby, I want to. Matter a fact, I want to turn you over and flip up your dress right now."

She shoved me playfully and looked around to make sure no one else heard me. "Isaiah!"

"Seriously, the last time I didn't feel right about doing it so soon. I felt like I dogged you. And I don't want to feel like that again. And I don't ever want you to feel like that's all I want from you, so I'm waiting for the right time to come around again."

"How will you know when it's the right time?"

I reached over and kissed her earlobe and whispered in her ear, "'Cause you're going to tell me. You going to come to me when you're ready."

"Oh," was all she said. Then she shivered.

I wrapped an arm around her. "You cold, baby?"

"No, I'm fine. It's just sometimes the things you say . . ."

I pulled her closer and kissed her.

A few days after our visit to the Farmers Market, Deyja told me to meet her at her house after she got out of church, which was around twelve. She then had me pulling up the weeds in her yard. Once I was done, I came in her house with just my pants on, sweating like crazy.

I knew I was buff from being in prison for the last seven years and she was admiring my muscles as she was in the kitchen making us some spaghetti for our lunch.

She smiled and said, "I'm almost done cooking."

"Okay. I'm going to go shower all this dirt and sweat off of me, if that's okay with you."

"Go ahead."

I went into her bathroom. Since I knew she was going to have me doing yard work, I had brought an extra set of clothes.

I turned on her shower and stripped down.

"Hurry up, Isaiah!"

"I'm coming," I yelled.

I lathered up quickly, washing my whole body and even washing my curly hair. I had just rinsed off when she knocked on the bathroom door.

"It's open," I said, turning the water off.

The door opened and she stepped in the bathroom.

"Everything okay?" I asked, shaking my wet hair in the shower.

She was silent.

I could only see her silhouette through the sliding glass door. I was curious as to why she was quiet and immediately thought something was wrong.

When I slid my face out. I was surprised to find her buck-naked and facing me. She said simply, "I think I want you to make love to me again, Isaiah."

That's all she had to say.

I tossed the shower door back and stepped out.

She turned her back to me and walked from the bathroom to her bedroom.

I stood for a moment and admired her as she walked. Deyja was bad. Her skin was flawless, waist was so small, her rump firm—and man, her thighs and calves. Instantly my dick was hard watching her walk her normal walk. The shit was sexy was hell to me.

She paused near her bed and turned to face me. I was still in the same spot, watching her from the bathroom door. Now I was hit with a view of her perky breasts and dark-colored nipples.

I licked my now dry lips.

She looked a little nervous and slipped under the covers of her bed.

I followed after her and got into the bed, spooning her.

I rubbed my hands alongside her bottom and her waist.

"Come here, baby."

She scooted closer to me.

"Can I see you?"

She nodded.

I peeled the covers back from her body. And this time I took my time looking at her. I stared everywhere, from her sexy lips to her perfect C-cup breast to her chocolate nipples. My eyes were then on her thighs and the span of her hips. I admired her pussy and her pink clit. I placed kisses on her stomach, taking the time to dip my tongue in her navel.

She moaned softly and her hands started playing in my still wet hair.

I grabbed a hand, one at a time, and sucked on each one of her fingers. Her eyes were half closed as she watched me. I eased myself down further until I was between her legs.

"Can I taste you, Deyja?"

"Yes."

So I did. I took her completely in my mouth and the taste was so sweet. I eased my tongue out of her and sucked on her clit.

She started moaning and thrashing her head from side to side. Her cries were making me crazy. I was already hard beyond means. I was sticking my fingers, first one, then two, inside of her hole all while I continued sucking on her clit. A free hand reached up and massaged her nipples that were as hard as rocks.

She was still so tight.

"Isaiah!"

"I know, baby."

I wanted to take my time and really enjoy her. And let her enjoy the things I was doing to her body.

But she was pleading with me.

I placed more kisses between her thighs, down to her knees, then back up again toward her pussy, and licked the juices that leaked there.

For a second I thought about going in her without protection and getting her pregnant so I could always have her in my life despite whatever happened between us. I had never had the desire to get a woman pregnant so soon. And I was about to take a gamble and do it because I loved Deyja. But before I could, she pointed at the nightstand.

So I edged my way toward it, pulled it opened and pulled out a condom she had resting on the top of bras and underwear. I ripped it open and put it on. Then I got back on the bed and pulled her body on top of mine so that she could ride me.

First she took her time and rode me slowly. But I started slapping her on the ass and pressuring her to speed up.

"Come on. Get that dick, baby."

That's when she got wild with it, thrusting up and down on me and twisting her body in a circular motion.

I reached up and grasped her breasts and started playing with her nipples, squeezing them between my fingers. Then I rubbed my palms across them.

I then gripped her and propelled her up and down on my dick so she could move at a faster pace.

Her moaning continued and I flipped her over so that I could hit it from the back.

But before I stuck it back in, I began eating her from behind while gripping her ass in my hands.

She pleaded with me. "Isaiah, please finish making love to me!" She was reaching behind her, grabbing my knees.

I reinserted my dick back into her.

"Get it," I told her, breathing hard.

She started bumping against me, making me groan as her pussy splashed against me.

I then started meeting her pace, ramming into her harder and harder.

I held onto my nut so she could get hers, but once she started convulsing and her pussy twitching on my dick, I let loose all up in her. Well, I wish into her, but into the condom.

The next thing I knew we were all sweaty in the bed. Despite the sweat and how hot we felt, we were still all on each other.

I played with her by saying, "You got wild with it, D," giving her a nickname.

She buried her head in my chest. "Oh god. I'm sorry!"

I wrapped my arms around her and kissed her on her head.

"Naw, it's cool. I liked it, baby."

She sat up in the bed. "Isaiah, all of this feels so foreign to me."

"What?"

"This. Do you know how long it has been since I have even dated, let alone had sex with a man?"

It couldn't have been as long as I had been waiting, I wanted to say, but I didn't.

"I honestly feel like I'm starting all over again, because for so long, I have been scared to see another man. But you, I don't know . . . there is something different about you, Isaiah. I feel safe on so many levels. It doesn't feel like I've known you a couple of months. And you have been in my head ever since out first date. And I think I want to explore where this can go."

It sounded so good to hear her say that.

But I was curious. "Why has it been so long since you have dated someone else?"

That's when she inhaled as if she was about to speak, then she stopped herself.

"I'm going to go and get the spaghetti served up for us."

Chapter 35

We made love four times that day.

Deyja pretty much had to push me out of her house. I didn't want to leave.

"If I don't get you out of here I'm not going to be able to get any work done!" she said as she pulled up to my hotel. I wasn't ashamed to show her where I lived, because she said my financial status and living situation didn't matter to her I wondered what *would* matter to her. What would be a deal breaker for us? And there were still things I wanted to confess to her, but fear of losing her wouldn't let me.

"Bye, Isaiah."

"Bye, baby." I kissed her sweet lips again and got out of her car.

I waved to her one last time before going into the building.

Once I got to my room I unlocked my door, walked in, and laid back on my bed, reliving the past couple days.

I had never fell for somebody so hard and so bad as this girl in my life.

"Man." I chuckled, thinking about her.

Then there was a knock on my door.

I figured it was Deyja. Maybe she changed her mind about work and wanted to play some more.

But when I opened the door, I saw Toi standing there.

I paused and stared at her.

She placed two hands up as if in surrender. "Before you think I'm stalking, let me come in."

No response from me.

"Can I come in?"

"No."

"Chance, you ain't gotta act like this, baby. Come home to me. And it can be like old times." She gestured toward my room. "You aint' gotta stay in no shit hole like this! Yeah, I'm back in the Springdales, but my crib is decked out. We can be like old times. Like no time has passed between us."

She reached out to hug me.

I took a step back, causing her hands to fall to her sides.

Her face turned to an ugly scowl. "Is it cause of that bitch who just dropped you off?"

"You need to stay out my business," I warned.

"Humph. I guess that fucking bitch got your nose wide open. With her stuck-up ass."

"Yeah? And what do you know about her?"

"That she is the bitch you chasing after. Keep on chasing after her. That's all you'll ever be able to do, 'cause I'm pretty sure she don't do convicts!"

Her head rolled around on her neck and she now had her hands on her hips. "I bet you ain't bothered to tell her you did seven years in jail for murdering a cop."

"You need to get the fuck on, Toi." I made a move to close the door in her face but her words stopped me.

"Maybe I'll just pay her a visit and tell her my damn self."

That's when I snatched her in the room and had her hemmed up against the wall.

I studied her face. First she seemed scared, then hurt, then angry. "Muthafu—"

But I was tired of her and her bullshit.

I placed a hand over her mouth. "Shut up." I stepped even closer to her and stared in her eyes intently. "Listen and listen well. What we had—is gone. I don't love you. I don't even like you. I don't want no parts of you. Get that shit through your fucking head! Leave Deyja the fuck alone, keep my name out your fucking mouth, and stop coming around here!"

Tears spilled from her eyelids onto my fingers.

When I released her, she slid to the ground, looking pitiful.

I turned my back on her and shook my head.

Then in a flash, before I could catch her, she ran to my kitchen area.

"Get the fuck out!"

Next thing I knew, she was rushing toward me with a knife in her hand, yelling, "Muthafucka!"

She aimed it toward my chest.

I moved over to the side and she blindly plunged it into the wall, putting a hole there. She spun back around, facing me. She paused as if she was deciding whether or not to go after me again.

Before she could make another move, I lunged for her, knocking her on the floor.

I used my strength to twist her body up like a pretzel with one hand and snatched the knife out of her hands with my other hand.

She started sobbing uncontrollably.

I didn't want to hurt her. But at the same time, like I said, I didn't want any parts of her.

"Chance, please! It's 'cause I love you so much, that I'm acting this way. I'm sorry I turned my back on you! Please give me another chance!"

I tossed the knife toward the kitchen and went to the door. I opened it and held it open for her.

"Get out."

She dragged her miserable ass out my door, sobbing all the way.

Once she was gone, I slammed the door shut and locked it behind her.

Chapter 36

The next day, Deyja ended up popping up at my job during my lunch break.

"Hi, baby."

"Hi," she said.

I studied her. Something didn't look right.

I came from around the counter and hugged her. "Everything okay?"

She pulled away. "Isaiah. I need you to go somewhere with me.

I closed the shop and called Zalman to let him know I would be gone a couple hours. He said it was going to cost me. I didn't care.

I was surprised when she brought me to an actual cemetery called *Forest Lawn*. I wondered what her purpose was bringing me there.

"Remember when you asked me why I hadn't been with another man in a long time?"

"Yeah."

We got out of her car and continued to walk past the cars down a path of tombstones.

"Well, I am going to show you why, today. Now."

We continued to walk down the path.

I glanced a few feet away from where we were, a huge group of people were gathered by a grave, looking utterly depressed.

Being there made me think of my mother.

I looked away but continued to follow her until she said, "Okay. Isaiah, here it is."

We stopped in front of a huge tombstone. I read the words engraved on them and froze in disbelief. *Devin Johnson, 1/1/1980–3/6/2003. Gone Far Too soon And Never To Be Forgotten.*

He was the man I went to jail for murdering.

"He was my fiancé. He was killed the night before we were supposed to get married seven years ago."

Tears slipped from her eyes as she relived it. "He was the love of my life. My everything. And after he died, I wanted to die. I couldn't imagine living in this world without him. He was all I had out here. My home, my comfort. When he died, I flew back home to Baltimore and stayed with my parents, wanting to get away from all the madness, all the memories of me and him. I knew I had to get out of the house that we shared because all it did was make me want to die. I would smell him, see him, and I thought I was going crazy. So I sold our house and left. But when I went back home, all I did out there was cry and cry. Everyone that I came into contact with who knew about what had happened to me, felt so sorry for me that even if I managed to make it through a day without crying they would make me cry all over again, by reminding me. So a year later, I came back to California. I thought if I kept myself busy with work the pain would be less. I threw myself into real estate so I had no time to think about anything else. I ended up doing so well and I became so busy that I opened up my own real estate office. It kept me busy but still nothing felt right anymore. I was unable to move on and love another man after him. And part of me felt like it was a betrayal to him if I did. During that time, I felt so empty inside." She smiled through her tears and cupped my face in her hands. "And now seven years later, I meet you. Isaiah, baby, you have shown me that I can. You—I don't know!" she screamed excitedly. "You don't know what you have done for me. There has to be something different about you. You woke me up. You make me smile and laugh. You make me feel good. And most of all, you make me feel like it is okay to love you." She wrapped my arms around me and sobbed into my neck.

I was still in shock and had a sick feeling in my stomach.

I continued to replay Deyja's words in my head at home and who she was at home.

I shook my head. The man I went to jail for murdering was the same man that Deyja was going to marry. To know this killed me and to know what I had to do at this point killed me even more.

She had been calling me nonstop since we had gone to the grave site. I ignored the calls out of fear that she would pop up at my job I worked at the other store. But when she showed up at my room, I knew what I would have to do.

I opened the door and simply started at her. I must have avoided her long enough, I thought.

"Hi," she said in a shaky voice.

My tone was flat, not loving like it used to be. "What's up."

"Can I come in?"

"Naw. I'm tired."

She looked at me, confused. "Isaiah, I have been calling you nonstop and a couple times I stopped by the shop and you weren't there. I got worried about you.

I asked Zalman what was going on but he was tight-lipped. What is this?"

I gave her a fake laugh. "Look, I think you got me misunderstood. What you looking for, I'm not. I'm not trying to be your man and you just a little too needy for me."

She whispered, "What?"

"I ain't looking for what you looking for, baby girl."

"But I—"

"Bitch. I don't want you! It wasn't never like that, so fall the fuck back!"

Her eyes teared up instantly and her shoulders begin to shake.

"Isaiah?"

I turned my back on her. "It was just pus—" my voice cracked. "Pussy to me."

Silence was all I got. All I wanted to do was take her in my arms, though. It crushed me to say that bullshit to her.

She turned and walked away.

I took a step to go after her, then stopped myself. I would rather break up with her then have her find out who I really was. What were the chances she would believe that I was innocent? None.

That night as I tossed and turned, I couldn't sleep for shit. I knew I couldn't let it stay that way. So I jumped out of bed, threw some clothes on, called a cab, and rushed over to her house.

When I got there, despite how late it was, I banged and banged on her door until I saw a light come on.

When she opened the door and saw me she immediately slapped the shit out of me.

I closed my eyes at the sting her little hand brought to my face. "I'm sorry, baby."

But she wasn't done. I let her beat on me because I deserved the shit. I took all her punches and slaps.

Soon the beatings stopped because she was now sobbing uncontrollably.

I pulled her into my arms.

I carried her to her bedroom, all the while repeating, "I was just scared, baby."

I laid her on her bed. She let me.

I proceeded to make love to her.

This may sound stupid, but I figured if I made love to her and if I was real good, it would correct the hurt I had inflicted upon her. And once I did serve her, I think that I did it right because once she came, she fell right asleep in my arms.

Chapter 37

I woke up the next morning to fingertips tracing my lips.

I kept my eyes closed but kissed them.

She started kissing me on my neck.

I still kept my eyes close but was relieved she was over how I had hurt her the day before.

"If my fingers and kisses can't get you awake, then maybe my hot breath will."

She sat on top of me and before she got a chance to, I rolled over quickly and straddled her.

She squealed.

I started tickling her.

She started screeching and fighting me but I kept going, getting her under her smooth arms and on her small waist.

"Isaiah, please stop!" she begged.

"Yeah? And what do I get if I stop?"

"A kiss."

"Nope." I kept going. "Your breath stank," I joked.

"I'll cook for you."

"I ain't hungry this early."

She laughed and looked at her nightstand where a book lay. "Wait! Wait! I'll read to you."

"You can read?" I joked.

She punched me in my shoulder, playfully.

"Get the book," I ordered, slapping her on her behind.

She leaped up quickly, laughing like crazy. She picked one of the books off her nightstand.

She remained standing and flipped through the pages. When she found what she wanted, she stopped. "These are poems by Jack Gilbert. Okay, I'll read this one. It's called 'The Great Fires'."

She took a deep breath.

I leaned back on the bed and listened to her recite the poem.

When she was done I clapped for her.

She tossed the book to me. I snatched it up and my eyes scanned the cover. The man on the cover looked so depressed. Who would have thought he would write a nice poem like that? I thought.

"After my fiancé's death I joined everything from a writers group, to mountain climbing. I rescued homeless dogs and cats, almost broke my neck in a yoga class, fed the homeless, took a sewing class, and joined a charity group at my church. For a while I was writing an inmate while he was in prison."

My heart sped up.

She didn't notice and sat back on the bed.

She smiled. "He was such a sweet guy in a really bad situation. He was in jail for murder. And you know what? Part of me believed he was innocent."

I smoothly changed the subject by holding up the book to her. "Looking at him I would think he would write the kinds of stuff that would make me want to put a bullet through my head!"

She laughed. "Well, then, I won't bother to read 'Harp and Boon' to you. I used to read that poem day and night after I lost my fiancé because the poem was about him getting over the death of his wife. I felt his pain because

I was going through the same thing that he was going through. We had both lost the loves of our life. Michiko was his wife's name and you could really tell that he loved her and was never the same after her death. My fiancé's death definitely changed me. I was depressed for so long. It was hard to find joy in things, in life. I always put on a fake smile for everyone else so they wouldn't bring it up. But I was so unhappy."

I looked away.

She caught it. "What's wrong?"

"Nothing."

She crawled over to me, stood on her knees, and cupped my face between both of her hands like she did that day at the cemetery.

"But now that I've found you," she said, chuckling, "I have that same happiness I had before I lost my fiancé, Isaiah. I have so much fun with you. You are . . . What's the right phrase? A long-awaited comfort."

I pulled away from her. I couldn't do this. I couldn't keep this shit from her. As a man, I had to tell her and pray, pray that she wouldn't end things between us.

I stood to my feet and took a deep breath. "Baby, listen. I have to tell you something."

She nodded and stared at me intently.

"Some years back, when you were a part of that charity group, writing someone in prison?"

"Yes. I did it for Mrs. Grace. He was such a sweet guy. His name was—"

"Chance. Deyja. I'm Chance."

Her eyes got wide and her head snapped back. Her mouth popped opened as if she wanted to say something, but she couldn't.

"But that's not the worst of it. Baby, you gotta believe me in what I'm about to say next." I swallowed hard. "I spent seven years of my life in prison for a crime that I swear to you that I did not commit. Murder. Deyja, the person I went to jail for murdering was your fiancé."

Her eyes closed at the impact of what I just said.

She stood to her feet, but once on her feet her legs must have gotten weak because she tried to back up from me and stumbled, bumping right into her nightstand. She then fell to the floor.

I rushed over to her to help her up.

Her hands shot up to block me.

Then they covered her face. She sobbed into her hands, all while screaming, "You killed Devin?"

"Baby."

She stood back to her feet and clutched onto her nightstand, backing as far away from me as she could.

"Oh, God, what have I done?"

"Deyja, listen."

She looked at me. "All this time it was you? You kissed me, made love to me, and all this time you were the man who took Devin's life? This was probably a game to you."

I shook my head. "Baby, no—"

"You are the one who ruined my whole world seven years ago. You killed a good man, my best friend, and you slept in his spot in my bed. Ate the food I used to cook for him. . . . "

She looked toward the ceiling.

"Deyja, I—"

"Get out."

"Just listen, baby, I swear I'm not lying to you."

"You have been lying to me this whole time. I feel so stupid. I'm so stupid! I spit on his grave sleeping with you. I'm so stupid!"

"No, baby, you're not."

"Get out!" she yelled through her tears.

I pulled on my clothes quickly.

Once I had them on I said, "I will go, but please listen to this. I love you. I feel like I fell in love with you before I even got the chance to actually meet you, Deyja. You gotta know that you are the reason why I'm still here. Your letters, your words. You helped me get through being in that box. When I thought I was going crazy, I thought about you and how you encouraged me to keep going. I owe my life to you."

I closed my eyes briefly and repeated, "I love you, Deyja." Tears were not running down my face.

I walked out of her bedroom, hearing her sob uncontrollably. The sound stayed in my head the whole ride back to my room.

Chapter 38

I called off work the next day. I couldn't go. I would have stayed in bed that whole day. I could not get over what happened between me and Deyja. I kept hearing her cry. I couldn't knock the image or her whimpers out of my head.

I knew she now hated me and didn't want anything else to do with me. To know that gave me that same sick feeling I had got the day she took me to that grave site. But I couldn't lie to her anymore. The guilt was eating at me. Now I felt totally wrecked. I had no appetite at all. I couldn't sleep. I just lay in bed.

Part of me regretted even telling her the truth. If I had just kept my mouth shut, I'd still be in her life. But for how long? Sooner or later, my past would have caught up with me. Eventually she would have asked me to meet her friends and her family. Maybe they would have found out who I really was, even if her family lived in another state. It was like Calhoun had said. "The way you get someone is the way you lose them." I had lied to her from the very beginning and my lies are what tore us apart.

I closed my eyes and reminisced about how good it felt being with her, talking to her. She was so smart and so sweet. Everything about her felt good, it felt pure.

My phone rang, taking me out of my thoughts. I thought it was Zalman, trying to get me to do a job, but when I saw the number was private I answered.

"Yeah?"

"We got 'em. Meet me outside in five minutes. If you have a gun, bring it for our protection."

It was Mateo.

Adrenaline immediately pumped through me as I threw on a pair of jeans, a black T-shirt, and some tennis shoes.

I pulled open one of the drawers in my room and grabbed the gun that Calhoun gave me, just in case.

I jogged outside and watched Mateo pull up to the front of the hotel. Even as I opened his passenger door and got in the car, I couldn't help but question if I should even go through with this. I didn't know this Ron Jasper at all and he obviously was a criminal.

The drive was silent for the both of us. Mateo headed over to the Imperial Courts in Watts. The whole time, all I saw was the man's face the day I was in that courtroom with my freedom on the line and he was the one who took my freedom with his fucking lies.

I balled and unballed my fist.

We pulled in the front entrance and rolled down a couple lots. Even though it was late, like any other typical projects, you had people outside hanging out.

"How is this shit going to work out?" I asked.

"His girlfriend knows we are coming. I had to pay her two hundred dollars to have him here. He doesn't know we are coming. By the way you gotta give me the two hundred back." He hit the steering wheel, yelling, "Bang. Bang!"

I shook my head. "How you even know he is going to be here?"

"He is there now. I wouldn't have brought you out here if it was bullshit. Easy. Easy."

I frowned. To me it seemed like he was just using me to play MacGyver and shit.

"You sure you ready for this, Chance?"

I didn't say anything. I just made sure the gun was still in my pocket.

I followed after him as he went to the back door. He held a finger to his lips.

I nodded.

Mateo slid open the unlocked door which had us in the kitchen We were ducked and waited a few seconds before moving on. Over the kitchen counter, I could see into the living room. It was empty as well.

"Where the fuck is he?" I demanded.

"In the bedroom," Mateo whispered. "Shut up!"

I followed behind Mateo, who didn't even have a fucking gun.

We both tiptoed out of the kitchen threw the living room up to the door he gestured towards and paused.

He snapped a finger and pointed to the door. Mateo gave me a nod.

I flung my left foot back and kicked the shit wide open.

When I saw a male leap from the bed and a female run out of the room, I rushed past the chick and toward the guy before he could get away.

"What the fuck is this?" he yelled and tried to run past me, but I was blocking him and Mateo was blocking the bedroom door. "Bitch, you set me up!"

I took my fist and slammed it into his forehead, making him fall backward on the bed.

"*Hola*, sweetheart," Mateo said, walking toward the bed. "I finally find you, *amor*."

When he tried to sit up, I yanked the gun out of my pocket and aimed it at his temple. "Lay back down, muthafucka."

He mean-mugged me but did it.

Mateo sat next to him on the bed.

I remained standing and leaned over him. "Do I look familiar to you ?" I asked.

"Man."

Mateo said calmly, "Maybe this will help your memory."

Mateo took one of his arms and twisted them back. It was a move I didn't know he had in him. The shit looked like it hurt and must have because he howled, fell back on the bed, and said, "You dirty muthafuckas! What the fuck y'all want?"

"We ask the questions, *mejia*." Mateo pulled him back to a sitting position on the bed.

"Get a good look at me, muthafucka. 'Cause I'm not going to ask you again."

He stared at me long and hard before smirking. "Yeah, man. I know who you are."

"Good." I punched the fuck out of his ass, knocking him off the bed. He flew into a lamp on the nightstand near his bed and came crashing down on the floor.

When he tried to get up, I pointed the gun at him again.

He froze in fear.

Mateo sang, *"Vido mas. Vido mas."* Then he whistled.

Ron's eyes flew from me to Mateo, then back to me.

"Since you know who the fuck I am, you mind telling me why the fuck you framed me for a murder you know I didn't commit?"

"Man, fuck you. I ain't gotta tell you shit."

I took the end of the gun and busted him in the mouth with it. Blood splattered.

"You gonna tell me, muthafucka, or your ass won't be walking out of here. You ruined my muthafucking life and you thought you was going to walk around like you ain't done shit?"

"Shit I did. Face it. You got played, nigga. I don't even know why you here for answers. Fuck you and your life. What, you thought you were going to come here and get an apology from me?"

I went crazy. I yanked his ass off of that bed and started fucking him up. Seven years' worth of misery, pain, and loss was taken out on his bitch ass. I tossed him all around that room.

He didn't even try to fight me back. I delivered punch after punch. And when my hands started aching from punching him, I started stomping him repeatedly until the pain in my hands dulled then I started strangling him with my bare hands. Despite how bad his breathing became, and how strong he clutched at my hands to loosen their hold on his neck, I wouldn't stop. I wouldn't release my hold. Truthfully, I wanted to kill his ass.

Mateo continued to call my name. "Chance! Chance! That's not why we came. You not going to get what you looking for if you do that."

But I continued until his arms started flapping at his sides. Each second that passed the flapping got weaker and weaker until he damn near couldn't get his arms back up. He was losing the strength in them as well as the rest of his body. Snot flew from his nose just like that skinhead that I had killed.

"Chance! Do you want to go back?"

It would be worth it for the shit that he had done to my life. I had lost everything. My beautiful mother was six feet under and she was never coming back. My child would be seven years old now. And my dreams. . . . they all out the window, thanks to this piece of shit. Everything that I had worked hard for. Yeah, for what I lost, his life was a fair trade. But then seven years of misery flashed right before my eyes. I couldn't go back there. I looked at Ron for a moment as he grew weaker and weaker. I loosened my hold on his neck little by little. Then I pulled my hands away.

He dropped to the floor. I landed a kick to his side.

He rolled onto his back and clutched his neck, struggling with his breathing.

I put the gun back on him.

After a pregnant pause while the nigga tried to get his breathing back to normal, Mateo said, "Chance, give me the gun."

I shook my head.

Mateo's hands closed over mine. "Give me the gun," he said quietly.

I let him slide the gun out of my hands.

My eyes burned into Ron. I was glad he was in pain. I was glad he was scared his life would end tonight.

I kicked him again, this time in the head. He howled and still held his neck.

From the corner of my eye, I watched Mateo slip something out of his jacket and slide it over the gun.

It was a plastic bottle.

He aimed it at Ron and fired.

The bullet shot through Ron's arm.

My eyes got wide. I wasn't expecting Mateo to do that. By him placing a bottle over the gun, it worked as a silencer.

Ron screamed loudly and clutched at his arm.

I snatched his ass up. "Why the fuck did you set me up?"

He still wouldn't say anything.

Mateo put the gun at his temple.

I punched him in the same arm Mateo shot him in. He yelled out in pain.

I snatched the gun from Mateo and punched Ron in his nose so his mouth shot open. Then I buried the gun in his mouth.

"Talk, muthafucka! Or I will end your shit."

Since Mateo had already shot him and I damn near strangled him to death, I guess he figured we wasn't playing with his ass.

He made inaudible sounds but held his hands up as if in surrender.

I slid the gun out of his mouth but still held it up to the side of his face.

"Okay muthafucka, you wanna know the truth? The truth is I ain't set up shit, I just did what someone else fucking told me to do."

He took a deep breath as his eyes burned into mine. He winced as blood oozed out of his arm.

"Keep talking ," I ordered, wondering where this was going to lead.

"You wanna know who set you up, nigga?"

He licked his lips and shook his head. "It was your fucking boy Calhoun!"

"Quit fucking lying!"

But even as I said this I was wondering how the fuck did he know Calhoun?

"You think I'm lying after all of this?" he coughed between words. "Ask him, my nigga. Ask him who really set you up. It was his ass. I put that on my life. And he sent me to your job to scare you so you would stop trying to find me. 'Cause if you found me you would find out the truth about your boy."

I shook my head at him and continued to aim the gun.

He stared me straight in my eyes.

Chapter 39

"Y'all just gonna leave me here bleeding, man?"

I did turn around, though, even Mateo was saying we had to go. But it wasn't to help Ron.

I walked back over to Ron and punched that nigga again in his mouth and this time I knocked him out.

Now I was riding in the car next to Mateo, knowing I wasn't even finished with this shit.

My chest was aching and my heart pumping from what we had just did. From what I had just learned.

I kept thinking of what Ron said. *You wanna know who set you up? It was your boy Calhoun!* I even thought about the fact that he said Calhoun was the one who had him come to my job with the gun to scare me and stop me from going back to the private investigator. Damn. If this was true Calhoun played it off real good, giving me that gun and all.

There was silence in the car as Mateo drove me home. I didn't know whether or not to believe it. A huge part of me did believe Ron was telling me the truth. I think the other part of me was in adamant denial. First of all, why would Ron just decide to lie on me? What would make him just volunteer himself for that, knowing that if he went to the police he would do time too? Last time I checked wasn't no nigga going to volunteer to go to prison for nothing. It was too many holes in his shit. And what he was saying about my friend. It was hard to believe. Calhoun was like a brother to me. I always thought we had a bond. We had more years of us hanging out and being a part of each other's lives than us not. To me that seemed unbreakable. I knew I had to hear it from him. And I hoped that he would tell me that what Ron had said was all bullshit.

"Do you believe him?" Mateo asked, breaking the silence.

I didn't respond.

"You want me to go with you to your friend's house?"

I shook my head. "Just drop me off at my room."

Once we got there, Mateo asked me, "You sure you going to be okay alone?"

"I'll be straight. Thanks, man."

"No problem. Call me if you need me."

I watched him speed away.

I knew I had to confront Calhoun no matter how much it would kill me to. And I didn't plan on searching for him either. I would make him come to me and tell me the fucking truth.

When I got into my room, I dialed his number on Zalman's cell.

When he picked up, he said, "Hey, what's up, Chance. Listen, I'm busy. Let me hit you—"

"I know."

A long pause. I grinded my teeth.

"Chance?"

"I know, muthafucka."

"You know what?"

Oh, he was gonna play that role?

"Ron."

Silence. I licked my dry lips and waited for him to speak.

"It's not what you think, man. Look, I will be over there in ten minutes."

Chapter 40

I waited. I couldn't keep still. I paced for the full ten minutes, wondering what he was going to say. I continued to glance at the time on Zalman's cell phone. Ten minutes had passed and he hadn't showed up. I continued to pace. Then I sat down on the bed with my head in my hands in utter turmoil. After exactly eighteen minutes, I grabbed my room keys, shoved the phone in my pocket, and walked toward the door.

I turned the knob and pulled it open to find Calhoun standing behind it.

We both froze, facing each other.

My eyes locked with his. My look was murderous. He looked away quickly.

He stood there, frozen for a moment, until I backed into my room.

He stepped in and closed the door behind him.

I stayed standing.

So did he.

"Listen, man. I don't know what you know 'cause I don't know what somebody told you. But it's more to this shit than you really think."

I exploded. "I grew up with you! We were boys. Tell me that this man is lying on you! That you wasn't involved in this shit, Calhoun!"

He shook his head, covered his face with his hands. He made inaudible sounds. When his hands moved away from his face I saw it was wet with tears and they continued to run down his face.

I started crying too. "Tell me the fucking truth, Calhoun! Were you a part of this shit?" Inside I was praying the whole time that he really wasn't. That it was all a big fucking lie when it was fucking obvious that the truth was staring me right in my face!

Silence was all he gave me.

I asked him again in a lowered voice, "Were you?"

"It wasn't just me, man. It ain't all what you think—"

Before he could finish, I grabbed him by his neck and slammed him up against the wall. "You ain't shit!"

"Chance!"

"Shut the fuck up!" I slammed him into the wall again with all my might. He didn't fight me.

That's when my room door flew open and Toi rushed in the room.

I released him for a second and raged at her. "Get the fuck out of here!"

She looked from me to Calhoun.

"I called her, Chance."

I released him, confused.

He pushed himself off of the wall.

My eyes shot to Toi, who had an unreadable expression on her face.

"On the way over here, I figured since the shit is out and you know, you might as well know the truth," Calhoun said.

"Yeah! Tell Chance how you set him up, how you lied and told Ron to say that Chance was with you the day you killed that man and not you!"

My eyes got wide. How the fuck did she know this?

"Bitch!" Calhoun took steps toward her, then stopped himself. He turned to me with a finger pointed at her. "Chance, this bitch is foul!"

"Fuck you Calhoun. You ain't shit!" She was pointing wildly at him. "You always been jealous of Chance and the fact that you couldn't have what he had and that included me."

"Naw, bitch. That ain't what went down." He turned back to me with a pleading look in his eyes. "Chance . . ."

"Don't believe what he says, he's lying, baby!" Toi screamed over Calhoun.

"What? Bitch, shut the fuck up. Chance, the truth is this! I know Ron from a stint I did in prison. We still kicked it from time to time. She set me and the homie Ron up! She made it seem like she had a lick for us to do, that dude was a dirty cop with dope and money on him that he kept when he took down a big-time dope house. She made it seem like we could have made fifty grand worth of dope and money, easily. But in the end *you* were trying to get us to kill that nigga." He aimed a finger at Toi.

"That's a lie!" she screamed. "Tell Chance how you was fucking me all this time too Calhoun, and you was mad that I wouldn't pick you over Chance!"

"Yeah, bitch, I was fucking you! And that cop, you was fucking him too! You got mad that he was marrying somebody else! And he got you pregnant and told you to get an abortion. I was there, bitch! I heard what he said. He said he didn't want you! He was marrying Deyja. Yes, Chance, all this time I knew who she was. And he gave Toi money to get an abortion. The whole time you was with Chance, you was fucking around on him!" He turned to me. "Chance, you wanna know who shot that cop? She shot and killed that fucking cop!"

Toi started sobbing.

"And she told us both that if we said anything she would lie and say that we did it. She knew I had two strikes, Ron had one strike, and she had a clean record and they wouldn't believe us over her. So I got scared and I told Ron to turn himself in and say that he was with *you*. At first he wasn't going to do it and part of me was glad that he wasn't because deep down I knew it was wrong to do you like that. But this bitch offered him money. That's why she sold your house, Chance, and kept the money. She used it to pay Ron off. He was a nothing-ass nigga. He didn't have shit and probably never would be that close to the money she offered. So he agreed and did it. He ended up only getting three years for his so-called involvement in that shit. And he got those three years because he took a deal to rat out the real killer. And he only served half of it. She paid him forty grand." He swallowed hard. "And they got you." He slapped himself upside the head. "But I didn't think that they would keep you, Chance. I mean, your record is squeaky clean. I thought they would release you on uncircumstantial evidence. But they didn't, man, and I'm sorry. I ain't never meant for this to happen to you, dawg. I love you like a brother. If I had known it would go that far I would have never—"

He walked toward me but I shook my head with a look of hatred on my face and backed up.

He sobbed and said, "I wanted to say something. But I was scared that would be it for me. And I didn't know about the blood, Chance. She had to be the one to plant it."

He was right. She was the only one who had an extra set of keys to my car and all this time it never occurred to me.

Toi had her back to us now and continued to bawl. "Chance, don't believe him," she pleaded.

"Bitch!" Calhoun yelled. He rushed toward her.

She spun around quickly; that's when I saw the gun in her hand. Without a second's hesitation, she fired several bullets straight into Calhoun's chest.

I watched horrified as the bullets sent him flying back into the wall. He then slid down to the door, covering the white paint with his blood. He landed on his stomach with his body slightly twisted.

I rushed over to him quickly and dropped to my knees near his body.

I turned him over to see if he was still breathing. He was. But his breathing was ragged.

Blood flowed out of his mouth as he attempted to talk.

My hands slid over his heart. His shirt was soaking up his blood. I almost didn't feel his heartbeat 'cause it was beating so slow and felt so faint. I felt for the bullets. Several were lodged in his chest.

"I'm sorry, Chance, so sorry," he said.

I reached for my cell phone to call 911.

"Put down the phone!"

I eyed Toi as I was about to dial the number. She now had the gun pointed at me.

Still, I took a chance to dial. Just as I pressed nine, the gun clicked.

I froze.

But it didn't go off. Her gun must have been out of bullets.

Without even looking her way, I dialed the rest of the numbers.

"Nine-one-one. What's your emergency?"

"Yes, someone has been shot." I placed my hand back over Calhoun's heart to feel it still beating softly.

"What's your address?"

Toi ran.

I could hear someone yelling, "Freeze! Put your hands up!"

Security in the building must have heard the gun-shots and went after her.

As I gave him the address to the hotel I could hear Calhoun softly saying, "I love you, man. I never meant to do you like this." Over and over he repeated the same thing.

"We will be there shortly."

I sat the phone down.

Despite what Calhoun did, I still loved him. He was the one who I had experienced so much with growing up. He was my boy, really my best friend. We had had so much history together. But he betrayed the fuck out of me.

"I love you, man," he repeated in a hoarse voice.

"I know."

"Aye. Remember when we broke into Fred Sanford's house and that crazy-ass monkey came out of the clos-et? You were shook."

I laughed as tears slid down my cheeks. "You always get this wrong. *You* were shook."

He gave a laugh and with it more blood flowed from his mouth. It trailed down his chin. His shirt was now completely covered. He saw it. It scared him. But he continued to talk almost as if he was in denial about the fact that he was dying.

"All right, man, I was scared. I'm only admitting that to you. I don't want to jack up my street cred."

I couldn't help but start sobbing as a glazed look came over his eyes.

"I sure miss Paul. Remember when he used to pop those wheelies in his wheelchair? He had some serious skills, man."

"He did them better than we did them on our skate-boards."

"Yep. He did."

There was silence for a moment.

"Guess I'm going to see him soon."

"Naw. Not yet." My lips trembled. "The ambulance is on the way."

"I always looked up to you, Chance. I always wanted to be just like you, despite all the shit I talked."

His heartbeat was fainter. "Like me. I'm the boring-ass square."

"Naw. You're somebody special, Chance. Don't forget that shit. You're too good for this world. I love you."

And it didn't matter if the ambulance had rushed through the doors in that very moment.

His heart stopped.

Chapter 41

Although it was against the law and a clear violation of my civil rights, luckily the hotel room had a hidden camcorder in my hotel room the whole time I was there. It was what I needed. With the camcorder hidden in my room it filmed everything that happened the night Calhoun and Toi came to my room. That included Toi shooting Calhoun and trying to shoot me. Once the case for Calhoun was tried, she received twenty-five years to life for first-degree murder. The case of Devin Johnson was reopened and she was then tried for the murder. Ron Jasper was also tried for perjury.

Deyja and I were both present for the Devin Johnson trial. Since Ron so easily lied on me, not caring about the fact that I was innocent, it felt good to see him go down. He received five years. Now seeing Toi go down . . . I didn't know how to respond to that or how to even feel. At one time, I deeply loved her. I had planned on marrying her. And I never really knew her at all.

After the verdict was read and the judge told her she was being sentenced to another life sentences she sobbed, standing next to her public defender.

As the two officers escorted her out of the courtroom, she caught sight of Deyja sitting in one of the rows of benches.

She tried to rush toward her but the two officers had a tight hold on her.

"You bitch! What the fuck are you doing here?" she demanded. "That's why I was fucking your fiancé!" she yelled.

Deyja didn't respond. She kept her face calm too, which I knew had to be hard.

That's when Toi saw me. She smiled and said, "Chance, I love you, baby! I still do!"

They had to drag her out of the courtroom; the way they had dragged my mother out the day I was sentenced.

Once Toi was gone and we were all able to leave, Deyja rushed right past me. I wanted to stop her but I figured she needed more time.

Now fuck that. I thought as I made it outside. I chased after her as she rushed to the parking lot.

Tears flew from her eyes.

I walked toward her and as she neared her car, I yelled, "Deyja!"

She froze in the spot she was in.

I did too, not knowing what the correct move to make was. And in a second I didn't have to do anything.

She spun around and walked toward me.

I started walking too, fast as hell.

Then she started sobbing and threw herself in my arms.

I grabbed her tightly and hugged her, stroking her back. "It's going to be okay, baby."

"I'm sorry I didn't believe you," she said, sobbing on my shoulder.

I kissed her on top of her head.

She pulled her face from out of my shoulder and looked at me. I started wiping the tears from her face.

"All this time I grieved for a man who was unfaithful to me."

I nodded.

There was a pregnant pause before she said, "This connection between us is so tainted, so ugly, so horrible. I don't think we should—"

I wasn't going to let her shoot me down.

"I don't know what to make of this all this crazy shit either. Our exes being involved with each other. Toi killing Devin, you losing seven years of being happy, and me going to prison for all their lies. But I know that us meeting wasn't just by chance. This was supposed to happen, baby. Deyja, there is something special about you. You saved me from myself. You were the hope I needed at a time that I didn't feel my life was worth living. I owe you. And I want to spend the rest of my life paying you back for that. I am sorry that your fiancé died. I hate the fact that I spent seven years in prison for his death. But all of this, these crazy-ass circumstances, brought to me to you. I want to be with you. Give you all the love you can handle. Because I do love you."

"I'm scared." Her bottom lip trembled.

"Baby, you done with all that. I swear no more harm will ever come your way. And I won't ever do anything to hurt you. Hurting you would be hurting a part of myself because as far as I'm concerned, you and I are one. Please let me back in. Let me take care of you."

She took a deep breath.

She then cupped both my cheeks in her hands, gave me that smile.

And I knew I was back in. In her life. Nothing felt better than kissing her lips and finally knowing I wasn't at risk of losing her again. Deyja was finally mine.

Epilogue

Turns out the ACLU launched a civil suit against the County of Los Angeles on my behalf. I won. I was awarded a total of seven million dollars. A million for every year I had spent in that prison. It turns out that there was reasonable doubt in my case and the district attorney was just in a hurry to finish my trial so he could go on vacation. So they used Ron as a witness although a polygraph test clearly showed that he was lying. There was also evidence that would have tied Toi to the murder scene, like her fingerprints and saliva on a glass. Also the fact that there were vaginal secretions on Devin due to the fact that she had had sex with him the night he was murdered. There was a Black & Mild with saliva on the tip that would have linked Calhoun to being there that night and Ron's fingerprints—which didn't matter because he had already confessed to being there. Since the case was reopened after Calhoun had died and you can only get DNA from a dead person up to a week after their death, they subpoenaed Calhoun's father into court and used his saliva to match Calhoun being there because of his saliva on the Black & Mild. DNA was something else. It's crazy that none of this was ever included in the first trial. They did not even have the proper record of who handled or even bagged all the evidence, which the courts called 'Chain of Custody', which was extremely important when

DNA evidence was being handled. The DA attacked the fact that there was a witness and blood in my car and left it at that. In addition to the seven million dollars I received, they also took the charge off of my record and it was back clean.

So of course I couldn't just keep the money for myself. I paid a visit to Delano Prison, a place I never wanted to head back to but I was coming back for a different reason than why I came before. I came to pay Lewis a visit. And sure enough, he was there. After he gave me a hug and asked what I had come up there for, I slid a check in his hand for a cool million dollars so he and his family didn't have to be prisoners to that hellhole any longer.

He started down at the check and his eyes got buck. "Shit, are you serious. Chance?"

"What you think? Get the fuck out of here, while you still got your health. Open up some type of business."

His lips trembled and his eyes were watery. "You just saved my family's life, man."

I smiled.

He hugged me.

When I pulled away I told him, "Stay in touch, man."

"I will."

I turned to leave that place but not before I heard, "Yeah, I quit, muthafuckas!"

I threw back my head and laughed.

I figured that God gave me that money to do something good with it. So I bought houses for both of Calhoun's baby mamas, gave them one hundred grand apiece, and set up savings accounts for both his kids so that when they turned eighteen their college was fully paid for and they would each have a car. Now they didn't have any excuse not to go to college and make something of themselves. I even kicked fifty thousand Mateo's way so he could open up his own office.

When I set the check in front of him, he couldn't believe the shit. He read it over and over again. Then after reading it for the fourth time he stood and sang, "*Vido mas. Vido mas!*" before giving me a hug.

"No problem, man."

"Let me have the waitress make you a *carne asada* burrito. For old times."

"Naw, I gotta go, dude," I said, laughing.

"If you need me you know where I am, Chance. And I always carry this."

I busted up laughing when I saw him pull half of a folded-up soda bottle out of his pocket.

My next plan was to open up a nonprofit law office to help inmates who are falsely accused of a crime and did not have the money or knowledge to fight the case.

I also paid a small chunk of money to have my mother's body moved to *Forest Lawn Cemetery* and for her to have a tombstone.

When they finally deposited her body in the grave, I remember feeling the same pain I felt when I had found out that she died. I cried and hugged her tombstone, wishing that she was still here, aching for her.

Except this time I wasn't alone like I was when I was in prison. I had someone offering me comfort, arms rubbing up and down my back, kisses and the promise that she would help me get through this . . . Deyja. She was now my family. Which meant I had to put a lid on things so I could move forward. So that I could be fully happy, be at peace.

Now I could let my mama rest in peace, because I was now at peace. *Trouble don't last always.* Mine was buried with Calhoun and resting in the cell with Ron and with Toi. It couldn't touch me or hurt me anymore.

Still, I needed closure. When we left her grave site, I started feeling like I had to put some things to rest. I decided to open up the package that Emily had given me when I got out of prison. I couldn't believe it had taken me so long to do so.

Inside were a bunch of pictures of me when I was a kid and some with my mother and me. There were even a few of Calhoun and me hanging out in the Springdales. I even found all the letters that I had written my mom while I was in prison. I was surprised to find one addressed to me but with Ellen's address on it. It was dated a week before my mother had passed.

I opened it up quickly.

Chance,
I pray that you are okay in there and I still don't understand this. You are not supposed to be there. I wish I was out and could help you, baby. Thing is, the doctors have told me that my heart is really bad. I don't know if I'm going to live to see you get out of there but I know one day you will get out.

I smiled.

But there is something that I need you to know before I do pass that you never knew. This is a secret that I have been keeping from you. I'm so sorry that I did. I hope you will in your own time forgive me for this. Years ago, I was pretty wild. I made a lot of bad choices, Chance. One of them was getting involved with a man I had no business getting involved with. But at the time, I didn't care. I had my own place in the

Springdales, felt like I was grown and could do grown things and it wouldn't catch up with me. My neighbor invited me to her home for a birthday party for her son and I met him there. From there we carried on an intimate relationship. The man I was sleeping with already had a wife and told me that if I ever got pregnant by him I would have to have an abortion. So when I did get pregnant with you I didn't tell him for fear that he would make me abort you. When he found out that I was pregnant I lied and told him that I had been sleeping with another man from the Springdales so he wanted nothing to do with me even though he would leave me on a regular to go home to his wife. He always told me that he loved me, but that his duty was to wife and that she came before me. He couldn't handle the thought of me being unfaithful to him and said that his wife was also pregnant and that she needed him. So he ended things with me. Chance, the man you thought was your father is not. Curtis Redding didn't claim you because you were not his. Your father is Tony Parks, Calhoun's father.

The letter dropped from my hands.

I shook my head and thought I hadn't read it right. So I snatched it up from the floor and read the words again. *Chance, the man you thought was your father is not. Curtis Redding didn't claim you because you were not his. Your father is Tony Parks, Calhoun's father. I hope you can forgive me for keeping this secret from you. Once you came into the world you became my meaning and my purpose. That's why I named you Chance. You were truly a blessing. Understand that once*

*you came into the world I tried to do the best that
I could to take care of you. And while providing
for you was a struggle, being your mother wasn't
because you made it so easy and joyous.*
      Love you with all I have in me,
      Mom

Tears streamed down my face. The revelation had me shocked beyond words. Calhoun was my brother. Tony Parks was my father.

I shared the letter with Deyja, who was sitting next to me at my house. A house that after I married her, I wanted to make her own as well. Her eyes were as wide as saucers, even though she tried to keep a smile on her face to keep me calm.

I stood up and went to the kitchen.

She followed after me as I grabbed my car keys off the kitchen table.

She hugged me from behind. I turned around and put one of her hands to my lips and kissed it.

"Where are you going, baby?"

"To see Tony Parks." I couldn't bring myself to call him Dad even though my mother said that is who he was. All this time. All this time, the man I always wished was my father really was?

"Do you want me to go with you?"

I turned around and kissed her. "I will be okay, baby."

I walked outside and got into my white pearl Cadillac Escalade.

I rolled over to Calhoun's parents' house, in shock the whole way there.

Once I got there, I hopped out of the car and went up to the steps. I had no idea what I was going to say.

The thing about my letter was my mom never mentioned if Calhoun's dad ever found out. Probably not.

When he opened the door I noticed his eyes were red and swollen. The last time I had seen him was at Calhoun's funeral. Maybe it was dumb that I went because he had betrayed me. But he was gone and I didn't want the bad to be my last memories of him. I thought of the bond we had shared. The good times, from rolling around eating chili cheese Fritos, to breaking into Fred Sanford's house and being attacked by that crazy-ass monkey, to losing Paul. Fuck all the other shit. He was gone and the wrong he did would be between him and his God. Not between him and me. He had lost his life behind the shit.

Tony Parks took me out my thoughts about Calhoun and to the present. The reason why I was there.

"How you doing, Chance?"

As I stood there, facing him, I scanned all the features on his face, noticing for the first time in my life that I did favor him. In all those times he came by to get Calhoun, why didn't I ever notice before?

I cleared my throat. "Fine, sir. Can I come in?"

He stepped back, giving me space to walk inside.

"How are you holding up since the funeral?" he asked me.

"Gets better day by day. Listen. There is something I wanted to talk to you about. It's about my mother."

I studied him and how the mention of my mother made him look even more depressed

"Before my mother died—"

A sob choked my words. "This is so hard."

His eyes narrowed at me as I managed to get control of my shaking shoulders and wipe the tears off my face with my free hand as they started to fall. My other hand held the letter.

I took a deep breath and continued. "Before my mother died, while she was in prison she wrote me a letter."

I handed it to him. "And I think you should read it."

He looked surprised, but he opened the letter and read it.

I kept my eyes on his face as he did. By the time he got to the end of the letter, his eyes were watering and his lips were trembling.

He dropped to his knees on the floor and shouted, "Dear God!" His whole body wracked with sobs. "I didn't know! I didn't know!"

I rushed forward and placed a hand on his back. He grabbed me and hugged me, sobbing and repeating the whole time, "I didn't know. I'm so sorry, Chance. I should have known! I should have known!"

I nodded and broke down crying, still hugging him.

And maybe, in that moment, I should have said, "Fuck you nigga, you knew! You never did shit for me!" Or, "Where were you when I needed a father? I'm grown now!" "Why you crying now?"

But why do any of that? Yeah, I never had a father but I'm not worse for wear. I'm okay. I grew up respectful, with morals and values. I was a black man who grew up in the projects and managed to not only graduate from college, but not break the law. I was blessed. I had more money than I ever thought I would. I had a beautiful woman who is so special and sweeter than any woman I had ever been with. And more importantly, I had my freedom. I considered myself to be pretty fucking lucky. Despite being innocent, there were so many black men in prison who would rot away there for some shit they never did. That made me a blessed individual. And after all I had been through, I was still standing like the man my mama raised me to be.

So I continued to hug him.

I hugged him like he had always been in my life . . .

About the Author

Karen Williams is the author of:

Harlem On Lock
The People Vs. Cashmere
Dirty to the Grave, and
"Diamond In The Sky", in *Around The Way Girls 7*.

She has her bachelor of arts degree in literature and communications from California State University Dominguez Hills. She works as a probation officer and has two kids, Adara, thirteen, and Bralynn, one.

Notes

ORDER FORM
URBAN BOOKS, LLC
78 E. Industry Ct
Deer Park, NY 11729

Name: (please print):_____

Address: _____

City/State: _____

Zip: _____

QTY	TITLES	PRICE
	The Cartel	$14.95
	The Cartel 2	$14.95
	The Dopeman's Wife	$14.95
	The Prada Plan	$14.95
	Gunz And Roses	$14.95
	Snow White	$14.95
	A Pimp's Life	$14.95
	Hush	$14.95
	Little Black Girl Lost 1	$14.95
	Little Black Girl Lost 2	$14.95
	Little Black Girl Lost 3	$14.95
	Little Black Girl Lost 4	$14.95

Shipping and handling-add $3.50 for 1st book, then $1.75 for each additional book.

Please send a check payable to:

Urban Books, LLC

Please allow 4-6 weeks for delivery

ORDER FORM
URBAN BOOKS, LLC
78 E. Industry Ct
Deer Park, NY 11729

Name: (please print):_____

Address: _____

City/State: _____

Zip: _____

QTY	TITLES	PRICE
	16 ½ On The Block	$14.95
	16 On The Block	$14.95
	Betrayal	$14.95
	Both Sides Of The Fence	$14.95
	Cheesecake And Teardrops	$14.95
	Denim Diaries	$14.95
	Happily Ever Now	$14.95
	Hell Has No Fury	$14.95
	If It Isn't love	$14.95
	Last Breath	$14.95
	Loving Dasia	$14.95
	Say It Ain't So	$14.95

Shipping and handling-add $3.50 for 1st book, then $1.75 for each additional book.
Please send a check payable to:
Urban Books, LLC
Please allow 4-6 weeks for delivery

ORDER FORM
URBAN BOOKS, LLC
78 E. Industry Ct
Deer Park, NY 11729

Name: (please print):_____

Address: _____

City/State: _____

Zip: _____

QTY	TITLES	PRICE
	A Man's Worth	$14.95
	Abundant Rain	$14.95
	Battle Of Jericho	$14.95
	By The Grace Of God	$14.95
	Dance Into Destiny	$14.95
	Divorcing The Devil	$14.95
	Forsaken	$14.95
	Grace And Mercy	$14.95
	Guilty Of Love	$14.95
	His Woman, His Wife, His Widow	$14.95
	Illusions	$14.95
	The LoveChild	$14.95

Shipping and handling-add $3.50 for 1st book, then $1.75 for each additional book.

Please send a check payable to:

Urban Books, LLC

Please allow 4-6 weeks for delivery

ORDER FORM
URBAN BOOKS, LLC
78 E. Industry Ct
Deer Park, NY 11729

Name: (please print): _____

Address: _____

City/State: _____

Zip: _____

QTY

Ship...   ...or
each...
Pleas...

Pleas...